Totally Bound Publishing books by Jasmine Hill:

From Leather to Lace
Serena's Submission
Roses are Red
Lillian's Light Horseman

LILLIAN'S LIGHT HORSEMAN

JASMINE HILL

Lillian's Light Horseman
ISBN # 978-1-78430-380-8
©Copyright Jasmine Hill 2014
Cover Art by Posh Gosh ©Copyright November 2014
Interior text design by Claire Siemaszkiewicz
Totally Bound Publishing

LILLIAN'S LIGHT HORSEMAN

Dedication

To my editor, Faith Bicknell-Brown—thank you for
your tireless analysis, your invaluable input and your
constructive criticism.

Prologue

Henry Baxter lit a cigar and relaxed into a wingback chair as he reflected on the day's events. It had been emotionally draining, but his decision to detach young William Cartwright from Lillian was a necessary evil.

He wouldn't soon forget the look of utter desolation and betrayal on Cartwright's face when he had informed the young man that he, Baxter, intended to resettle his family in England where his daughter Lillian was promised to a young man of established connections and family. He recalled the furious glint in Cartwright's eyes and the hard set of his jaw, as he had demanded to know when Lillian had agreed to a marriage. For a moment, Henry had felt a frisson of fear at the young man's vehement reaction at the news of Lillian's imminent departure and her promise to another, but just as quickly, Cartwright's anger had been replaced by resignation and an odd acceptance. Henry guessed that Cartwright knew his influence was minimal. After all, Lillian was only sixteen and required the consent of a parent or guardian for marriage, and Henry had no intention of giving his consent to a young man whose only claim in life would be that of a country solicitor.

Now, if William's older brother James Cartwright had petitioned for Lillian's hand, that would have been a different matter entirely. James would inherit all sixty thousand acres of the family's Mulga Creek Sheep Station and would make a formidable son-in-law and an excellent connection for the Baxter family. Unfortunately, James was aware of the affection his younger brother held for Lillian and would not play any part in being the cause of William's unhappiness. Henry knew this to be the case because he'd approached James with an offer of his daughter's hand, which the man had refused immediately in favor of his brother's feelings.

The most disturbing aspect of the day had been when he'd had to inform his daughter they would be relocating to England. He supposed he hadn't needed to follow that statement with the lie that William Cartwright was soon to be married. But it was imperative to Henry that Lillian relinquish all hope of a future connection with the young Cartwright. His daughter's desperate, anguished sobs at the news would live with him always. It had been heartbreaking for him to witness and know he was the cause of her misery, but he consoled himself with the idea that what he'd done, he'd done for the benefit of the Baxter name.

One of his most advantageous assets was his daughter. Her beauty, charm and wit were incomparable and he would not squander such a treasure on a lowly solicitor. Lillian was young and impressionable and she would soon outgrow her girlish infatuation with William Cartwright. Then Henry would be able to present to her a more favorable proposition.

He assured himself that his actions were not motivated by his dire financial situation but had everything to do with affection and concern for his daughter. He was a loving and considerate father, after all, and the well-being of Lillian was his top priority. If that meant separating her from Cartwright, unfortunately, that was what had to happen.

Chapter One

*The love of field and coppice, Of green and shaded lanes,
Of ordered woods and gardens, Is running in your veins.
Strong love of gray-blue distance, Brown streams and soft
dim skiesI know but cannot share it, My love is otherwise.*
My Country — Dorothea Mackellar (1904)

England
Ten years later

Lillian Hamilton packed the last of her belongings
into her trunk and prepared to leave her aunt's home
for the last time. She doubted that she'd return. Her
aunt had passed away three months before and now
there was nothing keeping Lillian in England. She
mourned her aunt dreadfully, her mother's sister. Her
Aunt Agnes had been kindness personified when
Lillian's father had died two years previously, leaving
Lillian destitute and homeless. She owed her life to the
woman and shuddered to think what would have
happened to her had her Aunt Agnes not swept in and
taken Lillian into her care. Not only had she given

Lillian shelter and affection, but she'd also suggested that Lillian take her last name of Hamilton. The Baxter name, thanks to her father's unscrupulous business dealings and gambling debts, was besmirched with suspicion and corruption, and no decent family or acquaintance would have their good reputation tainted by any association to it. Lillian's already fragile social status would have been irreparably damaged had she continued in English society as Lillian Baxter. As it happened, a change of county, social circle and name meant that Lillian's connection with her father and his dubious transactions was limited to those who knew the family personally. To all new acquaintances, she'd been largely able to start afresh, free from suspicion and conjecture.

It was a flight of fancy, however, to believe that she could continue to be untouched by her past. Angry energy rippled through her as she recalled the words of her aunt's attorney.

"I'm sorry to be the bearer of bad news, Miss Hamilton, but your aunt's estate is tied up in legal disputes. As you will be aware, your father left considerable debts and there are a number of creditors applying to Mrs. Hamilton's estate for reimbursement. You are her sole heir, but after legal damages and settlements, I fear that the lion's share of your inheritance will be consumed."

Lillian had been unprepared for the fury that had suffused her at the thought of her beloved aunt's belongings and home being sold to pay Lillian's irresponsible father's debts. Suddenly her aunt's asking Lillian to take her jewelry and hide it until such a time that Lillian could safely sell it didn't appear so odd. Her aunt must have been aware of her father's debts and Agnes' dying wish had been that her niece might have a little money before the creditors took everything.

Lillian had done what her Aunt Agnes had requested and as soon as she was able, she'd sold most of her aunt's jewelry and any dresses and outfits that served no practical purpose. If Lillian were careful, she'd have money enough to last her for some months.

Her mind drifted to her father — how he'd pushed suitor after suitor in her direction in the hopes that she'd make an affluent marriage, and how she'd spurned every attempt of his matchmaking.

Lillian had desperately wanted to please her father with a good connection, but she'd never been able to forgive or forget her first love. The inability of hers to obliterate him from her memory had made courtship with another man almost impossible. Even after ten years, just thinking his name made her chest constrict painfully. By the time Lillian had taken up residence with her aunt, she'd despaired at ever finding true love again. She'd received more than her fair share of attention from a number of eligible gentlemen, but not one had touched her heart. She knew that her view of marriage for love was silly and juvenile, that matches were often made less for love and affection and more for the social advantages of beauty and position, but she couldn't bring herself to relinquish her romantic notions and dreams. Now, at nearly twenty-six, she was left completely alone in the world with barely enough money to see her through to the end of the year.

Finally, she locked her trunk and walked from the room, checking the other chambers before she emerged into the hallway where she spotted the driver at the front door. She directed him to the bedroom to retrieve her belongings and took one last look around the home that had been her safe haven for the past two years. With a sigh and a heavy heart, she stepped outside, locking the door securely and with finality behind her. She would drop the keys at the attorney's office on her way to the port where she would board a ship—a ship due to sail later that evening. Soon she'd be on her way back to the country of her birth, a country that she had loved passionately—a country that she'd been told she'd never see again.

* * * *

As she sat waiting to board the vessel that would carry her to the next phase of her life, she reflected on the letter that had brought her to the decision to leave England. She retrieved the correspondence from her reticule, the paper now soft and fragile, the folds tearing slightly owing to her repeated examination. For what seemed like the hundredth time, she reread the words that had recently changed the course of her life so dramatically.

Dear Miss Hamilton,

I expect by the time this missive reaches you, your Aunt, Mrs. Agnes Hamilton, will have passed on. Please accept my sincere condolences for your loss.

I hardly know where to start so I shall start with the letter that I received from Mrs. Hamilton one month ago. She stated that she was very ill at the time of writing and expected to be taken into God's hands in the very near future but that she could not rest in peace until she'd done all she could do for her beloved niece, a Miss Lillian Hamilton (Baxter).

Mrs. Hamilton explained the death of your father with his subsequent debt and her concern for your welfare and well-being once she'd departed this world. It appears that Mrs. Hamilton was quite knowledgeable about your life in Australia before your family left for England, and in particular about your connection to Mulga Creek Sheep Station and the Cartwright family. I can only assume that your mother imparted this information to your aunt before she died.

Now I shall get to the heart of my reason for writing to you. Mrs. Hamilton asked if there might be a position for you at Mulga Creek station as governess to Mr. Cartwright's children. She'd heard that Mr. Cartwright's wife had succumbed to the Spanish influenza and, while she was deeply saddened by the news, your aunt hoped that your education and upbringing would be of benefit to the Cartwright children, particularly as their mother has been so cruelly taken from them.

I must confess that I too have been concerned about the welfare of the children. Their father, while a good and decent man, is very busy with the demands of the sheep station and while I was taught my letters and sums, I do not have the education or the time necessary to instruct children in a position such as theirs.

Mr. Cartwright's intention has been to engage a governess, so your aunt's communication was warmly welcomed as quite fortuitous. I must also confess that I hope you take up the offer, as I would enjoy seeing you once more at Mulga Creek. I remember you to be a warm-hearted, sweet child and a charming young lady, and your aunt assured me that you have grown into a thoughtful and lovely woman.

I must warn you, however, that I have not imparted all of this information to Mr. Cartwright. He only knows that a lady by the name of Miss Hamilton will be taking the position of governess. I have not conveyed to him the whole *truth of your identity. I will no doubt be chastised warmly for my duplicity but I believe that the past must stay in the past and that you should impart any explanations personally.*

There is something else you should know. Mr. Cartwright fought in The Great War and might seem a little changed from what you remember. I will say no more of this and leave it to your own personal observations if, in fact, you decide to accept the position.

Please respond in the quickest haste so that I may make the necessary arrangements.

Yours sincerely,
Mrs. Millie Thompson
Head Housekeeper – Mulga Creek Sheep Station

Lillian reflected yet again on the letter's contents. She'd read it so many times that she could quote it verbatim. Unfortunately, it raised more questions than it answered.

When had her mother spoken to her aunt about their life in Australia? Lillian had never mentioned that time. She preferred to forget it in order to attempt to move on. She'd been deluding herself, of course. It had been ten years since she'd seen William Cartwright, and still his image haunted her dreams. Then there was James Cartwright's fighting in the war. How much had those experiences changed him? And had the death of his wife affected him terribly, perhaps adding to the change in character that Mrs. Thompson thought necessary to allude to? And where was William? Mrs. Thompson had not made mention of him in her missive, yet she must be partly aware of the connection that she and William had shared. A connection they'd had, at least until Lillian's father had relocated the family to England shortly before

William had married. Just thinking of William married to another sent a deep ache lancing through her. After all the years the pain had not lessened, but rather had morphed from an intense, overwhelming sensation into a dull, aching throb.

She shook off her momentary melancholy and thought about Mulga Creek Sheep Station, wondering if it had changed a great deal. It made sense that James Cartwright would require a governess. The property was too large and too isolated to enable the children to attend a standard school and she imagined that they were too young for boarding school. She pondered what James' reaction would be when he learned that Lillian Hamilton was, in fact, Lillian Baxter. She could only hope that his reaction would be favorable. She'd always liked William's older brother and she had to have faith that the feeling was mutual. At least if her correspondence was anything to go by, she would have an ally in Mrs. Thompson. She remembered the housekeeper as a kind and very capable woman who was much respected in the Cartwright household.

Lillian was risking considerable emotional distress by traveling back to Australia and opening herself up to a whole world of potential hurt, but her options were limited. She had no connections or dependable income to keep her in England.

No, she had no real choice but to take a chance and start afresh in Australia.

Chapter Two

I love a sunburnt country,A land of sweeping plains,Of ragged mountain ranges,Of droughts and flooding rains.I love her far horizons,I love her jewel-sea,Her beauty and her terror – The wide brown land for me!
    My Country – Dorothea Mackellar (1904)

Australia
August 1921

Lillian stopped and looked around Coolabah train station as she waited for her trunk to be offloaded. She was beyond weary. Between the lengthy sea voyage and the journey from Sydney to Coolabah, she'd been traveling for nearly two months and she longed for nothing more than a warm bath and a soft bed.

She stood uncertainly on the dusty platform, unsure as to how she was to get from the station to the property. A moment later, she had her answer when a tall, wiry-looking man dressed in dusty work attire strolled purposely in her direction. Removing his bush hat, he bowed slightly and introduced himself. He was one of the Mulga Creek station hands come to collect her. Within minutes, he had her trunk secured in the buggy and they were on their way.

Lillian was relieved that she'd been picked up in a buggy and not an automobile. It meant that she'd have more time to prepare herself for seeing Mulga Creek and all it represented. It would give her a period to reconnect with her surroundings and hopefully allow her some reprieve until the bittersweet memories, bubbling just below the surface, would rear up and take her under assault.

As they traveled along the dirt road, she took an avid interest in the environment. Recollections from ten years before swirled through her mind and brought with them overwhelming feelings of both happiness and sadness—memories of a previous life and her only love.

She'd forgotten the desolation of the Australian outback—how dusty and dry it was and how unbearably hot it could be. She was lucky that she'd arrived in winter but the days in the outback, even in winter, could still be warm. She knew that her clothes would be impractical for the environment but there was not a lot she could do about that. Her wardrobe was designed for English weather and she knew that as the days grew warmer, her dresses and skirts of durable, heavy European fabric would be oppressively uncomfortable.

They drew nearer to Mulga Creek Sheep Station and her nervousness increased, making her palms damp and clammy. She'd spent the past ten years trying to forget about William and her memories of their time together, first as childhood friends then as childhood sweethearts, only now to put herself into a position where those bittersweet memories would be thrust to the forefront of her consciousness. She wondered where William was living and whether he bore any resemblance to the young man of nineteen he had been when last she'd seen him.

The buggy rounded a bend in the road and the homestead finally came into view. The house was newly painted white and glowed welcomingly in the midday sun. A garden fronting the residence was filled with hardy, durable flowers and plants — the only type to survive in such a dry and unforgiving climate. Geraniums and wattle bordered a pathway that led to the front door and an extensive vegetable garden took up the right side of the house adjacent to the kitchen.

The sight of the homestead and the sudden pang of *déjà vu* that it brought with it took Lillian's breath away, and all too soon they were pulling up in the long drive and the station hand was unloading her belongings.

"I'll take your trunk inside, miss. Mrs. Thompson has gone into Bourke to run errands. She asked that you wait in the drawing room for the boss. I'll let him know that you're here."

Lillian's anxiety deepened. She'd expected that Mrs. Thompson would be at the homestead to greet her and had hoped that she'd be present to ease any awkwardness that might arise when James Cartwright discovered her identity.

Lillian followed the station hand into the house and stopped in the hall to assess her reflection in the mirror. The image that greeted her made her gasp in shock. Her hair, which she'd styled so carefully that morning, was coming loose from its chignon and fell in dusty ringlets around her shoulders. And her face, usually of a peaches and cream complexion, was caked in a fine layer of red outback dust. She stepped back and surveyed her traveling attire, unsurprised to find that her skirt and jacket were creased and covered in fine ocher-colored powder. She'd forgotten how quickly the outback dirt permeated everything—even her mouth was gritty with the stuff.

She couldn't meet James Cartwright looking like she did. She needed to freshen up. Making a decision, she left the hall and went in search of someone to assist her. Finding a maid in the kitchen, she requested a basin of water and a cloth and quickly scrubbed her face and hands. She scraped her hair back and re-pinned the escaped tendrils as best she could. There was nothing much she could do with her attire, so she settled for patting herself all over liberally with the damp cloth. It would have to do. One more inspection of her reflection in the hall mirror confirmed that she looked moderately better.

Taking a deep breath to steady her nerves, she made her way to the drawing room. There were subtle changes in the décor. The furniture had been re-upholstered and beautiful hand-worked cushions dotted the room, giving it a comfortable and cozy feel. She picked up a gilt-edged frame and examined the photograph. It was of a woman, not conventionally beautiful, but she was handsome and radiated strength of character through a strong jaw and direct gaze at the camera.

"This must be James' wife," she mused aloud then replaced the frame on the mahogany table top and turned to survey the rest of the room.

Spying the piano, she walked to it, running her fingers over the polished wood, remembering when she used to sing and play this same instrument and recalling how William would sit and listen to her with a rapturous expression. She hissed in a breath and drew her fingers back from the piano sharply, not wanting the hurtful reminder of happier times.

Turning, she went to stand by the window, her back to the door, and took deep breaths to quell her anxiety. As she gazed out at the garden, she heard footsteps in the hall then the unmistakable sounds of someone entering through the door behind her.

"Miss Hamilton," a deep voice greeted her. "My apologies for keeping you waiting."

She turned to offer a greeting of her own and stopped abruptly, gasping in shock as she faced the man standing in the middle of the room. Her hand flew to her mouth and she swayed slightly, her equilibrium tilting.

Standing before her was not James Cartwright, as she'd expected, but his younger brother William.

Lillian stared at him in mute astonishment, her mind whirling and her heart thumping a rapid drumbeat against her ribcage. A range of dormant emotions bubbled fiercely to the surface of her consciousness. Her anguish at his betrayal of their love, the terrible hurt he'd caused her and—strongest but hardest to cope with—the deep feelings of devotion and affection that she still held for him.

She was awash in sensations—shock, disbelief and uncertainty. She'd neither seen nor heard from him since that day ten years ago, when her father had informed her that William was to marry another and that Lillian would be leaving Australia for England.

Wariness and the ultimate need for self-preservation overtook her and she pulled herself together. She stiffened her spine and raised her chin. Looking him in the eye, she waited for him to make the first move.

She saw her own shock and disbelief reflected in his face, but he quickly masked his emotions, expertly affecting an impassive expression as he stood quietly assessing her.

"Well, well, this *is* a surprise. To what do I owe the pleasure of this visit after so many years?" he asked, his tone mocking and cold.

Lillian was taken off guard. How could he sound so bitter and accusing when it was *he* who had betrayed *her*? And how could he look so calm and collected when her emotions were spinning out of control? She studied him, trying to regain some of her composure.

The years had changed him—he was still devastatingly handsome but more masculine and powerful. He had lost the leanness of youth, his body now strong and muscular and there was a hard edge to his chiseled jaw. His brown hair, burnished copper from the sun, was too long for fashion and fell just below his collar. An unruly lock flopped over his forehead, imparting a rakish air, and his hazel-green eyes held a hard intensity that had not been there before, giving the impression that he'd seen and experienced things that made him view the world differently.

She thought fleetingly of Mrs. Thompson's letter and her mention of the war and wondered if it had been William to whom she'd been referring. He crossed his arms over his chest, his posture rigid as he waited for her to respond to his question.

"I was expecting your brother," she said quietly. "I'm the new governess for your brother's children."

He raised an eyebrow, a look of surprise crossing his features. "That's very interesting considering that James has been dead for five years."

Lillian gasped in dismay but before she could respond, he continued to speak.

"My brother was fatally injured when he was thrown from a horse. The children to whom you refer are *mine* and I take it that you are Miss Hamilton?"

"Yes, I'm Miss Hamilton, the governess."

Lillian was reeling from this latest information. She'd assumed when Mrs. Thompson had written of Mr. Cartwright that she'd been referring to James, the older brother. She hadn't for a second thought that Mr. Cartwright, owner of Mulga Creek Sheep Station, was William. She needed time to think and reassess her situation but she suspected that William was not about to give her that luxury.

"And why do you go by the name Miss Hamilton? Was it to misrepresent your identity?" He cocked his head to one side and studied her. "Or is it the name of your husband and you have represented yourself as unmarried in order to seem a more appealing prospect for the governess position?"

It appalled her that he'd think or even suggest she would be so deliberately deceitful. She was shocked by his accusations and realized that what she had hoped could be a new beginning would bring her nothing but further heartache. It was very clear that William did not want her at Mulga Creek and genuinely believed that she'd been duplicitous in her application for governess. She doubted she could find suitable words to explain her situation. Her thoughts were in turmoil and she suspected a form of shock was setting in. No, there was nothing more for her to say. She needed to leave as soon as possible – only then could she take stock of her circumstances and plan a way forward.

Summoning an inner strength she didn't know she possessed and struggling not to break down in front of him, she straightened her spine and looked William squarely in the eye.

"Please accept my sincerest apology, *Mr. Cartwright.* I was led to believe that it was your brother who required the services of a governess. I would not have accepted the offer had I known that it was for the *younger* Mr. Cartwright. I must impose upon your hospitality this evening. I will arrange to leave first thing in the morning."

Before her stiff façade crumbled and she fell into a quivering heap on the floor, she swept out of the drawing room, maintaining a dignity that she didn't feel under the circumstances. Upon entering the hallway, she stumbled down it in a desperate quest of an exit. She needed to find somewhere quiet and isolated where she could think and give vent to her anguish and astonishment.

Chapter Three

William didn't try to stop Lillian when she fled the drawing room. There was no point. She couldn't go anywhere and she obviously needed to be alone—as did he.

His heart rate raced with the effects of seeing her again, his pulse roaring in his ears. He'd managed to keep his emotions in check though while outwardly he'd looked composed, inwardly he was in turmoil, his reaction to her presence so visceral that he felt lightheaded.

When she'd turned from the window and he'd caught sight of her for the first time, he had initially thought he was imagining things. It had taken some moments for his mind to catch up with his eyesight and assert that what he was seeing was real and not a vision.

He shook his head, trying to clear it and make sense of the situation. How had it occurred that Lillian would apply for the governess post? Of course she'd expected to see James and she'd made it very clear that if she'd known that it was he—William—who required the governess then she would not have accepted the position. And where was the husband and why in God's name had the man allowed his wife to travel unchaperoned across to the other side of the world? The last he'd heard was that she was resettling in England with an eye to marry a more prosperous prospect, as if she were a gold-digging floozy. He'd never understood it. Those actions were not the actions of the girl he'd admired and loved. Just the thought of her deceit, even so many years later, made his blood boil.

Cold, hard fury swept through him. How dare she re-enter his life when he'd worked so hard to forget her? He clenched his fists in frustration while he regulated his breathing. Shoving a hand through his hair, he propped his other against the wall over the mantel, pondering what to do. His head was telling him to send her on her way and wave her cheerily goodbye while his heart was insisting that he keep her with him — to lock her up — if that was the only way to make her stay.

To make matters worse, her beauty was undiminished and had only grown and enhanced as she'd matured. He'd barely stopped himself from reaching out to caress her flawless skin. He'd wanted to grasp her lush body and lock her against him. And the sight of those wide green eyes, looking so confused and anxious, had nearly undone him.

"Oh God," he groaned aloud with suppressed desire. He rested both hands on the mantelpiece and hung his head, emotions warring a fierce battle within him.

Even her scent was the same — a hint of apples had wafted to him when she'd swept past, punching him in the gut with a feeling of *déjà vu* so intense that it had taken his breath away.

He'd never forgotten the rich color and texture of her hair — a beautiful auburn — a shade he'd never seen on anyone else. And that body! She no longer had a girl's slight figure but ripe, sexual curves that he could discern clearly beneath the drab fabric of her traveling attire.

William thought about her husband and a surge of jealousy twisted his insides. The fact that the man was able to touch and caress those luscious curves when he, William, should have been the first and only one to do so had a haze of red suffusing his gaze.

How had she even learned that he required a governess and why on earth would she apply for such a post? He hadn't given her a chance to explain, although what she could say that would justify her actions of ten years ago, he didn't know.

What should he do now? He was terrified of being hurt again and his gut told him that if he allowed her to stay, that's exactly the path he'd be heading down — one of heartbreak and anguish.

Lillian had inflicted feelings of betrayal and guilt on him for ten years — betrayal at her desertion of their love and the guilt of never having fought for her. There had been other feelings of guilt too — the guilt of never having been able to love his wife enough. Ruth had been a good and caring woman. However, he'd *never* been *in* love with her. He'd cared for her deeply and respected her immensely but his heart had only ever truly belonged to Lillian. And now that Lillian had walked back into his life, William was afraid for his sanity *and* she supposedly belonged to another. But what if he couldn't let her go a second time? What would become of him then?

Ten years ago, he'd been a young man of nineteen, barely out of boyhood and still too emotionally immature to have questioned the actions of Lillian and her father. If he had that time over again, he wouldn't have stood for it. He would have fought for her tooth and nail. Time and experience had toughened him and instilled in him strength of character. He knew that his tendency to command and dominate was not always a benefit, but he liked to think that he would never again be weak-willed or exploited.

He sighed heavily in exasperation. He couldn't send her away. There was some reason she was here and he wasn't so vindictive that he would cast her out to find her way alone. No, he would speak to her and reach an agreement.

Now she knew for whom she'd be working. If she'd be willing to stay on, he wouldn't ask her any questions about her life and he wouldn't pry into the reasons behind her return to Australia. It was none of his concern and he suspected that further elaboration would only serve to embarrass her and hurt him.

He stared into the empty fireplace and assessed the circumstances. *Perhaps if I keep my distance and maintain a purely professional relationship with her, it could work.* Even as he told himself that, he knew deep down that he would struggle to remain detached. But keeping his guard up was essential if he wasn't prepared to risk more despair and betrayal, because if that happened, he didn't think he would survive it a second time.

* * * *

Lillian found herself in the backyard. She'd fled the house so quickly, her eyes blurry with unshed tears, that she hadn't realized where she was even heading. She made her way over to a tall Coolabah tree and sank to her knees beneath it, swiping angrily at the tears coursing down her cheeks. She was mortified and furious at William's unfair accusations. What made him think that she was married? Was it just the name change or was there something else?

She had to leave the following morning but where she would go she had no idea. She drew in a sharp, shuddering breath in an attempt to calm her shattered nerves. She'd appreciated that her decision to return to Australia was a risk but she hadn't considered the possibility of being without shelter and financial stability so quickly.

Determined not to weep any longer, she took a few moments to collect herself before she stood and made her way back to the house. She'd come this far, so she wouldn't crumble under pressure from the unknown. She'd survive as she always did and she *would* get by. She would speak to Mrs. Thompson when she returned from running the household errands. Perhaps the housekeeper could offer some advice regarding other possible positions.

As Lillian stepped into the hall of the house, William appeared in the doorway of the drawing room.

"Miss Hamilton, please may I speak with you a moment?"

Lillian paused, wondering what more he could possibly say to her. Curiosity overcame her wariness, however, and she followed as he led the way to his study. He stopped and sat behind a large mahogany desk. She stood facing him uncertainly.

William gestured for her to take a seat opposite him. "You've been crying. I'm sorry to have caused you so much distress. I apologize for my less than civil behavior earlier. Your appearance caught me off guard."

She perched on the edge of her chair and gave him a curt nod in acceptance of his apology.

"I would like you to assume the governess position. I understand if—after my behavior—you wish to leave, but I would like you to listen to what I have to say."

Lillian willed herself to meet his gaze and lifted her chin. "Go on." She was amazed at the steadiness in her voice and gave herself a mental pat on the back.

He cleared his throat. "I think that if we can forget the past and focus on the future and maintain a professional relationship, then I don't see any reason why this can't work. I have two children—Edward, who is seven, and Clara, who is five. They are good children and need a governess to see to their education and, to a certain extent, their upbringing regarding etiquette and appropriate behavior. You will be satisfactorily paid and, of course, you will have room and board. I have set aside a small room upstairs to serve as a classroom. I think your instruction would be beneficial for them and I know that your education is more than sufficient for the role. I won't ask anything about your life, since we knew each other before. Your past is your business and your business alone. I don't know the circumstances that brought you here but I won't see you put out if you require a position and shelter. I'm definitely not that vindictive."

Lillian needed a moment to process his words. He was studying her intently, trying to read her features for a reaction.

She stood and paced to the window to think. While she was thankful that William had given her a chance to stay, his words—so devoid of emotion—left her feeling cold and desolate. But the inescapable fact was that she had no other options. She must stay and make the best of a bad situation. The children were the priority and should provide a much-needed diversion and keep her busy enough that she wouldn't think too often about William and their past. And provided they kept out of each other's way as much as possible, she might minimize any additional hurt that being so near to him again would surely bring.

She turned to face him and her breath caught as she was struck yet again by how handsome he was. He'd always been a good-looking young man and he'd grown into a strikingly attractive gentleman. But there was also a harder, more uncompromising quality about him that at once intrigued her and made her slightly nervous. She shrugged off this last thought and came to a decision.

"Thank you for your offer, Mr. Cartwright. The children, of course, must be the priority and as you believe me to be capable of performing the governess role then I will accept."

He nodded and Lillian thought she detected a quick flash of relief cross his features before he rearranged his face once more into an impassive mask.

She felt that she had to offer her condolences and before her courage failed her, she resumed speaking. "I'm very sorry for the loss of your brother and your wife. It must have been a terrible time for you and the children."

He gazed at her intently for a moment and Lillian felt her stomach bottom out at the intensity of his stare.

"Thank you," he responded finally. "James' death was a shock to us all. It was a freak accident that took us all by surprise. It happened just before I left for the war. It was some relief, however, that he didn't leave a wife or children. My wife had been ill for some time and while her passing was extremely distressing, it was not wholly unexpected. We all miss her terribly, particularly the children."

He turned away from her quickly and looked at his pocket watch. "Mrs. Thompson should be returning at any moment. She will show you to your room and assist you in getting settled. The children are currently with her in town. You will meet them tomorrow."

He stood and moved toward the door then turned to look at her, a softness crossing his features. "I'm glad that you've decided to stay," he said quietly then left the room.

Lillian sank onto the window seat and let out a deep breath as she reviewed their conversation. William had been cool and impersonal, but at least she had somewhere to live indefinitely. It would take some time to become accustomed to the formality of the situation, but she agreed with William that it was for the best for both of them to maintain a distance — professional and aloof.

Chapter Four

The evening was chilly and peaceful. Lillian had forgotten how solitary and quiet the nights were in the outback and how beautiful and clear the sky was—a vast, ebony blanket dotted with twinkling lights. She'd finished her unpacking and had come outside for a moment of quiet contemplation before she retired.

She reflected on her conversation with Mrs. Thompson when the housekeeper had returned to the property. Mrs. Thompson had said that she'd assumed, based on the letter from Lillian's aunt, that Lillian knew to whom she'd been referring when she had written about Mr. Cartwright. She hadn't intended to be deceitful. There had just been a miscommunication along the way.

Lillian had no idea how her aunt had come across the information about the death of William's wife and his subsequent requirement of a governess but it mattered little. She was at Mulga Creek now and she had to make the best of her situation.

She took a deep breath and inhaled the unique scents she had only ever experienced in the outback. The aroma of eucalyptus and campfire smoke that drifted to her on the evening breeze brought back fond memories from childhood and she smiled wistfully as she recalled a time full of laughter and carefree days. She drew her gown closer around her and leaned against the side of the house, taking comfort in the solitude and the familiar.

She was studying the stars and re-familiarizing herself with the southern hemisphere constellations when she heard the sound of running water from the other side of the house. She tiptoed to the end of the deck and, conscious of her stark white nightgown, stayed in the shadows peering over the railing to investigate the noise.

Her breath caught in appreciation as she spied William. Naked from the waist up, he stood by the yard water pump. She had thought he looked good with his shirt on, but nothing could have prepared her for the sight of his bare torso. She studied his physique with fascination, enjoying the way his hard, spectacular chest muscles rippled in the moonlight as he bent to scoop water over his head. His dusty bush hat and equally dusty work shirt lay next to his booted feet, indicating that he'd just come in from working the paddocks. Water drops clung to the fine sprinkling of dark chest hair that followed the lean trail of his washboard stomach. Her gaze lingered over the defined V of his abdomen then dropped lower, following the V as it disappeared beneath the waistband of his trousers. His overly long, wavy hair glistened wetly in the moonlight and dripped water over his back and shoulders.

She knew she shouldn't be watching him. It wasn't proper, but she couldn't tear her eyes away from his muscular form. She wondered what it would feel like to have that hard body pressed against hers, to have his strong arms enveloping her and offering her comfort and protection. A warm glow flared low in her belly and a clenching beat started between her thighs.

She drew her breath in sharply and in doing so, drew William's attention to her.

He spun around quickly, narrowing his eyes as his gaze alighted on her shadowed form.

"What are you doing hiding there in the dark, Miss Hamilton? Come out where I can see you."

Lillian took a tentative step forward, then another, until she was no longer shrouded in darkness. As she drew closer to William, she saw his mouth curve in amusement.

"Enjoying the show?" he asked, his tone low and mocking.

Lillian's cheeks burned with embarrassment. She was mortified that she'd been caught spying on him and was unable to invent a reasonable explanation.

"I'm sorry. I'll let you have some privacy."

She turned to go, but he stepped toward her and grasped her wrist.

"Not so fast, Lilly."

She jumped at the unfamiliar use of his pet name for her and swung around to face him. He was so close that his body heat permeated the soft fabric of her nightgown and sent warmth radiating through her limbs. He tugged her closer, pressing her breasts against his damp chest, then slipped her dressing gown from her shoulders and tossed it aside.

Her breath caught at the feel of his damp skin through the filmy fabric of her nightdress.

"Do you like what you see?" he whispered in her ear. His warm breath sent shivers through her, hardening her nipples to taut points.

"I think you do," he continued. "I feel your arousal."

Lillian struggled against his hold, appalled at her body's embarrassing reaction to him.

"Turn around," he rumbled in her ear, spinning her so that his front was snug against her back. He splayed one large hand over her throat and tilted her head back, resting it on his shoulder. Her heart beat a frantic tattoo against her ribcage and a tightness coiled heavily in her loins. She knew that her reaction to William was wrong, but she couldn't help her primal response to him. Only in her dreams had she ever imagined their two bodies being so close again.

Keeping his left hand at her throat, he ran his right down her shoulder and arm until he reached her breast. "Let me touch you."

She shivered at his illicit caress and a soft moan escaped her. When she made no move to pull away, he cupped her right breast and ran his thumb over her erect nipple then rolled it between thumb and forefinger. She gasped and wriggled against him.

"Shh, my sweet," he murmured at her ear, eliciting another shiver from her traitorous body.

He palmed her right breast before moving to her left, running his palm across that nipple softly, testing its stretch. "So responsive. So ripe." His voice vibrated hoarse and hot against her flesh.

She groaned and arched her back to press her breast harder into his hand.

"Feel how heavy your breasts are? It's your desire that makes them so full and weighty." He ran his left hand down to join his right and cupped heavy mounds, weighing them and using his thumb and forefinger to tug on each of her nipples.

The sensations were so unfamiliar, so intense. Her insides quivered and a liquid heat suffused her limbs, turning her weak and pliable. She slumped against William in total supplication as he continued to work her nipples into impossibly hard points. A whimper left her throat and she rubbed against him, gripping his strong forearms to steady herself. She could feel the hard length of his arousal against her lower back. It should have shocked her but it only inflamed her further and made the deep ache in her belly throb more insistently.

"*Please.*" She was unsure what she was begging for but understood that she needed some relief from the sensations that were swamping her.

"Please what, Lilly? What do you want?"

"I... I don't know," she stammered.

He ran his hands lower to her hips and started to draw her nightgown up slowly until she felt the cool evening breeze against her fevered flesh. She was aware of the dampness seeping between her thighs and she pressed her legs together, trying to give herself some relief from the feelings roiling low in her belly.

"I know what you need. Let me feel you," he said, his voice low and husky. "Let me feel that hot, wet pussy of yours."

Lillian gasped in shock at his crude words but spread her legs wide, not able to stop her body operating automatically to seek alleviation from the needy, throbbing sensations that were overwhelming her.

"That's it, my sweet," he coaxed. "Open wide for me."

He swept his hand from her hip to curl in the soft hair between her thighs. "So wet and ready." He slipped a finger inside her. "So hot and tight."

She groaned loudly and thrust against his hand as he caressed her. Never had she felt such pleasure—the internal quivering of her muscles was almost too much to bear and she tried to close her legs, but he was ready for her. He made a soft *tsking* sound in her ear and gripped one of her thighs, widening her stance and preventing her from closing her legs. He caressed across her folds, finding her clitoris. He pressed down, thrusting two fingers into her channel and stroking her inner wall.

"Just here," he murmured.

She cried out, her body convulsing against his. Sudden waves of pleasure pulsed through her, her vision blurred and she seemed to float outside of her body. She'd never felt such a sweet euphoria like had just surged through her from head to toe, leaving her weak and lightheaded.

She slumped against William in confusion and lethargy as he continued to caress her most intimate place.

"Christ, you're responsive," he groaned, his voice full of reverent wonder. "Just one touch and you're coming apart in my arms."

He banded a muscular arm tightly around her waist while with the other he thrust one, then two fingers roughly inside her, pushing deeply.

Pain shot through her at the cruel invasion and she cried out and struggled in his grasp.

William froze. "Fuck, Lillian—you're a virgin?" He pushed her away and turned her to face him.

Lillian didn't want to admit that she was. William thought that she was married—or at least had assumed that she'd *been* married. And she wanted that shield—needed that protection. The fact that she'd been married meant that she hadn't been pining away for ten years thinking about William with his wife. It was proof that she hadn't turned away every man because of the unrequited love that she harbored for another.

She thought quickly, trying to come up with a reasonable excuse.

"No, I'm not a virgin," she proclaimed, using her best indignant voice. "I've been married."

William narrowed his eyes and cocked his head to one side studying her.

"I don't believe you," he said eventually. "I'm quite experienced where women are concerned and I know a virgin when I come across one."

"Of all the insolent, arrogant things to say," she hissed. "I don't care what you believe, *Mr. Cartwright.* I don't have to explain anything to you."

"You're correct. You owe me no explanations. I'm just glad that things didn't go any further. I can't believe that I've already broken the rules that I laid out so carefully this morning. I'm sorry. Please forgive me. It won't happen again," he promised.

He stooped to collect his shirt and hat and with a quick bow in her direction, he turned abruptly and stalked toward the house.

Lillian breathed out a sigh of frustration. She'd forgotten how good he could make her feel. She'd never felt as alive as she had just now in his arms. Her skin still tingled deliciously from their connection, as though her every nerve ending was a charged wire.

She bent to pick up her dressing gown and slipped it on, pulling it tightly around her body as she walked slowly to the house. She hated the sense of remorse and sadness that swept over her. A cold, heavy feeling settled in her chest at the thought that she would never again feel the delicious pleasure that he had elicited so easily with his touch.

Chapter Five

William strode into his study and poured himself a hefty slug of whiskey from a decanter on a sideboard. He swallowed the liquor in one gulp before pouring himself a second, less generous serving. He shoved a hand through his hair in anger and sank into a wingback chair. He couldn't believe what he'd done with Lillian. What had possessed him? He supposed it was the fact that she'd been watching him with obvious desire that had spurred him to his impulsive and careless behavior.

He groaned aloud with pent-up longing and frustration. *Fuck.* Never had a woman felt so good in his arms. Those lush curves and her silky skin had made him heady with lust.

Thinking about her breasts, so heavy with desire, and her tight little nipples made his cock throb with insatiable need. To make matters worse, her scent was all over him, the proof of her pleasure and lust enveloping him in a sweet, aromatic cloud that was doing nothing to abate his relentless hard-on.

"Christ," he muttered in agony. Staring into the crackling fire, he took another swallow of whiskey.

The feel of Lillian's hot, tight little notch clenching around his fingers had nearly unmanned him. Never had he wanted a woman as he'd wanted her at that moment. He thought about her assertion that she'd been married and was sure that his initial impression had been correct and that she was, in fact, untouched. But if that was the case, why the hell had her marriage been unconsummated? No man he could imagine would be resistant to her charms and beauty, particularly not if they belonged to him.

He was unprepared for the fierce anger that swept through him at the possibility that she might *not* be a virgin. His body shook with the sheer vehemence of his emotions as he thought about another man touching her. No, he would not contemplate the image of her being intimate with another. Of course, for years he'd assumed she was married and had tormented himself with thoughts about her in the arms of her husband, but after what had just transpired between them, he wasn't so sure about anything.

Her body's natural response to him had been amazing. She'd been open and uninhibited and she'd been so wet with desire that he'd wanted to sink to his knees and lose himself in her scent and her taste. His mouth watered as he envisaged spreading her sweet folds and thrusting his tongue deep inside her. A fierce shudder rocked through him, his cock straining against his pants at the image. *Fuck.* He had to think of something else before he blew his load like an inexperienced schoolboy.

Abruptly, thoughts of his wife crowded his mind and swiftly his raging erection deflated. He sighed deeply as a vision of Ruth intruded upon his thoughts. Ruth had always been obliging in the marital bed, but he'd suspected that she hadn't overly enjoyed the act of lovemaking and she most certainly had never responded in the brazen and needy fashion that Lillian just had. His very thoughts about such a matter left him riddled with guilt but he couldn't help but compare the two. He'd loved his wife with a steady loyalty. However, theirs had never been an all-consuming, passionate union but a solid and dependable association that had suited them both.

Lillian had changed in the ten years since he'd seen her. She was still beautiful. In fact, she was even lovelier than he remembered, but it was the change in her character that was most notable. She was no longer a sweet, flighty girl but a mature, almost solemn, young woman. He wondered what had happened, what she'd endured to take the sparkle out of her exceptional emerald eyes. It killed him that he didn't know anything of her immediate past and cut him to the core that something had occurred to affect her so deeply. He clenched his fists in impotence and frustration.

Now that she'd re-entered his life and he'd so carelessly given in to temptation and had tasted the forbidden fruit, he feared for his sanity and well-being even more. If he'd kept his distance as he'd promised himself he would, then his head wouldn't now be filled with libidinous and lustful images — images unfortunately he knew would never leave him, making him more determined than ever to re-establish the professional boundaries between himself and Lillian.

* * * *

Lillian hadn't slept well. Thoughts of William and his dexterous and experienced fingers had haunted her dreams and left her feeling tired and fractious. Luckily, William's children provided her with a welcome diversion and she was delighted when they enthusiastically showed their excitement at having a governess. They were also polite and respectful and Lillian looked forward to teaching them. She suspected that the poor little things had been left largely to their own devices since the passing of their mother and she threw herself into the role of caregiver, educator and friend with relish and enthusiasm, and was pleased to discover that their mother had progressed their learning quite substantially.

Lillian had not spoken to William all day. She'd watched out of her bedroom window when he'd ridden out early that morning and had marveled at the site of him on his horse. She could see how dashing and distinguished a Light Horseman he would have been. He handled his horse so confidently and he looked so handsome astride the large animal while he trotted around, ensuring that the men knew their duties. She could only imagine how commanding and formidable he would have looked in uniform.

William had not joined the household for lunch. Mrs. Thompson explained that he'd be out all day, driving the cattle from one paddock to another, and wouldn't be arriving back at the homestead until later that day.

When he'd not appeared at dinner, she suspected he was avoiding her. She should have been grateful but she was surprised at the hurt his evasion caused her.

Later that evening, sitting by the fire with Mrs. Thompson in the kitchen darning the children's socks, she heard William arrive home. A moment later, his footsteps sounded on the stairs as he made his way to the children's room to kiss them goodnight. She couldn't help her sharp intake of breath as she acknowledged his presence in the house. Mrs. Thompson looked up from her work and gave her a sympathetic smile.

"Why don't you talk to him, Lillian?" she asked gently.

"I can't. He's made his feelings very clear," she responded softly. "He is determined to keep things between us professional, which I respect and I agree with. I just don't understand what I did to make him dislike me so much."

Mrs. Thompson gave her a compassionate look. "Perhaps you both need to talk things through," she suggested. "I think there must be a lot of things left unsaid and unexplained between you. Nothing will be resolved if you don't communicate."

Lillian sighed heavily. "You're right, of course, but I don't believe William agrees with you."

"Give him time, Lillian. Your return to Mulga Creek has confused him. He's accustomed to controlling every aspect of his life, and the fact that he obviously has unresolved feelings for you is upsetting his equilibrium."

Lillian arched an eyebrow in surprise. "I'm obviously upsetting his equilibrium but I don't believe it's due to unresolved feelings."

Mrs. Thompson smiled and patted her hand. "You'll work things out. I remember how close you both were when you were younger. A friendship like that can't be so easily disregarded. You also have to keep in mind Mr. Cartwright's experiences in the war. He was a very well-decorated and respected Light Horseman, although he doesn't speak a great deal about what happened over there. There is no doubt that he was a changed man when he returned. More somber...and he can be quite controlling at times. I think he became so used to giving orders that it's hard for him to let go. But don't you worry. I have complete faith that everything will work out," she finished brightly.

Lillian wished she had half of Mrs. Thompson's faith and she wondered, not for the first time, how much the woman knew of their childhood intimacy. She finished neatly sewing closed a small hole in Edward's sock when her thoughts drifted to William's wife and her desire to learn more about the woman who had stolen William's heart.

"What was Ruth like?" she asked.

Mrs. Thompson raised her eyebrows in surprise and thought a moment before answering. "She was a good woman—loyal and faithful and a loving mother. She doted on the children. Her death was extremely hard on them and they are only now just starting to come to terms with their loss. I do believe your presence here will be good for them, Lillian. They need a young woman in their life—not to take the place of their mother, of course, but to provide them with love and affection and guidance. I love them like they're my own, but I'm more of a grandmother figure to them."

Lillian considered Mrs. Thompson's words. "They *are* lovely children and I can see myself becoming attached to them."

"Ruth would approve of you," the other woman stated matter-of-factly.

"Was she beautiful—Ruth?"

Mrs. Thompson frowned. "Not in the traditional sense. I believe she would have been described as handsome. She had good, strong features and a lovely nature, which made people *think* she was beautiful."

Lillian nodded. "I would have liked to have met her. I only hope that I do her memory justice and teach her children as efficiently as she has done."

The other woman smiled. "I'm sure that you will. In fact, I'm positive of it. Now, while I remember, I should tell you that Mr. George Dawson, who owns the property adjoining ours, is hosting a dance and supper tomorrow evening with his daughter, Margaret. It will do you good to get out and socialize and it will also be a good opportunity for you to meet some of the local families."

Lillian wasn't sure if she felt much like mingling with new people but she supposed Mrs. Thompson was right. Admittedly, she was curious about their neighbors, and perhaps some dancing and music would lighten her spirits, helping her to forget William, even if only for a short while.

Chapter Six

Lillian assessed her reflection in the bedroom mirror. She'd dressed with care in her one and only decent dress. It was a long-waisted velvet gown in emerald green that plunged quite daringly in the front. She was beyond thankful that she'd had the forethought to keep it when she'd sold the remainder of her gowns. She'd wrapped a matching green scarf around her head, turban-style, and she wore her only necklace, a set of long pearls, which she'd knotted at her breasts. They'd belonged to her mother and she hadn't been able to part with them. When she'd sold the majority of her aunt's jewelry, she'd kept her mother's pearls and a delicate gold filigree bracelet belonging to her aunt. She stepped into her only pair of evening shoes of black velvet and twirled in front of the mirror. She was happy with her appearance. The deep emerald green of her gown matched her eyes and highlighted them perfectly. She wrapped an ornately crocheted woolen shawl around her shoulders to ward off the winter evening chill and picked up a black velvet drawstring bag.

Lillian made her way downstairs and met Mrs. Thompson in the hallway, looking very smart in a navy blue wool dress and matching hat.

"Lillian, you look beautiful," she cried enthusiastically. "You will be beating the men away with a stick!"

Lillian laughed delightedly and followed the sounds of excited children into the drawing room. She'd dressed the children earlier that evening and was relieved to find that they'd managed to stay relatively neat and tidy.

"You look so pretty, Miss Hamilton," Clara stated, her eyes wide with awe and admiration.

Lillian bent and gave the child a peck on the cheek. "Thank you, my darling."

As she straightened, she came face to face with William. Their gazes locked and they stared at each other, quietly assessing. They'd not spoken since their encounter in the back garden and there was a moment of awkward silence until William addressed her.

"You are looking lovely this evening, Miss Hamilton." He bowed slightly in deference.

"Thank you, Mr. Cartwright. You too look quite dashing, if I may say so," she said, blushing.

He did look good—very good. His black evening jacket fit his broad shoulders perfectly and his trousers were expertly tailored to emphasize his narrow waist and lean hips while hugging his derrière deliciously. She was pleased to see that he'd left his hair to wave naturally and forgone the slick, greased-back hairstyle that was so popular among men of the day. The sudden urge to run her fingers through his unruly locks overwhelmed her and she clasped her hands behind her back before she could act on the impulse.

William gifted her with a tight smile before he grasped his children's hands.

"Come, little ones. There is a party awaiting us," he announced theatrically, sending the children into fits of laughter. Turning, he stepped aside and inclined his head in invitation for Lillian and Mrs. Thompson to precede him through the door and out into the waiting automobile.

* * * *

The party was in full swing when they arrived at the Dawson property. The large wool shed had been gaily decorated with lanterns and garlands. Tables, covered in crisp white cloths, lined the entirety of the back wall and were laden with punch bowls, sandwiches, cold meats and salads. Chairs and round tables sat scattered about the vast space, offering cozy areas where guests could relax and rest their feet. A band was playing popular dance tunes. The whole ambience was one of merriment and fun, and Lillian found herself smiling widely at the infectious mood.

The children squealed in delight and ran off to join their friends as Mrs. Thompson moved off toward a group of older ladies, leaving Lillian and William alone.

Lillian looked up at him and thought yet again how good he looked in a dinner suit—suave and sophisticated. He was easily one of the handsomest men at the gathering. Already he'd drawn the attention of several ladies and men. It was not only his looks but also his presence, she reasoned. He was so formidable and held himself with such an air of authority that it was impossible to overlook him.

"It was good of you to invite Mrs. Thompson and me tonight," she commented. "I wouldn't have expected to come. After all, we just work for you."

He looked surprised. "Why wouldn't I invite you both? As far as I'm concerned, Millie is part of the family—even more so since her husband died. You know she's been with our household since I was born, and it was a good opportunity for you to meet some of the local families."

"All the same, thank you for including me."

He nodded, his hazel eyes burning into hers. "Come. Let me introduce you to some people," he murmured, placing his palm on her lower back and gently propelling her forward.

William looked down to where his hand rested on the small of Lillian's back and battled the urge not to drag her hard against him. He'd barely been able to contain himself when he'd first seen her that evening at the house. He'd at once wanted to ravish her and lock her in her room so other men wouldn't be able to look upon her. She looked so stunning it was all he could do not to drop his head and lose himself against her creamy throat and lush cleavage.

He steered them in the direction of George Dawson's group with the intention of introducing Lillian. He looked around as they traversed the room, furiously noting the attention she was receiving from all the men in the gathering. He gritted his teeth and pretended not to notice when a young man deliberately brushed against her. He tried hard to look impassive when other men stooped low to bow to her in awed admiration and, no doubt, he thought, to get an eyeful of her bountiful bosom. He looked down at Lillian to gauge her reaction at all the attention she was receiving and was pleased to note her blushing with such a self-effacing attitude as to make her even more appealing.

Finally, after what seemed like an eternity, they reached Dawson.

"Sir, thank you for hosting the dinner dance this evening," William stated and bowed in greeting. "Please allow me to introduce Miss Lillian Hamilton, my children's new governess."

Lillian took Mr. Dawson's extended hand as he murmured a welcome. She didn't miss the fact that his eyes seemed glued to her décolletage and for the first time, she wondered if her dress was too daring for the likes of an outback dinner dance. She straightened and pulled her shawl tighter around her shoulders, noting William's scowl in George Dawson's direction. William tugged her closer to his side and introduced her to the other guests in the circle. Something in his voice made Lillian glance at him when he made the introduction to Miss Margaret Dawson and she couldn't miss the young lady's blush and averted gaze when William looked upon her.

She was very pretty—plump and vivacious with a sleek cap of blonde hair cut into a fashionable bob, which was no doubt considered highly irregular in the outback community. It was a cut that Lillian had considered, but she hadn't had the time or the inclination to indulge in a new hairstyle while her aunt had been so sick.

Could it be possible that William and this Miss Dawson had some sort of connection? She hoped fervently that she was mistaken but she planned to study the pair some more during the course of the evening to determine if there was any affection between them.

She was pondering the question when a young man materialized before her, introduced himself as Mr. John Steele and asked her to dance. She glanced to her side and noticed that William was deep in conversation with Margaret and Mr. Dawson. Seeing that she wouldn't be missed and glad of the diversion, she accepted. Smiling, the young man escorted her onto the dance floor and whirled her into a fast-paced waltz.

Lillian exhilarated in the music and the dancing. It had been a long time since she'd been able to enjoy herself. Her aunt had been sick for so long, and afterward, she'd had the worry and responsibility of managing the will and discharging her father's debts so she couldn't remember when last she'd been able to relax. And young John Steele was an enjoyable dance partner. He was enthusiastic and danced with a practiced confidence that made Lillian all the more at ease with her own ability.

He looked down at her and twirled her effortlessly around the floor. "So I hear that you're Cartwright's new governess. Do you know the family well?"

"I knew them a long time ago, before my family moved to England. "

"How well do you know William Cartwright?"

The question surprised Lillian and she wondered if there was more to his inquiry. She decided that she'd play down her previous association. "We were childhood friends but as I said, we've not seen each other for ten years."

She looked up at him and wondered at the play of emotions crossing his features.

"We served together as Light Horsemen, which was quite common, given that we're all excellent horsemen here in the bush," he said with a self-effacing laugh. "He was an officer in my regiment, a good military man." He grimaced. "He was well decorated but you wouldn't want to get on the wrong side of him."

Lillian frowned in puzzlement. She hadn't known William ever to display a particularly bad disposition but then everyone knew that the war could change people.

"I hate to mention anything—what happens away, stays away and all that—but I just think that you should be careful around him. He has quite a temper. Let me just say that his boxing skills are legendary and there has been more than one man on the receiving end of his fists."

Lillian stiffened at his allegations of William's violence. She wondered what it was all about but dismissed it as inconsequential. She wouldn't take anything that this stranger said at face value. "Thank you for your concern, Mr. Steele, but I can look after myself," she said coolly, effectively drawing a close to the topic of conversation.

Chapter Seven

William listened to George Dawson as he watched John Steele twirl Lillian elegantly onto the dance floor and hold her too closely for William's liking. He excused himself politely from Dawson's presence and cursed under his breath at the unfamiliar stirrings of jealousy.

He ran a hand through his hair in frustration and strode to the bar, trying unsuccessfully to divert his attention away from Lillian and Steele. He couldn't have chosen a worse dance partner for her if he'd tried. He had history with Steele but he couldn't cause a scene by yanking Lillian from the man's embrace.

He had to get a hold of himself *and* his emotions. Lillian had been gone for ten years and his feelings toward her should have diminished to fond sentiment. Instead, he was being reduced to acting like a jealous, overbearing paramour.

How had he expected that the sight of Lillian in another man's arms would not disturb him, particularly a thug like Steele? The vision of her being whirled around in his tight embrace had him practically wanting to beat the other man to a pulp.

His restless pacing brought him into the path of Miss Dawson, who curtsied prettily to him. This was what he needed—a distraction only a pretty woman could provide. He bowed briefly and offered her his hand to dance. Two could play at this game, he thought grimly, as he placed his palm in the small of Miss Dawson's back and pulled her to his chest.

He looked down into her upturned face and didn't miss the flirtatious fluttering of her eyelashes as she gazed up at him. She was very attractive and he'd thought so for quite some time. She had that rounded plumpness that was appealing to hold, and her face, while not beautiful, was charmingly pretty.

Perhaps Miss Dawson was the diversion he wanted. He pulled her body tighter against his. He knew her father would be more than pleased if he and Margaret formed a connection and William had been visiting the Dawson property with that thought in the back of his mind. But Lillian's reappearance had altered things considerably and while he was attracted to Margaret, he didn't feel anything like the passion and lust he felt when he looked at Lillian. Those feelings, however, had given him nothing but heartache in the past so it was best to harden himself against them.

Perhaps if he tried harder with Margaret, he would, over time, develop similar feelings for her. He gritted his teeth as another bout of anger swept through him at Lillian's untimely and irritating return to his life.

He smiled down at the young woman in his arms and tried to work up some enthusiasm for the dance, but perhaps some quiet time was what they really required, time away from the crowd of people where they could talk.

When the band ended the music with a flourish and the couples started clapping politely, he grasped Margaret by the hand and pulled her in the direction of the door.

Lillian watched William lead Margaret Dawson outside and away from the party revelers. She wanted to follow them and, taking her hand from Mr. Steele's, she asked if they could get some fresh air. The young man was obviously delighted with the prospect of being alone with her and complied with alacrity, unwittingly following William and his lady friend, as he steered Lillian outside.

The evening had grown quite chilly and the young man wrapped an arm about Lillian's shoulders as they strolled. She knew she should shrug off his attentions but she was cold and wanted the comfort of his proximity. They walked and chatted about the dance. She was trying to calculate the direction that William would have taken when she heard a woman's giggle and a man's deep voice. Her chaperone, also having heard the couple, drew up short of a building and pulled Lillian close as they peered around the corner.

There, bathed in the moonlight, stood William and Miss Dawson. She was leaning back against a wooden fence, gazing up into William's face and laughing at something he'd said. Lillian's breath caught and her heart rate thumped a tattoo in her chest. It was clear that Miss Dawson obviously felt some attraction to William, but William's feelings toward the woman were less obvious. She couldn't bear to watch anymore, in case she was to witness William kiss her. She couldn't believe he would so brazenly seek out this young lady after what he'd done with her only two evenings before. She felt terribly betrayed by him yet again. He was obviously nothing but an exploitative cad.

Lillian whirled around and started back toward the wool shed. She'd forget about William Cartwright and any feelings she had once had for him. As she reached the door, Mr. Steele caught up with her and, grasping her around the waist, he turned her to face him.

"Where are you going?" he breathed in her ear.

"I'm sorry but I'd like to return inside," Lillian muttered, pushing against the man's weight.

"Don't I get a kiss?" He cupped her chin to hold her head in place. "After all, I thought that was why you wanted to take a stroll outside."

She could have kicked herself for her stupidity. In her haste to spy on William, she hadn't thought about the consequences of stepping out of doors at night with a strange gentleman.

She tried once again, unsuccessfully, to struggle out of his grasp and raised her voice, not giving him any room for misinterpretation. "Please, let me go."

Suddenly William was there and Steele's body weight lifted off her. William grasped him by the throat, spun him around and pushed him hard up against the wall.

"It's not polite to force a lady's hand, Steele," he snarled. "Leave, now, before I'm forced to do something that you and I may regret!"

Lillian watched in apprehension as Steele flexed his fists by his sides and glowered at William, weighing whether to retaliate.

Anticipating Steele's actions, William spoke again. "Don't try anything. You know who the loser will be."

She watched Steele struggle with his decision then he abruptly pushed William away. He turned toward

Lillian, gave her a slight bow and a tight smile, then whirled on his heel and stalked inside.

William turned his murderous gaze on Lillian. "What do you think you were doing out here with a man you've just met this evening?"

"I wonder that you think to question me, Mr. Cartwright," she jeered. "When I noticed you with a young lady of your own."

"Miss Dawson and I have long been acquainted," he replied sharply. "And I'm not about to manhandle her as John Steele was about to do to you. I know him, Lillian, and I know that his intentions toward you would be less than honorable."

"Well, I thank you for your concern but I'm quite able to take care of myself," she said stiffly then turned to make her way back to the party.

William remained outside, trying to rein in his temper. The sight of that young prick pushing Lillian against the wall had sent him into a murderous rage. Steele was lucky that he'd maintained enough control to keep from punching him in the jaw. It was appalling behavior toward a lady—behavior he wouldn't tolerate.

He looked at his watch and decided it was time to leave. He'd had enough of watching all the men in the gathering slobbering and simpering over his governess. He would think twice before inviting her to such a function again. If he did, he would personally inspect her intended outfit before he would allow her to step one foot out of doors.

Chapter Eight

Lillian was happy that there were no lessons for the children the day following the dinner dance. They'd played games in the morning and done some painting before they'd stopped for lunch. Now Clara was taking her nap and Lillian had left Edward struggling sleepily with the novel *Robinson Crusoe*.

She'd decided to do some exploring in the afternoon. It had been too long since she'd investigated the delights of the Australian outback and its many flora and fauna. A long walk would give her some much-needed exercise and clear her head.

She was annoyed with herself for acting so sillily the previous evening when she'd seen William with Margaret Dawson. What had she expected? Of course women would be interested in William—he was not only handsome but also an extremely prosperous catch. It hurt her to acknowledge it, but she had no right to be jealous or upset by his attentions to other women. She needed to remember that she was just his employee and to act with a cool and professional approach to all things. It was much easier said than done, however.

She changed into an old dress and sensible shoes and tied a sun hat on her head. She wrapped some biscuits in a handkerchief and found a leather canteen in the kitchen pantry that she filled with water. She informed Mrs. Thompson that she was off to do some exploring around the station and set off along one of the many dirt tracks that wound around the extensive property.

She'd been walking for half an hour when she caught sight of a joey. It was a delightful creature and thoroughly enchanted her as it hopped along, nibbling the underbrush. She was overjoyed at once again experiencing the local wildlife and decided to follow the creature in the hopes that it would lead her to the adult female. She didn't think that a kangaroo that young would stray far from its mother.

She'd been following the little animal for quite a way, relishing its antics and playfulness. It had to be aware that Lillian was nearby but it had displayed no fear or concern at her presence. The joey rounded a tree and a large female came into view. Lillian stopped in her tracks, not wanting to antagonize the mother, and watched as the joey bounded over to nuzzle at its mother's pouch, requesting access. There were several other large adult kangaroos grazing and lazing in the shade of the trees. Lillian observed them for a moment longer then turned to find her way back to the dirt trail she'd been following, thinking that it was high time she made her way back to the homestead.

She walked a little way before she realized with a sinking dread that in her distraction with the joey she'd lost the track she'd been following. Wandering desperately in search of the trail, she tried to quell her rising panic. If she couldn't find it, she'd be hopelessly lost. She could kick herself for having been so careless. She remembered that it was too easy to become lost in the outback. There were very few unique landmarks and the vast expanse of space made losing one's way a very real possibility.

An hour later, she had to concede that it was a hopeless task. By the height of the sun and the diminishing daylight, she judged the time to be at least four p.m. Her only hope was to stay where she was and try to ride out the night. She was concerned about the cool winter evening ahead but with no matches, she had no way to light a fire. She walked to a nearby tree and collected some foliage and underbrush to pile into a makeshift pillow then sat to wait. She didn't expect anyone to find her quickly and she pushed to the back of her mind the possibility that she might not be found at all. Mrs. Thompson would notice her absence at dinner and raise the alarm. She could only sit, wait and try her best not to panic.

* * * *

William returned from mustering the sheep in time for dinner at six p.m. He cleaned up in the yard under the water pump and entered the kitchen to find a distraught Mrs. Thompson pacing by the slow-combustion stove.

"Mr. Cartwright, thank God you've come home this evening," she cried, wringing her hands in worry.

William's first thought was of the children but before he could voice his concern, the housekeeper anticipated him.

"The children are fine," she assured him quickly. "It's Miss Hamilton!"

William froze in place as a cold fear gripped him. "What's happened?" he demanded.

"She went for a walk earlier today, just after lunch, and she's not been seen since!"

The fear that had initially struck him took root and spread throughout his body. All manner of things rushed through his mind, not the least of which was the fact that Lillian was out alone, at night in winter and there were literally thousands of acres in which she could be.

Galvanized into action, William instructed Mrs. Thompson to organize food packages while he rushed to the Jackeroo and station hand quarters to round up the men.

Half an hour later, he sat astride Victory, his stock horse, and addressed the men, explaining the situation as Mrs. Thompson passed around food packages of beef jerky, biscuits and cheese.

He organized the men into two groups to head in different directions. Adoni, his good friend and one of the best Aboriginal trackers he knew, would ride with him.

"If you find anything, organize one of you to locate the others. You all know the direction in which we are each heading and you all know this land like the back of your hand. Remember, Miss Hamilton is on foot, so she can't have traveled too far."

The men gave him a salute in acknowledgment of their orders and turned their horses' heads in the direction of the search.

Fear gnawed at William's gut. Already the evening temperature had started to drop dramatically from that of the day. He knew that Lillian wouldn't have any warm clothing, nor would she have matches to light a fire, so it was imperative that they find her quickly. The dark would make it difficult for Adoni, but he was an excellent tracker, and William had faith that the man would soon pick up her trail.

He and Adoni gave the horses their heads and whipped them into a gallop as they sped across the nearest paddock toward the outer, larger enclosures where they would start their search.

* * * *

The evening cold relentlessly seeped into Lillian's bones. She'd tried to keep active by jumping up and down and maintaining her blood flow but she'd started to tire. It was too dark to keep wandering about. Besides, if there *were* people searching for her, she didn't want to run the risk of going in circles and walking back on herself, which would only confuse matters. No, she had to have faith that someone would find her soon. She started to shiver—hard, racking shudders that sent her teeth chattering noisily.

In the distance, she heard an owl hoot, a lonely, haunting sound in the absolute blackness that did nothing to quell her nerves.

She squinted and tried to peer into the inky depths that surrounded her and added shudders of fear to those of cold, as a low howl rent the night. She'd heard stories of dingoes and how they sometimes attacked humans. Her predicament suddenly presented another, more sinister element.

"Oh God, please help me," she prayed fervently, wrapping her arms about her bended knees and rocking back and forth in an effort to ward off her rising panic.

* * * *

William and Adoni had been riding hard for over an hour. They'd stopped a couple of times for the tracker to search the earth for signs of Lillian. Half an hour earlier, he'd found a footprint and signs of crushed undergrowth. Lillian had obviously been following a trail, but what had possessed her to wander from it, William had no idea. Adoni was walking his horse, stopping frequently to study the ground for clues of Lillian's movements while William held aloft the hurricane lamp to cast light on his search area. William willed himself to remain patient and allow the tracker to do his thing. He knew that Adoni would not be rushed and William wouldn't want to risk losing her trail by trying to hurry.

His concern was growing by the minute as the evening temperature dropped to what he reckoned to be forty degrees Fahrenheit. Adoni had picked up the tracks of dingoes not far behind those of Lillian. The wild dogs could be stalking her. They'd been known to do such things and, like any wild predator, they possessed a sixth sense where vulnerable prey was concerned—particularly if they were traveling in a pack.

He waited impatiently for Adoni to indicate the way forward and urged his steed into a canter when the tracker gesticulated urgently. A moment later, a high-pitched scream pierced the night, a sound so full of terror that it raised the hairs on the back of William's neck.

"Fuck!" he shouted, urging Victory into a gallop and racing toward the sound. He prayed with everything in his being that he wasn't too late.

* * * *

Lillian prayed for rescue or daylight—whichever came first. The profound darkness and utter isolation was alarming and heightening her panic level to the extreme. She took deep breaths and gave herself a pep talk, willing herself not to overreact. She strained her ears for any sounds, any noises to indicate that someone might be on their way to her rescue, and that's when she heard it—the frantic scrabbling in the underbrush nearby. She snapped her head around, searching for the cause, and saw them—four pairs of glowing yellow eyes, creating a menacing spectacle in the blackness.

Her heart stuttered in fear when she realized the eyes belonged to dingoes. Her blood ran cold and she screamed—a long, terrifying sound that sent roosting birds screeching into the night sky. Through her anxiety and dread, she heard the thunder of hoof beats heading in her direction then the loud crack of a rifle shot. She turned desperately in the direction of the horses and caught the unmistakable cry of William's voice.

"Lillian!"

She managed to stumble into a standing position as William's horse galloped toward her.

"William!" she screamed.

He reined his horse in hard and vaulted from the saddle. She ran into his embrace, sobbing in relief as she felt him band his strong arms around her protectively. He hugged her to him quickly before gently pushing her back to run his hands up and down her body, checking for injuries.

"My God, you're frozen," he said into her hair, encircling her once more in his arms.

The adrenaline left her body and shock started to set in. She slumped against him, her teeth chattering uncontrollably as shivers racked through her.

William spoke to Adoni above Lillian's head. "I won't be able to take Miss Hamilton back to the homestead yet. Find the others and tell them that she's suffering from shock and exposure. I'll build a fire and we'll shelter here until she's well enough to travel."

Adoni gave a brief nod of acknowledgment and set off at a gallop to meet up with the others.

"The d-dogs," she stammered between chattering teeth.

"The commotion and my rifle shot have scared them off for the time being," William soothed, wrapping her in his oilskin coat. "The fire will ensure they keep their distance. I need to get you warm before you die of hypothermia."

He unslung his .303 rifle from his shoulder and rummaged through a saddlebag then passed Lillian a blanket. "Here, wrap this around you while I light a fire."

She draped the rough wool about her shoulders gratefully and watched William set about collecting kindling and branches for a fire. He finally set the wood alight and blew gently until the flames took hold.

He sat, tugged Lillian down into his lap and enfolded her in his arms. She tried to stop shivering but she still felt so cold. She continued to shudder and William pulled her tighter against his body, rubbing her arms briskly.

"Oh, Lillian," he sighed heavily into her hair. "I was so worried about you. We could tell that you were following the trail but then we saw that you left it and wandered into the bush. What were you thinking?"

"I was following a joey. I just lost track of my surroundings. I know it was silly and stupid of me. I just wasn't thinking. I'm so sorry for all the trouble I've caused you," she sobbed into his chest.

"Hush now. The only trouble was to my peace of mind. I was going insane with worry. I think the men were quite thrilled with the opportunity to perform a search and rescue. This is the most excitement they've had in a while. You definitely know how to shake things up," he said in a mock stern voice, trying for levity.

"I was so scared," she whispered. "Well, I wasn't doing too badly until the dogs came." She shuddered at the memory. "Until then, it was just the cold and dark, but the thought of what those dogs could do to me frightened me more than anything."

"It's over now and you're safe. Try not to think about it," he crooned against her ear as he rocked her gently.

Gradually, she started to feel better and the shivers racking her body began to subside.

William deposited her gently beside him and moved to get supplies from the saddlebag. "I'm going to brew some tea. You need to drink something warm and sweet."

A few minutes later, the water finished boiling. He put tea leaves into a mug then added a few teaspoons of sugar. "Here, drink this. It will make you feel better," he said handing her the mug of tea before making one of his own.

Lillian took the tea gratefully and wrapped her fingers around the hot cup to inject some warmth into them.

William studied Lillian in the firelight as she sipped her tea and was relieved to see some color returning to her cheeks. The blanket lay draped around her shoulders and she clutched it to her with one hand while she tipped the mug to her lips with the other. Her disheveled hair fell in tangled ringlets around her face and shoulders, the firelight highlighting the brilliant auburn of her tresses. Her green eyes were wide and ringed with dark smudges. His gaze drifted to her full lips, made redder from the warmth of the tea, and he imagined kissing her, imagined taking that pouty mouth and nibbling on it until she moaned.

He gave himself a mental shake and gulped the remainder of his brew, anxious to change his train of thoughts and distract himself.

"How are you feeling?" he asked.

"Much better now, thank you. Although I can't seem to totally shake this cold feeling."

"The temperature is low, particularly with nothing to protect you." He fingered the fabric of her dress. "This might be adequate for the day but will not keep you warm during an outback winter night."

She nodded, put her tea to one side and crossed her arms around herself in an obvious bid for additional warmth.

William couldn't stand to see her suffer and he couldn't deny himself the feel of her body any longer. He needed to reassure himself that she was here with him and in one piece.

"Come here," he ordered softly, opening his arms in invitation.

She hesitated briefly before she scuttled over and into his waiting embrace. He tugged her onto his lap and circled his arms around her, relishing the feel of her lush body against his.

After a moment, she relaxed against him, her head falling back on his shoulder as she sighed deeply. He kissed the top of her head and massaged her arms in order to assist the blood flow to her limbs. Her slender back was pressed against his chest and he felt her shudders start to abate until eventually they stopped completely.

"Better?" he asked softly against her ear.

"Much, thank you." Her voice was low with fatigue.

That husky voice and the fact that her gorgeously rounded backside was currently perched in his lap sent him wild with need for her. He couldn't seem to stop his rising erection. He tried desperately to think of something else but his cock was growing harder by the second. He moved restlessly in an attempt to relieve some of his discomfort.

"Am I too heavy?" Lillian asked, mistaking his agitation and trying to struggle out of his lap.

"Not at all." He grasped her around the shoulders to stay her retreat. "Your proximity is just making things a little...uncomfortable."

She wriggled her bottom then gasped as realization obviously dawned.

"I'm sorry, my sweet," he mumbled into her hair. "It seems to have a mind of its own."

He knew he should release her, understood that it was the right thing to do, but her scent combined with her curvaceous body pressing so close to him was like a drug, making him heady with lust for her. He'd thought, after her father's revelations all those years ago, that he'd never see Lillian again, let alone have the opportunity to hold her so close. Now feelings of fear and possessiveness had suddenly hijacked his common sense.

He sighed deeply and tried to regain control of his raging emotions to work up the determination to remove Lillian from his lap. Then, as he was about to do just that, she sighed in contentment and relaxed into him further.

He stiffened when the scent of apples wafted on the air, tickling his subconscious and searing him with a fierce sense of *déjà vu*. Fuck, she'd always smelled like apples. It was forever a scent he'd associate with her and with it, a dozen bittersweet memories washed over him.

"William, are you all right?" she asked softly, turning her head so she could look at him. "I'm sorry. I shouldn't have just called you William, it's just…" She made her own attempt to extricate herself from his hold.

"Lilly. Don't," he said roughly, tugging her back. It was no use denying his feelings. It was killing him. So was the fact that she'd just apologized for using his given name. "I want you to call me William," he murmured and wrapped his arms tighter around her. "I like the way my name sounds on your lips. I always have."

"Oh."

He could sense her confusion and hesitancy and he needed to make her feel secure, to make her feel safe in his arms. "Please, Lilly, I need you near me right now. It scared the hell out of me when you went missing."

The only sounds in the stillness were the hiss and crackle of the fire as he waited with bated breath for Lillian to say something.

Chapter Nine

I should keep my distance and protect my heart. But even as those words rang through her head, Lillian felt herself relaxing into William, seeking comfort from his embrace. It felt too good to be in his arms. The feel of his solid chest against her back was making her belly flutter wildly and she was suddenly very warm, her skin flushed and feverish. Perhaps she could let him hold her for a while. She needed the physical contact after her frightening experience. In fact, she realized with a jolt, she hadn't had any physical contact since her aunt had died. There'd been no one to offer her sympathy or a friendly shoulder to cry on. It had simply been her and her aunt's lawyer. All of their friends had distanced themselves when her father's debts had become public knowledge.

Sensing her change in mood, William nuzzled her, his voice soft at her ear. "Are you all right?"

She sighed and attempted to stop the weepiness that threatened to overwhelm her. Tears started to form as she thought of her aunt and everything she'd experienced since her death. Quickly, she swiped them away. "I'm fine," she said quietly. "Just hold me, please."

Air hissed between his teeth as he pulled her closer. His warm breath at her ear sent little shivers rippling down her spine and heat flaring low in her belly.

"You're warmer now," he commented.

Unfamiliar sensations swelled deep within her. "Oh, my," she whispered as her nipples pebbled into hard points and her breathing grew erratic.

William tensed for a moment then swept his mouth from her ear to her neck, kissing the delicate skin then licking a slow, deliberate path to her throat. She arched her back and pressed her neck closer to him, desperate for more of the feelings that were raging madly through her body.

He groaned, swept her up into his arms and stood in one swift movement. Lillian gasped at the unexpected motion and his strength to hoist her so easily. He brushed a feather-light kiss over her lips then allowed her to slide down his body until she found her feet. He pulled the blanket from around her shoulders and laid it on the ground in front of the fire, which had banked to a low, steady glow. Then, removing the oilskin coat, he added it to the blanket and pulled her body to his. The feel of his muscular chest flush with her breasts had her nipples peaking once more and her eyes widened at the sensation as she gazed up at him. She could just make out his features in the firelight, his chiseled jaw rigid with tension, his hazel eyes heavy-lidded and intense.

He caressed her cheek gently and ran his thumb along her lower lip. Grasping her hip with his other hand, he pulled her hard against him. She closed her eyes and melted into his touch, moaning at the contact. When he rolled his pelvis into her, she could feel his pulsing erection and she shivered at the sensation, both delighted and intimidated by its size. Dipping his head, he swiped his tongue lightly along the seam of her lips. She grasped his upper arms and let her head fall back in supplication, totally immersed in his kiss.

"Open for me," he demanded, swiping his tongue across her lips once more. "Let me in."

She opened her mouth to him and he tightened his embrace, crushing her body to his. Smoothing his hands down either side of her torso, he grasped her buttocks and pulled her pelvis tight toward him. He licked his tongue into her mouth, caressing her before he took the kiss deeper, becoming more demanding as he slanted his lips desperately across hers. He was taking her, branding her mouth with his own. Her insides liquefied and she became boneless and pliable in his arms, giving herself up to the sensations swamping her. She was no longer cold, but hot and feverish everywhere William touched her.

He broke away from their kiss, panting heavily and she swayed at the loss of his strong body.

He chuckled. "Open your eyes, Lillian. I want to see those lovely green pools."

She fluttered her eyelids open and focused unsteadily on him. He made a low growling sound in his throat then gently lowered them onto the blanket.

"I hope this dress isn't a favorite," he said huskily, kneeling over her. Grasping the fabric at her collar, he rent the material down the middle, exposing her chemise. He swept his gaze over her hungrily and her nipples puckered at the force of his intense scrutiny.

"So beautiful." He dipped his head and took one of the erect little tips into his mouth, sucking through the sheer fabric. She gasped and arched her back, pushing her breast farther into him. The feel of his hot, wet mouth on her nipple sent delicious quivers straight to her loins and she groaned in pleasure as he took a long, drawing pull on the tight nub.

He lifted his head and she gazed at him, marveling at the heavy-lidded look of ravenous lust that he gave her before he bent to take her other nipple into his mouth, sucking deeply.

Lillian curled her fingers into his hair and tugged him into her, trying to get closer and needing to relieve a dull throb that had started low in her belly.

He tore his mouth away from her and quickly divested himself of his clothing, his chest heaving with his ragged breaths. He shrugged out of his jacket and shirt then tugged off his boots, trousers and undergarments until he was standing gloriously naked over her.

She gasped, her attention traveling the length of him, drinking in his sculpted chest and rippling abdomen. She dropped her gaze lower, stopping at the solid shaft of his thick erection, which strained up to his belly button and seemed impossibly large. Her eyes grew wide as she thought about what he would do with that piece of his anatomy.

He joined her once more on the blanket and covered her body with his own, kissing her gently, almost reverently then sweeping a soft trail of kisses from her lips to her ear. "God, I want you," he rasped and suckled gently on the delicate skin of her neck.

She was desperate to get closer. Grasping his upper arms, she shuddered beneath him.

William drew away from her and, keeping his eyes locked on hers, moved slowly down her body. He removed each of her shoes and dug his thumbs into the arches of her feet, sending shooting sparks of pleasure straight to her groin.

He dragged the remnants of her dress from her shoulders and tugged the garment down her legs. "Fuck, too many clothes," he grunted, ripping her chemise in two and tearing through her undergarments until she was lying completely naked beneath him. He reared back, settled himself between her legs and studied her body intently in the firelight, making her blush hotly under his examination.

"Don't be shy, my darling," he said softly. "You're beautiful"

He started a slow caress from her throat as he gazed at her adoringly. "Your breasts are perfectly rounded. Perfect for me." He cupped each globe and thumbed her taut nipples.

She whimpered, his touch sending sharp quivers deep into her core. He smiled lazily and dipped his head once more to kiss a leisurely trail from her breasts down to her belly. He dipped his tongue into her navel, tasting her before continuing a path from one hip to the other.

Lillian squirmed in delight as he drifted his lips softly over her skin, flicking his tongue over her flesh and sending goosebumps flaring across her body. She was desperate for something more and she thrust her pelvis against him in a frantic attempt to relieve the ache that was flaring low in her belly.

"Please, William," she begged. "You're torturing me."

He chuckled. "I'm preparing you, sweetness." He slid his lips lower along her belly. "I'm preparing you to take me."

"Oh." She panted, watching him sink farther down her body. Realizing his intention, she gasped. "No, William."

"Hush, my sweet. I want to taste you." He gripped her hips to still her, then closed his mouth over her sex, delving his tongue deep inside her. The feel of his lips at her most intimate place was like nothing she'd ever experienced. In an instant, she forgot her inhibitions and shamelessly thrust against his mouth, desperate for more of him.

He growled low in his throat and swept his lips down her inner thigh. "I can taste your arousal, darling. You taste so sweet." He breathed against her sensitive flesh then flicked his tongue up to lave her cleft.

She cried out in pleasure when he added a finger to his thrusting tongue, then pressed his thumb to her clitoris and pushed, massaging the little bundle of nerves. The myriad sensations in her belly coalesced and grew into a roaring inferno, tightening her insides. She held her breath and tensed as waves of pleasure swept through her, racking her body with shudders and hazing her vision in blinding white. He continued to suck at her pulsing core, working her slowly down through her intense release.

She lay panting heavily, covered in a fine sheen of perspiration, when William crawled lazily back up her body. "You. Are. So. Fucking. Responsive," he spoke each word against her mouth.

He kissed her, running his tongue along her lips. "Taste yourself on me," he demanded, kissing her deeply. She should have been scandalized by the act but she kissed him back desperately, probing his mouth with her tongue. She arched into him and curled her fingers in his hair to hold him to her, relishing the salty tanginess of her own arousal. He pulled away from their kiss when they were both breathless and ran his lips down her neck, biting the flesh where her shoulder met her throat, sending jabs of pleasurable pain through her.

He thrust his hips into hers, rubbing his solid length against her belly. She needed more, needed to feel him inside her. She grasped his shoulders, curving into him, and whimpered in complaint at his denial. He rested his weight on one elbow and snaked one hand beneath her buttocks to pull her to him, grinding his rigid shaft into her pelvis and rolling his hips. He found her lips again and kissed her fiercely, desperately. She gasped into his mouth and he swallowed the sound, growling low in his throat.

He drifted his hand from her buttocks to her thigh as he ran his mouth down her throat, then slid his fingers slowly into her channel. She whimpered and thrust her hips up.

"You're very wet, my sweet, and swollen with desire," he rasped against her neck. "I think you're ready for me."

"Yes, please. I need…something," she panted.

"I know what you need. You need me, inside you." He pushed his fingers a little deeper and scissored them. Then he hovered over her, supporting his weight by one arm as he grasped his cock with the other and settled himself snuggly between her thighs. He rubbed his shaft against her cleft, then he reared back and pushed forward hard, sliding into her swiftly and deeply.

She went rigid and cried out as he pierced through her maidenhead. He stiffened then stilled and she felt his hot breath hiss against her ear. "Relax, my sweet."

She squeezed her eyes shut and breathed deeply, adjusting to the feel of him inside her. He brushed his lips over hers and pulled out fractionally before thrusting in a little farther. She relaxed beneath him, the stinging abating and replaced by a warm glow. He caressed her forehead with his lips then swept across to the sensitive skin below her ear.

"Let me in, Lilly—just a little more."

She couldn't believe that he wasn't in all the way— she felt entirely filled with him! She spread her legs wider and thrust up to meet him.

"That's it, sweetness," he crooned, slipping inside her and seating himself to the hilt. They groaned together as he started a gentle rhythm, pulling out entirely then driving back into her in long, slow glides. She gasped and clutched him tighter, new sensations taking hold and warming her insides. She felt a mad fluttering start deep in her core and she moved with him, matching his tempo. He swept his hand down her side and gripped her bottom once more, forcing her into his pelvis and tilting his hips, demanding that she take him deeper.

She threw her head back, the pleasure overwhelming her at his hard and fast strokes.

"Yes—God, yes," she panted, the fluttering in her belly quickening. At her cries, William wrapped an arm behind her head and took her mouth violently, thrusting his tongue into her in time with his pumping shaft. He moved his other hand from her backside, over her hip then between them to her clitoris. He found the little bundle of nerves and massaged the nub until she bucked beneath him.

"Come on, Lilly," he demanded against her mouth. "Let go!"

At his desperate plea, she did. The tightening and the quivering of feelings at her core intensified until suddenly all the sensations coalesced into one wave of pleasure that roared through her, making her toes curl and her back arch almost painfully. She cried out, shuddering and quaking through the throes of her orgasm.

William thrust hard twice more then his body went rigid. She felt the warm, pulsing rush of his release gush inside her and she watched with blurred vision as his face contorted and he growled out a long sound of pleasure.

Panting, she relaxed beneath him, her body made limp and pliable through her exertions. William buried his head in the crook of her neck and kissed the skin beneath her ear, stilling a moment before he heaved himself off her and swung a leg over her hips. He tugged her closer, one arm resting over her chest, the other cushioning her head.

Abruptly, Lillian felt shy and vulnerable. After such intimacy, she wasn't sure what to expect, and wondered in the back of her mind where they would go from this point. She stiffened in William's arms, unfamiliar and awkward with a lover's intimate embrace.

William removed his arm from under her and rested his head on one hand, his arm bent at the elbow as he looked down at her suspiciously. "You were a virgin, Lillian," he stated bluntly. "Why did you lie to me?"

She tried to struggle upright but he kept her immobilized.

"Don't," he ordered curtly. "I want you to answer me."

She huffed out a breath and stilled beneath him, trying to avoid his burning gaze, then sighed. "It's a long story, William. Perhaps it will be better told under different circumstances."

He eyed her a while longer then acquiesced and loosened his hold. "You're right. I need to get you back to the homestead." He rose quickly and started to dress.

Lillian sat up and tried unsuccessfully to pull the tattered remnants of her clothing around her. She blushed furiously when William stood over her and blatantly assessed her nakedness.

He chuckled at her embarrassment. "I didn't think this through particularly well."

"This is not funny, William," she said hotly. "How am I to return to the house looking like this?"

"Come." He grasped her hand and pulled her to her feet. Collecting his oilskin, he held it open for her. "Hands in the holes," he ordered then buttoned the too-large jacket all the way down the front. Stooping, he retrieved the blanket, shook it out and wrapped it around her. He gathered her tattered clothes and undergarments then shoved them into his saddlebag before extinguishing the fire with a dousing of sand.

He held her shoes out. When she took a step toward him, he knelt and grasped one of her ankles then slipped a shoe on one foot. He obviously wasn't going to bother with her stockings, which had been balled up and stuffed away with her other clothing. She steadied herself by grasping his shoulders.

"I can put my own shoes on, William," she muttered in irritation.

He just ignored her, dropping her foot and grasping the other one to fit that shoe into place too.

He stood swiftly, circled an arm around her waist and tugged her to him, dipping his head to her ear.

"You *are* going to tell me what's going on and I don't want you to lie to me."

Her nipples hardened at the sensation of his warm breath on the delicate skin of her neck.

"I've just taken you. I was your first. That means that you belong to me now, Lillian."

She shivered at the possessive edge to his voice then wondered what on earth he was talking about. He didn't give her the opportunity to respond to his high-handed attitude before he drew away from her, grasped her hand and tugged her toward his horse.

He grasped her around the waist and swung her up onto Victory, arranging her sidesaddle style on the horse's back. He lithely mounted the animal and settled behind her before kicking Victory into a gallop across the hard terrain and heading back to the homestead.

Chapter Ten

William clutched Lillian to him and rode them hard toward Mulga Creek. Her face was pressed to his chest and her slight arms were wrapped about his waist while he had one arm banded around her protectively. His mind was running through the consequences of what they'd just done. He'd known, deep down, that his first instincts had been correct and that Lillian had been a virgin, and given that he'd unceremoniously just taken that from her, he now felt a greater responsibility to her.

He'd known, yet he'd still pretended to himself that the act was not new to her. Fuck, his crassness knew no bounds. He'd just de-flowered his governess because he couldn't help himself—couldn't stop himself from possessing her as he'd wanted to possess her ten years earlier. Not the least of his worries was the possibility that she could become pregnant from their encounter. He could kick himself for his recklessness. He was the experienced one. He should have ensured that he was more careful. He could only pray that his seed wouldn't take root.

He was relieved when the homestead came into view. Lillian would need a warm bath, then they could talk.

His immediate concern, however, was how to get Lillian past Mrs. Thompson, who, he could see by the dim light cast by the verandah lantern, was waiting for them on the front steps clad in a nightgown and a sleep cap. He couldn't allow her to see that Lillian was naked underneath his oilskin coat and he didn't have to stretch his imagination to guess what else she was covered in. No, he had to get Lillian past his intrepid housekeeper before she suspected anything untoward. While Mrs. Thompson was one of his staff, he'd also grown up with her and consequently he knew that in formidable mode, she was a power to be reckoned with. He felt Lillian stiffen in his arms and guessed that she was having similar thoughts.

"Let me do the talking," he whispered in her ear as he reigned in Victory just short of the front steps.

"Oh, Mr. Cartwright, thank God you found her. Is she well?" Mrs. Thompson asked, not waiting for him to swing himself down from his mount. The soft light of the verandah lantern illuminated the lines of worry etched into her forehead. He smiled reassuringly at his housekeeper and, supporting Lillian's slight weight easily, he vaulted from his horse.

With Lillian in his arms, he strode up the front stairs and into the hallway, Mrs. Thompson hot on his heels.

"I have a bath ready for Miss Hamilton in the kitchen," she informed him, following down the hallway.

"Miss Hamilton's dress is torn and quite filthy from her ordeal. She will need to change into something else," he said over his shoulder, climbing the stairs to the second level.

"I can assist her, Mr. Cartwright."

"I'm fine, Mrs. Thompson. Please wait for us in the kitchen."

"William!" The sound of the name she had used for him in childhood froze him to the spot. "It is not proper for you to take Miss Hamilton into her room."

He turned on the stairs so that he could face her. "Miss Hamilton is tired and weak from exposure, Millie. As you cannot possibly carry her up the stairs, I will do so. I would hate for her to fall. I assure you that her modesty will remain intact. We'll be back in a moment, then you can see to her."

He turned away from her and recommenced his journey to Lillian's room, breathing a sigh of relief when his housekeeper didn't follow them. He looked down at Lillian and didn't miss the furious blush that flushed her cheeks.

"Don't distress yourself," he admonished gently. "She would much prefer some impropriety than for you to risk falling."

He deposited Lillian in her room, ensured that she was well enough to dress herself then closed the door.

William paced in the hallway waiting for her. He was anxious for them to talk but knew that he had to deal with Mrs. Thompson and allow Lillian time to bathe before they would have the luxury of conversation. He looked at his pocket watch. It was only ten o'clock but it felt much later. So much had happened in the span of time since he'd left the homestead in search of Lillian.

He was tucking his pocket watch away when her door opened and she stepped into the hallway, dressed in a long, thick dressing gown, the buttons fastened to her chin. He made a move to pick her up but she stepped aside. "I can walk on my own, William," she said quickly.

"I'm sure you can, but I insist. Please, allow me for my peace of mind." He ignored any further protestations and, sweeping her into his arms, he started downstairs in the direction of the kitchen.

Mrs. Thompson was waiting for them. A bathtub had been established in the center of the room in front of the slow-combustion stove, which was emitting a soft, warm heat.

"My poor child," she murmured as William deposited Lillian gently on her feet by the bathtub.

"I'll give you some privacy. I'll be in my study," he muttered, departing the room and leaving the door ajar.

From the hallway, he listened to his housekeeper speaking soothingly to Lillian and hoped fervently that the woman didn't suspect anything. A moment later, he heard Mrs. Thompson leave the kitchen and close the door behind her.

"Is everything all right?" he asked, as she was retreating down the hall.

"Everything's fine. Miss Hamilton just asked for some privacy. She assured me that she is quite well, so I'm going to retire for the evening. I've told her if she needs anything, not to hesitate to wake me."

William waited for the telltale click of her bedroom door latch before he stalked back in the direction of the kitchen. He knocked once lightly then strode through the door to find Lillian naked and on the verge of stepping into the tub.

She gasped in surprise at his arrival and tried to cover her nakedness. "William! What are you doing?"

"Don't be shy, Lilly." Fuck, she was so beautiful. The soft light of the kerosene lamp highlighted her gentle curves, so lush and ripe that he had to physically restrain himself from reaching out and clutching her to him violently. He stepped toward her, took a deep breath to calm himself and allowed his gaze to wander over her body. He blanched when his eyes rested on her blood-streaked thighs and he realized then why she'd asked Mrs. Thompson to give her privacy. God, he hoped he hadn't hurt her.

She stood frozen to the spot as if his gaze held her spellbound, until he placed his hands on her shoulders and gently pushed her into the bath. She sank below the water, wincing slightly, then closed her eyes and rested her head against the back of the tub. He kneeled behind her and reached for the soap and a washcloth.

"You shouldn't be in here, William. What if Mrs. Thompson comes to check on me?"

"She's in bed and she's a heavy sleeper. She won't be disturbing us. Trust me. Just relax and allow me to take care of you," he replied softly.

He dunked the washcloth in the water and soaped it up before wiping it along the back of her shoulders and around her neck. She sighed and leaned her head to one side, allowing him to access her throat. He moved downward, across her clavicle then over each of her breasts. The sight of the pale, full globes bobbing in the water had his cock hardening instantly. He watched, mesmerized, as each of her nipples puckered and strained at the friction of the cloth. Seeing her breasts and delicate nipples tightened his insides and sent hot lust burning through him. He gritted his teeth and steeled himself against the sensations, wanting only to cherish her and look after her. He moved the washcloth lower over her belly then gently swiped it between her thighs. She gasped and tried to squeeze her legs together but he resisted her efforts.

"Shh, darling. Let me wash you." He continued leisurely to cleanse between her thighs, willing her to relax. "Are you very sore? Did I hurt you?" he asked, praying that he hadn't.

"I'm a little tender," she admitted softly. "But it's just a small ache. It's not very bad."

He kissed behind her ear and nibbled on her earlobe. "I shouldn't have taken you like that, Lilly," he mumbled against the skin of her neck. "I'm sorry. I should have waited and made it special. Hell, I shouldn't have done it at all." His last words ended on a strangled note.

She stiffened under him and made a move to get out of the tub but he stopped her with slight pressure to her shoulders. "No, stay and finish bathing. Meet me in my study when you're ready." He planted a soft kiss to her crown then stood and left her to finish her ablutions in private.

* * * *

Lillian drew out her bath but she knew that William wouldn't rest until they had spoken. He would demand to know why, if she'd been married, she'd remained a virgin. She was in a lie of her own making and she knew that it would be easier just to admit the truth. She supposed that she could fabricate an older husband who'd been physically incapable of consummating their marriage, but why would she do that? There was no real reason to continue her deception. She'd only done so because that was what William had believed. To have him believe that she'd been married had meant that she could pretend she'd not been pining for him for the previous ten years.

She sighed in remembered pleasure as she thought about their lovemaking. It had been everything that she'd dreamed it would be — even more so. She'd had no idea that the human body was capable of such wondrous feelings, and the fact that William had so easily and skillfully elicited those feelings from her made her tummy flutter delightfully.

She recalled his words to her before they'd returned to the homestead. *"You belong to me now."* A warm feeling engulfed her. To belong to such a man sent euphoria singing through her veins.

She'd never belonged to anyone, not through love nor through familial association. Her father had treated her as a commodity to be offered and bartered to the highest bidder, and her mother, until her death, had appeared to agree with him.

She'd lingered long enough in her bath and knew that William would be getting anxious. If she didn't meet with him soon, no doubt he would stride back in, demanding to know what she was doing.

She climbed out of the tub and dressed quickly in her dressing gown. She brushed her hair and plaited it neatly before sliding her feet into her slippers. Taking a deep breath, she went to meet William.

She knocked softly on the door of his study and entered on his invitation. He was standing in front of the fire holding a tumbler of what appeared to be Scotch.

"Come and sit, Lilly," he invited, indicating a large chair in front of the fireplace. He poured her a glass of sherry and pressed it into her hand. She took a sip gratefully, relishing the warmth the alcohol provided.

He stood quietly assessing her for a moment then took a seat facing her, resting one foot across his opposite knee. The tumbler dangled from the fingers of his right hand as he ran the fingers of his left back and forth across his lips and gazed at her thoughtfully.

Lillian eyed him impassively and clasped her hands in her lap, waiting for him to speak first.

"I know that I initially suggested that our relationship should remain professional and that your past would not influence our employer–employee association. However, in light of what happened this evening, I think we can safely say that premise can no longer continue." He took a sip of his Scotch and studied her over the rim of his glass.

Lillian maintained a blank expression, even though her heart raced with anxiety. She couldn't begin to guess where William was heading with this conversation and she hoped fervently that he wouldn't throw her out of the house for being wanton and loose. Just when all of her dreams of having William, of being in his arms, had come true, they looked close to crumbling. She'd feared this would happen. She'd dreaded being hurt and having her heart broken a second time.

Only this time a lot more than my heart has been broken.

"I keep trying to tell myself that I didn't know that you were innocent, that you'd been married and therefore were experienced in the art of lovemaking, but I'm merely being self-serving and grossly unfair to you. I knew after our liaison in the yard that you were a virgin, yet I didn't pursue any explanation from you. I did this for two reasons — even though at that stage I had far surpassed the edicts of propriety, I still wanted to believe that we could maintain a professional relationship and I told myself that your past was none of my business. Second, I wanted to harden my heart against you and protect myself from becoming involved too deeply and risk being hurt by you a second time."

Lillian was flabbergasted. Why would he need to protect *himself* against *her*? She was speechless and she could only stare at him incredulously as he continued.

"I acted rashly and carelessly this evening. I'm ashamed of myself for taking advantage of you and your situation." He spoke quietly, looking at her intently.

And her heart broke a second time. How could he feel ashamed of an act that she felt had been so beautiful and loving?

A low sob escaped her and she pushed a hand against her mouth to stifle any further outburst but her eyes filled with water and tears flowed down her cheeks as his hurtful words pierced her chest.

William was out of his chair in a second and kneeling before her. "Please don't cry, my darling," he pleaded. "I'm so sorry that I hurt you. I would give anything to take it back." He cupped her face in his hands, swiping the tears from her cheeks with his thumbs.

"That's just it, William," she sobbed. "I don't want to take it back!" She watched through blurred vision as various emotions crossed his features—regret, pain, longing. He stood, scooped her up and settled her in his lap, clasping her head to his chest with one hand and stroking her hair with the other.

"I'm sorry I've upset you," he observed. "God, I can't seem to do anything right."

She relaxed into his embrace and her tears subsided as his gentle caresses soothed her. He kissed the top of her head then stood and gently deposited her onto the seat before he reclaimed the opposite one.

She felt weary and emotionally exhausted by the day's events but she knew that she owed William an explanation. She looked across at him expectantly and waited for him to ask the ultimate question.

"Are you, or have you ever been, married, Lillian, and if so, why was your marriage not consummated?"

She took a deep, tremulous breath. "No. I'm not married, nor have I ever been." She looked up at his sharp intake of breath. He was staring at her intensely, his fists clenched as he rested forward with elbows on his knees.

"Hamilton is the name of my maternal aunt. I assumed her last name when my father died two years ago. When Father passed away, he left behind numerous debts and many unhappy creditors. His reputation and the Baxter name were in ruins. My mother died not long after we arrived in England and after Father's passing, I was left destitute."

She paused in her recounting and looked across at William. He was staring into the fire but she could see by the rigid set of his jaw and tense posture that he was angry. She took a restorative sip of her sherry and continued.

"My only surviving relative was my mother's sister, my Aunt Agnes Hamilton. After my father's death, she came for me and helped me organize the funeral and sell the house so we could pay off some of his debts. She took me to live with her and suggested that I go by her name. The Baxter name was too sullied by my father's disrepute to be welcome in polite society. Aunt Agnes was like a mother to me. She gave me shelter and love when I had no one." Lillian could feel tears starting to brim again and she wiped her eyes and took a shuddering breath.

"Five months ago, my aunt died after a lengthy illness. She'd left all her worldly possessions to me, having no children of her own. Her lawyer informed me soon after that my father's creditors had applied to the estate for reimbursement of monies owed. Fortunately, Aunt Agnes had the foresight to have me hide her jewelry before her death. After selling her jewelry and my clothes, I had enough money set aside to last some months. It was also around this time that I received a letter from Mrs. Thompson. Apparently, my aunt had written to her before her death regarding a governess position. I took the Mr. Cartwright mentioned in her letter to be your brother, James. I had nothing and no one to keep me in England, so I wrote to Mrs. Thompson accepting the position and... Well... Here I am."

She looked across to William and was surprised to note the look of fury that suffused his features. His jaw was hard, a tic pulsing rhythmically in his cheek as his eyes glinted with steel.

"You mean to tell me that your father left you destitute? With no provision for your financial or personal security?" he asked, aghast.

Lillian gave him a small smile. "I'm sure that he didn't plan to die the way he did. He was mugged walking home one evening and expired through loss of blood. Although, given the things that I've learnt since his death, perhaps his murder was not a random act of violence but rather one of vengeance."

"Still, the man should have left you provided for," he snarled.

"You knew my father, William. He was always involved in some scheme or another, something that was bound to make us rich. I'm sure that he planned to arrange for my welfare at some point."

"You give the man entirely too much credit," he muttered angrily. "You must have been distraught to have been left in such a position."

"I wasn't a child, but neither had I sought any employment up until that point. My father required my assistance at home, so I had no income of my own. I was lucky Aunt Agnes came to my rescue. She and my father had never seen eye to eye, so I was thankful that she helped me. I owe her my life," she said simply.

William swore softly and scrubbed a hand across his face. "I can't believe I treated you so appallingly when you arrived, particularly after everything you've been through. I feel like a complete arsehole." A swift look of contrition flared in his eyes then distrust shadowed his features. "But speaking of schemes to get rich," he continued, "what of the man who you were promised to when you left Australia for England? Why did you not marry him?"

Lillian looked up sharply. "What are you talking about?"

William scrutinized her. "Well, that's the reason for your family leaving Australia after all, so you could marry who your father termed a 'young man of established family and connections'."

The blood roared in her ears as she listened in disbelief to what William was saying. She heard his words but the import was not sinking in. "I d-don't understand."

"Your father" — he sneered — "told me when I asked for your hand in marriage that you were already promised to another."

Lillian stood on shaking legs, unsure what she intended but needing some answers, as if she could walk to the next room and demand from her father to know what William was talking about. The room started to tilt and grow dim. She swayed. Distantly, she heard William demanding to know if she was all right. She saw him step toward her before the world went black and the last thing she remembered was William's arms around her.

Chapter Eleven

For the second time that day, Lillian had scared the hell out of him. His heart had stopped in his chest when he'd watched, as if in slow motion, her sway and start to fall. Thank God he'd only been a step away from her and had been able to catch her before she'd hit the floor.

He looked down at Lillian lying in bed, where he'd carried her and tucked her in after she'd fainted. She looked so beautiful and fragile, like an angel with her auburn hair fanned out on the pillow and her lush lips red and slightly parted in sleep. He brushed a lock of hair off her forehead and caressed her cheek gently. He could kick himself for the way he'd handled things, or, more to the point, *hadn't* handled things.

He'd been correct in his suspicions that she'd experienced hardships. No wonder she always looked so serious, so forlorn. His beautiful girl had been alone, had been left destitute by her bastard of a father. His chest physically hurt when he imagined what she'd gone through and he sent up a silent thank you to her dead aunt for rescuing her and providing a safe haven. He didn't want to envision what could have happened to her if Agnes Hamilton hadn't stepped in. Young women in Lillian's situation didn't have too many options and the alternatives didn't bear thinking about.

Playing through his mind over and over was her reaction to his question about her intended husband — something wasn't right.

He groaned when he recalled how he'd told her he was ashamed that he'd made love to her. What bastard told a woman that? Of course she was upset, particularly as he'd taken her virginity at the same time. It wasn't what he'd meant, but it didn't change the fact that he'd sounded like a callous arsehole. He needed her to wake up so that he could explain himself.

As if in answer to his silent prayers, she stirred beneath his caress and opened her eyes.

"William?" she asked tentatively, her gaze roaming his face.

"I'm here, darling," he said, softly stroking her hair. "You fainted. I've put you to bed. You've had a big day and you must be exhausted."

She furrowed her brow in confusion and he watched her warily.

"Don't distress yourself. Just relax," he murmured.

He could tell the moment she recollected their conversation — her green eyes grew wide and focused on him.

"William, why did you say that about me wanting to marry another?" Her voice trembled and her bottom lip quivered as she searched his face for an answer.

His chest tightened at her obvious distress. He hated to see her cry and over the past week, he'd caused her enough tears to last a lifetime.

"Hush, Lilly. We'll talk tomorrow. Just rest now," he soothed, caressing her cheek.

"I need to know now. *Please* tell me," she begged and struggled to sit upright.

He gripped her shoulders gently to stop her efforts.

"All right, I'll tell you, but please calm down. I don't want to upset you any further."

She took deep breaths to compose herself then settled back against the headboard and looked at him expectantly.

"Before you left for England, I went to your father and asked his permission to marry you. He told me that he was resettling the family in England, where you were to marry a young man who apparently had more money and better prospects than I did."

He could hear the bitterness in his voice but he couldn't help it. Even after ten years, he still felt anger and betrayal at Lillian's decision.

He watched her intently as a range of emotions crossed her face. Her green eyes were wide and confused and she shook her head obstinately.

"There was no man I was to marry," she said softly. "Why do you say that?"

"Because that's exactly what your father told me," he responded coolly. "I was destroyed, Lillian. I thought you loved me."

"No!" she whispered brokenly. "He can't have done that. I can't believe he would do that to me—to us!"

It was William's turn to look confused. "What are you talking about?" he demanded as a sick comprehension started to take hold.

"Father. He told me that he was moving us to England right before he told me that you were going to be married! I cried for weeks. I was devastated."

A cold, hard fury overtook William. He clenched his fists as a desperate need to hit something—to inflict damage—swept through him. He took deep breaths and counted to ten in an effort to regain his self-control.

"I only met and married Ruth after you'd left—after I thought that you were promised to another."

He grasped Lillian's hands in his and gazed into her eyes. The stark anguish and hurt he saw reflected in her emerald pools rocked him to his core. He wished with a desperate fervency that her bastard of a father were still alive so he could kill him all over again. How could he do that to his own daughter? The depths of the man's depravity knew no bounds.

"I've always loved you, Lillian. Words can't describe how I felt when you left. It was as if you took a part of me with you. I was devastated and furious—furious that you'd betrayed us and betrayed our love."

He studied her as she came to grips with what her father had done to them all those years ago.

"I can't believe he did that," she said, her gaze unfocused. "I knew that he wanted me to make what he considered a good match—he threw enough men in my path over the years—but I would never have believed he could have been so heartless."

William's vision hazed in red and rage gripped him anew at the thought of the men that Henry Baxter had pushed at his daughter. He was astounded and relieved beyond measure that Lillian had been able to resist her father's demands for as long as she had.

"I was also to blame," he said quietly. "I should have fought for you. I'm ashamed at how quickly I capitulated and I've been swamped with feelings of guilt ever since."

He sighed heavily, the full import of his failure hitting him hard. They'd lost ten years together and spent ten years each feeling the betrayal and heartache of a lost love. Of course he could console himself with the fact that if things hadn't occurred the way they had, he wouldn't have his children and he wouldn't have had the years spent with Ruth. However, those facts didn't ease his anger and fury at the injustice of Henry Baxter's deceit.

"You weren't to know that my father was lying, William. We were adolescents and I was too young to be married without my parents' permission. There was nothing that you could have done. My father manipulated the situation to serve him and his future plans. I knew that he was capable of deceit and immoral acts. The years before his death showed me exactly how unscrupulous he could be. But I would never have believed him capable of hurting *me* for monetary gain!"

William's heart wrenched at the tears that were flowing freely down Lillian's cheeks. He couldn't begin to understand how she must be feeling at the full realization of her father's depravity. He stood and moved to sit beside her on the bed.

"Come here," he ordered softly and pulled her onto his lap. "It's done now. Let's leave the past in the past and focus on the future." He rocked her gently in his arms.

Slowly, her tears abated and he felt her start to relax against him. Exhaustion over the day's events had finally taken its toll and she'd fallen asleep. He held her closely for a few minutes, not wanting to wake her. When he was sure that she was in a deep slumber, he lifted her gently and placed her back on the bed.

He drew the covers up to her neck and tucked her in securely, placing a kiss on her forehead.

Taking the lamp, he left Lillian's bedroom and made his way to his own. A sudden weariness overwhelmed him. He needed to sleep on everything that had occurred that day and he was sure that a way ahead for them would present itself to him in the morning.

There was one thing on which he had no doubts — he wouldn't allow Lillian to leave him again.

Chapter Twelve

When Lillian awoke, the sun shining brightly in her bedroom told her it was much later than she usually arose. She checked the bedside clock and was startled to find that it was just past ten a.m.

As she struggled to wake fully, the events of the previous day crowded her foggy mind until sudden comprehension had her instantly alert. Through all the events and emotions that had unfolded, she felt as if she'd lived an entire lifetime in the span of twenty-four hours. She couldn't quite believe she'd experienced so many intense reactions—fear, panic, lust, love and sorrow—in such a short period of time.

She recalled making love with William and her body tingled deliciously. Never had her immature fantasies come close to touching on the reality of what she'd experienced with William. She blushed fiercely, remembering what it felt like to have his mouth on her—everywhere. She couldn't believe that she'd done those things—and enjoyed them.

Too quickly, her thoughts turned to William's proclamation that he'd felt ashamed and it was as though a bucket of cold water had been poured over her. Of course he was ashamed. She shouldn't have acted like she had—wanton and immoral. It was little wonder that he regretted what they'd done. Worse still, she had no idea how she should behave around him from this point forward and that made her nervous. She was so inexperienced with the act of lovemaking that she was clueless about his expectations and their current relationship status.

Her thoughts then brought her full circle to what her father had done to them all those years ago and a fresh wave of pain stabbed her. She understood that her father had always been somewhat disreputable, but the things she'd discovered since his death had her realizing that she hadn't really known him at all.

A soft knock on her door startled her out of her reverie and she turned to see Mrs. Thompson bustling into her room bearing a tray laden with tea and bread.

Lillian sat up quickly and shuffled back to rest against the headboard. "Mrs. Thompson, please, you don't have to do this," she said in embarrassment. "I'm quite capable of coming to the kitchen. In fact, I should have been up and about hours ago."

"Nonsense," the older woman declared and placed the tray on Lillian's lap. "After the ordeal you had yesterday, you must rest. You could have caught your death out there in the cold." She reached across to lay a hand on Lillian's forehead.

"I'm quite well," Lillian assured her. "Just a little tired."

"It's no wonder. Now I want you to stay put and eat something. Food will do you a world of good."

"But the children—"

"The children are fine. At the moment, they're in my kitchen helping me bake bread and scones and having a world of fun doing it," she said with a laugh. "Take your time. Eat something and join us downstairs when you're ready."

With the conversation obviously over, Mrs. Thompson bustled back out of the room, leaving Lillian to her breakfast.

Lillian smiled to herself as she poured some tea and buttered a slice of freshly baked bread. For so long she'd looked after other people — her mother when she was sick, to a certain extent her father, then, after him, her dear aunt. It was nice to be looked after for a change, even if only for a little while. She still felt guilty about being in bed when everyone else was up and about, but she consoled herself with the thought that the longer she stayed in her room, the longer she could put off seeing William and delay what was sure to be an uncomfortable encounter.

She was finishing her breakfast and preparing to face the day ahead when she was startled by a sharp rap on the door. Before she could say anything, the man whom she'd so recently been distressing over strode casually into the room. Her breath hitched and her heart rate beat in double time when she took in his magnificent physique. He was dressed in fitted jodhpurs and a blue cotton shirt that stretched across the hard muscles of his chest and shoulders.

Nerves and a rippling current of desire had her hands trembling as she placed the breakfast tray on her bedside table. She sat back in bed and trained her eyes on her lap, trying to regulate her breathing.

"How are you this morning, Lilly?" he asked.

His deep voice washed over her like a sensuous caress, pebbling her nipples and sending shivers rippling down her spine.

"I'm very well," she muttered, still averting her eyes. She felt him move closer to the bed and she stiffened in alarm. She had no idea how to behave after the intimacy between them the previous evening and a deep flush suffused her cheeks.

She heard William drag a chair closer to her bedside and settle himself into it, but still she refused to look at him.

Moments passed in silence, making the air between them heavy and awkward. Lillian picked nervously at a stray thread on her counterpane as she waited for William to say something. When he did, it was so sudden and harsh that it took her breath away.

"Look at me, Lillian!" he demanded.

She snapped her head up and her eyes shot to his in surprise.

"Are you *that* ashamed of what happened between us last night?" he asked, his eyes narrowed.

"N-no," she said breathlessly. "A little embarrassed perhaps. It was very" — she waved a hand in the air, searching desperately for the right word — "intimate."

Her face flushed hotly at the admission. She hadn't ever expected to *talk* about what they'd shared, but obviously, William had other ideas. She dropped her head once more to stare at her clasped hands.

William cupped her chin and tilted her head up so that she was looking into his eyes.

"There is nothing to be embarrassed about, Lilly. If anyone is to be embarrassed, it should be me. I shouldn't have lost control. I shouldn't have taken you like that. I can't regret it, however. You've been in my dreams for a long time and last night I selfishly took what I've so long desired."

Her breath caught in her throat. "I thought that you were ashamed of what we did — of me."

He sucked in a sharp breath and his eyes glinted dangerously.

"Don't ever think that," he bit out. "I've wanted you for as long as I can remember. I would *never* feel ashamed of you. I'm ashamed of myself for not taking more care."

He was still grasping her chin, refusing to allow her to look away from him.

"When are your courses due?" he asked quietly.

If Lillian had felt embarrassment before, she now felt acute mortification. Her body trembled with the sensation and she flushed a deep scarlet.

"P-pardon me?"

"I realize that the question seems...indelicate, but I need to know," he said gently.

Sudden realization dawned and she was astounded that she hadn't thought of the possibility herself.

"They've just passed—one week ago," she whispered.

He breathed a sigh of relief and finally released her. "It's not infallible, of course, but chances are that we're safe."

She nodded numbly, not really sure herself about the possibility of pregnancy, and wondered idly how William was so knowledgeable.

"Are you very sore?"

Oh Lord, can he be any more personal?

"A little, but nothing that I cannot bear," she answered and looked once more to her lap.

"Good. Although I'd like to check for myself," he stated in a matter-of-fact tone.

Lillian's eyes shot once more to his and opened wide in astonishment. Just when she had thought he couldn't possibly embarrass her further, he amazed her with this scandalous request. She could only stare at him mutely as words failed her.

He stood, strode to the door and locked it before returning to her bedside and whipping down her covers.

"William!" she cried, finally finding her voice. "What are you doing?"

"I told you, Lilly, that I want to check you myself. I saw the blood streaking your thighs last night and I'd like to reassure myself that I didn't injure you. Remember also that I'm responsible for you. Until last night, it was the responsibility of an employer to an employee," he said quietly. "Now it extends to the responsibility of a lover. When I took your virginity, I also took accountability. Now we can do this the easy way, or the hard way," he finished, furnishing her with a long look.

Lillian stared at him in dismay and realized he was completely serious. She shuffled down until she was lying flat on the bed, ensuring that her long nightgown continued to cover her modestly. When she was fully prone, she lay stiffly and stared up at him, waiting for whatever William had in store for her.

He chuckled and clucked his tongue. "So shy, my darling. You know that I will need to lift this lovely nightgown?"

She nodded, blushed and cursed inwardly at her inability to face anything remotely embarrassing without flushing cheeks. As if reading her thoughts, he smiled and kneeled bedside the bed.

"I love that you blush so easily. Your innocence disarms me. How did you remain so untouched and unsullied in light of your father's debauchery?"

It was a rhetorical question, so she remained silent while he continued to study her.

"Lie across the bed, facing me."

She sat up and scooted sideways so that she was lying across the width of the single bed with her legs dangling awkwardly off the side.

He grasped each of her ankles and lifted them so her feet were flat on the mattress and her legs bent at the knee. He gripped her hips and tugged her down until her backside rested on the edge of the bed. It was an alarmingly vulnerable position and she tensed uneasily.

"Just relax, my sweet," he whispered, drawing her nightgown up her thighs until it was bunched around her waist.

She could feel his breath whisper against her inner thigh as he leaned closer. Her nipples puckered and her breathing hitched, desire flaring low in her belly. She recognized the feeling now, the clenching of her internal muscles and a light, quivering sensation in her loins that signaled her longing for something more. She couldn't quite believe that laid bare as she was, exposed and vulnerable, her desire outweighed any embarrassment.

She felt William's warm hands on her inner thighs where he gently caressed her before nudging her legs farther apart.

Dampness flowed between her thighs, warm and moist, and she tried unsuccessfully to close them.

William hissed a breath between his teeth. "You are so wet, my love," he rasped, gently stroking his fingers through her damp folds.

She couldn't see his face when he bent to examine her, using his fingers to sift through the furrows of her sex. She held her breath as his caresses sent sharp quivers of desire straight to her core. Her face flushed and her breathing grew ragged. She wriggled under his administrations.

"Stay still," he ordered, gripping her hip with his right hand. "I'm not finished."

She stilled and worked to regulate her breathing as he recommenced his explorations between her legs. His fingers entered her and she gasped, more tender than she'd initially thought. His delving produced a slight twinge of discomfort.

"Does that hurt?" he asked huskily, pushing his finger deeper inside.

"A little," she breathed and tried not to tense.

"Hmm." He withdrew his finger and circled her clitoris slowly. "I might have to kiss it better."

Lillian whimpered involuntarily. She recalled what he'd done to her with his mouth the previous evening and the memory sent more flutters erupting wildly in her belly.

"Does that please you, my sweet?" he asked, continuing to circle her clitoris with his finger and slowly working her into a delirium of building sensation.

"Oh, yes," she whispered, rocking her hips in rhythm with his rotating finger.

"You are so moist and swollen with desire, Lilly. I can tell that you need me to make it better. Would you like that, my love? Would you like me to ease the ache?"

His voice had grown deep and rough. He continued to massage her sex, intensifying the throbbing of her internal muscles to desperate proportions.

"Please, William," she begged, understanding that only he had the power to relieve the pressure building inside her.

She watched him under lowered lids as he gazed at her intently, studying her face and the effect that his ministrations were having on her. He smiled, a slow, mischievous curl of his lips. "You are far too tender for penetration, but perhaps a massage?" He dipped his head between her legs.

Lillian gasped, feeling his lips on the inside of her thigh. He kissed a slow trail north, grasping her knees to keep her legs parted widely.

"Your skin is so silky soft, so sweet," he muttered against her and continued his relentless path toward the apex of her thighs.

She felt his warm breath blow over her damp folds and she stiffened, her toes curling, then the delicious sensation of his tongue swiping leisurely through her center. She fisted the sheet in her hands and struggled to maintain control of the myriad sensations flowing through her. Her insides clenched and her breathing grew labored as he continued to assault her sex with his tongue, circling her relentlessly, probing and licking, then nipping gently on her clitoris, making her arch desperately into his mouth.

The feeling was indescribable and when he pierced her deeply, she erupted around him with a cry, her internal muscles tightening and pulsing as her body shuddered in blissful release.

She continued to tremble as William lapped at her gently, working her down through her orgasm.

She stared blindly at the ceiling, willing her heart rate to regulate and her vision to clear. *Will I ever get used to this euphoric feeling?* She hoped not.

She shifted her head and looked down her body to where William still rested between her thighs, a smug smile on his lips.

"You're so responsive, my love. Just one touch and you're coming apart." He licked his lips lasciviously. "Do you feel better?" he asked, rising swiftly to his feet.

She didn't answer, her voice momentarily lost when she caught sight of the very large bulge at his crotch. She hadn't seen it properly last night, but she recalled the feel of him when he'd entered her, and by the evidence now very clearly in front of her, she imagined him to be quite large. She wasn't sure what she could do to relieve his discomfort but she thought that perhaps she could do something similar to what he'd just done for her. Besides, she was beyond curious. She wanted to know what he would feel like in her hand, in her mouth. Before her courage failed her, she waved a hand in the direction of his prominent erection.

"Can I help with that?" She tried to sound seductive but thought that she'd only managed tremulous.

He hissed a breath and narrowed his eyes on her.

She steadied her gaze on his handsome face and watched a muscle in his rigid jaw tic.

Chapter Thirteen

William stared at Lillian in shock. "Have you done that before?" he demanded.

"Of course not," she gasped in mortification.

He mentally berated himself for asking the question but his immediate reaction had been one of surprise, followed instantly by the insidious thought that she *had* done it before. He knew he was being an arsehole, but he couldn't help the surge of irrational jealousy that had gripped him at the mere thought of it.

Of course he'd love her to relieve the painful ache in his balls and soften his throbbing erection but he wondered was it too soon? Was she ready for such an act?

He studied her carefully. She looked hesitant and was no doubt regretting her impulsive offer but he knew he was going to take her up on it. He couldn't help himself. The thought of her soft hands and plump lips wrapped around his cock had him pulsing in discomfort. Besides, he'd wanted her forever and she was his now. In his opinion, the moment that he'd taken her virginity had made her so.

He would be careful with her and ease her into it gently. He would give her every possible consideration that he could offer.

He studied her. She chewed on her bottom lip and stared into her lap.

"Look at me, Lillian," he said softly and stretched a hand forward to stroke her cheek.

She snapped her head up and he drew his breath in sharply when her emerald eyes met his, their green depths swimming with uncertainty and instilling in him a burning need to protect her and assuage her hesitation.

"I won't hurt you, sweetheart," he promised. "You're curious?"

She continued to worry her bottom lip then nodded slowly.

He stepped closer to her, nudging her thighs apart until he was standing between her legs. He framed her face with his palms, brushing his thumbs over her cheeks as he tilted her head back.

"Unzip my trousers, Lilly," he murmured, maintaining eye contact with her and caressing soothing circles on her cheeks with his thumbs.

He stiffened when she brushed his crotch and fumbled with the zip, dragging it down. He struggled to regulate his breathing as her small hands rubbed against his erection. *Shit, if she keeps doing that, I won't last long.*

He hissed in a breath. "Easy, Lilly, or you'll unman me."

She dropped her gaze to his crotch and was inspecting the bulge there with avid fascination.

He swept his hands to her shoulders and massaged her gently.

"Now reach in and take out my cock," he demanded huskily.

She gasped at his crude words, but he wanted to shock her. He wanted her to fully comprehend exactly what she was about to do.

He continued to knead her shoulders gently while she reached into his trousers and tentatively felt around.

Fuck. Her touch is sending bolts of pleasure straight to my balls.

He looked down at her from under hooded lids and watched her withdraw his throbbing member. He was so hard it was painful. The pleasure her gentle touch was inciting had his stomach muscles tightening and quivering in anticipation.

She looked up at him in wide-eyed fascination as she handled his erection. "It's very big," she whispered, running her fingers up and down his shaft.

He chuckled. "I'm rather large, but as you discovered last night, you stretch to accommodate me."

"It feels soft but hard, like velvet over a steel rod," she mused.

She ran her thumb over his glistening tip and he groaned, tightening his hold on her shoulders.

She looked up at him with worried eyes. "Did I hurt you?"

"No, sweetheart. That feels very good—too good. The tip is very sensitive. Similar to a certain place on your anatomy," he responded with a wicked grin and was rewarded with her fierce blush.

"Wrap your fingers around me and move them up and down, like this," he demonstrated for her.

She grasped his cock around the base with one hand and wrapped the fingers of her other hand above it and started to pump him up and down as he'd shown her.

The sight and feel of her small hands on his steel-hard shaft was heating his blood to boiling point and he groaned loudly, tensing his thighs and tightening his grasp on her shoulders.

"That's it, sweetheart." He started to thrust his hips in rhythm with her pumping hands.

He gazed down at her face and watched her work him over with a little, thoughtful frown. She was focused on her task and concentrating. Her breathing had increased and was creating little gusts of warm air over his throbbing erection.

He felt the pressure building in his groin, starting to work closer to release, but he didn't want to go yet. The feel of her hands on him, and watching her fascination, was something he wanted to prolong.

"Is this right?" she asked huskily, licking her lips and gazing up at him.

Her flushed cheeks and ragged breathing told him that she was aroused by what she was doing to him.

He growled and pumped his hips harder. "That's just right, sweetheart. Can't you tell what you're doing to me?"

Sweat dripped from his brow and his neck muscles locked, as he worked to maintain control. He needed her to experience the full impact of how she affected him. He wanted her to appreciate the fact that just her touch could make him rock hard and swell agonizingly.

He gazed down the rippling muscles of his abdomen to see her rubbing his pre-release all over his cock, lubricating him and creating a sight so erotic he knew he'd never forget it. Then, to his stunned amazement, she dropped her head to his shaft and flicked him a quick glance under her lashes, seeking his permission. He nodded once, barely registering her intentions, and held his breath as she closed her mouth around the bulbous head.

"Oh fuck, Lilly," he grunted, grasping her hair in one hand and sweeping his other hand up to cup her cheek. He was fast losing control and had long since given up on maintaining polite niceties.

He knew he wouldn't last long now. The feel of her hot, succulent mouth and lips wrapped around his cock was incredible. She hesitantly ran her tongue up and down his length, lapping at his pre-cum and fisting the base of his shaft. God, if he didn't know better, he'd think she'd done this before.

She took his tip into her mouth once more and he groaned, fisting her glorious hair tighter and manipulating her head gently. "That's it, sweetheart. Wrap those plump lips around me."

She gazed up at him under her lashes, her eyes seeking his guidance and reassurance.

"Relax your jaw, Lilly. Take me in farther," he said softly, caressing her cheek in encouragement.

She opened her mouth wider, wrapped her lips around her teeth and took him deeper as he gently guided her glide up and down his length.

She moaned, the action sending delicious vibrations rocketing through him until he was clenching his teeth so hard his jaw ached. He looked down to watch her slide his cock in and out of her mouth and the sight of his shaft, coated in her saliva and his pre-cum, gliding through her swollen lips had his balls drawing up and his abdominals clenching tightly.

His breath was coming in quick, short bursts as he struggled for control. Her mouth was so warm and wet that he wanted to bury himself there forever.

Knowing that he was the only man who had ever taken that beautiful mouth had him reeling with such violent possessiveness, the feeling staggered him.

She sucked on him greedily as he gripped her hair even tighter and splayed his other hand behind her neck. When he felt his cock brush the back of her throat, he was done for. His climax was on him and the build-up of pressure clamored for release.

"I'm going to come, Lilly," he said urgently but continued his rapid thrusts. He vaguely registered that he needed to warn her, to ready her to let go. "Do you know what that means?" he asked between gritted teeth.

He was on the edge and it was taking every element of his control not to blow her head off.

Potent lust curled talon-like down his spine. She looked up and slowly drew her lips back until she released his cock with a loud popping sound.

"I want to taste it," she pronounced softly.

"Oh fuck," he grunted and thrust back in between her waiting lips. It was too much — *She wants to fucking taste me!* Those erotic words, spoken out of her sweet, innocent mouth had him plummeting over the edge immediately.

He gripped her head and thrust hard one last time then threw his head back and roared as his pent-up release jetted out of him in long spurts and streamed into her.

He panted heavily and took a moment to gather himself before he gently extracted his still-erect cock from her mouth. He released his grip on her hair and massaged her scalp gently as he looked down upon her upturned face. She looked so breathtakingly lovely with her flushed cheeks and puffy, just-fucked lips that she took his breath away. He noticed a drop of his semen at the corner of her mouth and felt his cock twitch and surge to attention once more. *Christ, I've never seen anything so sexual, so purely carnal as my cream on that succulent, sweet mouth.* He reined in his raging erection and wiped her lip with his thumb.

"Are you okay? I didn't hurt you, did I?"

She smiled shyly and shook her head. "I liked it. Did I do it properly?"

Fuck, she liked it! She's going to kill me. He caressed her cheek with his knuckles. "I'm glad you liked it, my sweet. Many women don't and yes, it was perfect."

A small frown crossed her pretty features and he guessed it was due to his reference to other women. He didn't want to go there. It was neither the time nor the place.

He tucked himself in and re-zipped his trousers. "I'll give you some privacy so you can wash and dress." He dropped a chaste kiss on her lips before leaving her alone.

Chapter Fourteen

Lillian washed and dressed quickly. She was anxious to be up and about and to see that the children didn't interfere too much with Mrs. Thompson's housekeeping activities.

When she descended the stairs, she heard the children in the kitchen and followed the sounds of laughing and chatter to find them standing on chairs at the large, oak kitchen bench where they were rolling dough and scattering flour throughout the large space. Mrs. Thompson, flushed from the heat of the stove, was stooping to check on her baking bread.

"Good morning," Lillian greeted them brightly.

A chorus of cheerful hellos welcomed her and her heart warmed at the sight of the homey kitchen scene.

She collected an apron from a hook on the wall and tied it around herself before joining the children at the bench and assisting in the rolling and cutting of the scone dough.

She mused as she helped and wondered just where her relationship with William stood. She was also worried about the possibility that she could be pregnant. She couldn't believe that she hadn't considered the prospect before William had brought it to her attention, but then she supposed that she hadn't had much time to think about anything outside the events and revelations made the previous evening. Now she had one more thing to worry about. She could only pray that William was correct in his estimation that the timing of her courses would prevent a pregnancy.

She had to admit that being with William was beyond her wildest fantasies. She'd never have believed that her body was capable of such physical responses, but she supposed that her love for him had something to do with the way she reacted to him so readily. She flushed when she recalled what they'd done in her room that morning and that she'd enjoyed it. The odd sense of power she'd felt was extraordinary and she loved the fact that she could produce in him the sensations that he so easily elicited from her. She looked forward to an opportunity when they could once more be alone together. And they did need to be alone, if for nothing else than to talk. She desperately needed to hear from William where their relationship stood. She loved him—she always had— but she'd long ago given up any hope of their being together. Now, at any moment, she expected to wake up and find that the last twenty-four hours had been just a fanciful dream that she'd awake from, once more alone and heartbroken.

She could continue as if nothing had happened between them, but she knew she'd only be able to keep up the pretense for so long. No, she determined that she would seek William out and ask him frankly what he saw in their future.

* * * *

Lillian had half expected William to be out working on the property, so it was with some surprise, as she drifted down the hallway later that morning, that she heard the deep rumble of his voice from the drawing room. He was obviously in conversation with someone. Not wanting to intrude, she stopped just shy of the doorway and peered in to ascertain his visitor.

Standing in the drawing room with William was a woman. She was statuesque and handsome and looked to be his age or slightly older. It was immediately obvious to Lillian that the two knew each other well.

"It has been a long time since you visited me, William," the woman admonished.

She walked toward him, a gentle sway to her generous hips, and placed a hand on his arm in a familiar gesture. "Perhaps you can find time for lunch next week?" Her voice was soft and seductive and promised an invitation for more than food.

Lillian wasn't sure if it was her newfound sexuality or just an innate woman's sixth sense, but she realized instantly that William and this woman had been intimate. The knowledge sent a wave of nausea through her and she had to grip the doorframe as she swayed unsteadily. The movement caught the attention of the two in the drawing room and William was by her side in an instant.

"Lillian, what is it? You look pale." He grasped her around the waist and helped her into the room before lowering her into a chair.

"I'm fine," she muttered apologetically. "Just a little faint. I'm sure it will pass."

William knelt in front of her, his handsome face creased in concern, and took one of her hands in his. She looked past William to the woman standing behind him and almost flinched at the venomous daggers the woman was shooting in her direction.

"This must be the little governess," the woman commented waspishly, as she stepped forward and placed a hand possessively on William's shoulder. "Perhaps the outback air doesn't agree with her. The poor thing looks a little peaked."

William shrugged off the woman's attention and stood to face her. "I won't be able to make lunch next week. Thank you for the invitation, but I'm otherwise engaged."

He stretched an arm out in the direction of the door, a signal that the visit was over. "Thank you for the deliveries, Mrs. Simpson. I'll show you out."

Lillian heard her speaking in a hushed tone to William as they made their way to the front door, but she was unable to make out anything that was said. A moment later, William was back, closing the door behind him, then he returned to a kneeling position in front of her.

"Who was that woman?" Lillian asked, her head cocked to one side.

William pushed a hand through his hair then stood to take a seat opposite her. "That was Mary Simpson. She runs the local store and post office. She stopped by to deliver some mail."

Lillian snorted derisively. "One hardly 'stops by' the property, William. Surely she made a special trip?"

"Yes, she did. She was concerned because she hadn't seen me for some weeks and she wanted to extend an invitation to lunch the next time I was in town."

"Is she married?"

William shifted uncomfortably. "She's a widow. Her husband was killed in the war."

"You two seemed to be quite close," she commented, assessing him carefully.

He stood suddenly and paced to the window where he stopped with his back to her and stared for a moment through the glass. Then he turned and rested his hands behind him on the windowsill and fixed her with a long look. "Mary and I have, in the past, kept each other company," he explained in a low voice.

"Did that 'keeping each other company' involve a bed?"

William's countenance turned grim. "Yes, as it happens. We were both adults and both in need of physical company. It wasn't anything more than that."

"I think it definitely felt like *more* to her," Lillian argued. "She was positively venomous toward me and very possessive of you."

"Lillian," he said sharply. "I didn't give her any indication that it would be more than a casual, physical affair between us. She's a widow, hardly an inexperienced maiden."

"Unlike me," she responded softly.

His eyes grew wide as he realized the significance of his last words. "Yes," he muttered. "And there's a difference. I told you this morning that I'm responsible for you. Mary Simpson is an experienced woman who has her own life and livelihood. She's not in need of my protection—nor does she want it. I, however, have put *you* in a precarious position and I intend to make things right."

She'd no idea what he meant by 'making things right' or how he intended to go about doing it, but it didn't appear that he was going to enlighten her any time in the near future. Another aspect regarding his last words bothered her. "Is that what this is, William? A sense of obligation—of duty—toward me?"

He reclaimed the seat opposite. "No," he bit out. "I told you that I've wanted you forever—that you should have been mine ten years ago—but for the disgraceful deeds of your father!"

"But do you really like Mary Simpson and will you continue to...see her?"

"Is this what caused your little swooning episode?" he asked with a slight smile. "That you recognized something between Mary and me?"

Suddenly uncomfortable, she clasped her hands in her lap and stared down at her entwined fingers. "It was a shock, that's all. I could tell, by the way she moved and touched you, that you'd been intimate."

She looked up to see him nodding thoughtfully. "I didn't realize it was so obvious. In any case, I won't be seeing her again in that way. I'd just finished telling her that when you overheard her invitation to lunch." He grinned. "Mary is nothing if not tenacious. She's not particularly happy that our weekly rendezvous will be coming to an end."

Lillian was aghast. "Weekly?"

William sighed heavily. "Yes, Lilly. We met weekly. You must understand that I'm a man with needs. She had similar needs. It was an association that worked for both of us, and I reiterate that no promises were made on either side."

"So what now?" she asked the question uppermost in her mind.

"I can control myself, Lillian. I don't go running around the countryside finding skirts to lift! And control myself I must, because there will be nothing physical happening between you and I in the foreseeable future."

Lillian gaped in dismay. She wasn't sure what she'd been expecting, but it definitely hadn't been that.

He smirked. "I'm gratified by your apparent disappointment. But you'll be tender for some time and, of course, I will not risk you becoming pregnant."

"Is there not something we can do to...?" She waved a hand in the air.

William spoke before she could continue. "To prevent pregnancy?" he asked with a raised eyebrow.

She nodded.

"My, my," he chuckled. "You are becoming quite the temptress *and* a demanding little thing with it." He leaned toward her and dragged his thumb over her bottom lip. "*My* sweet, demanding little thing."

Her pulse leaped and a dozen butterflies fluttered to life in her belly at his sensuous touch.

He sat back in his chair once more and stared at her thoughtfully. "There are things that we can do," he said slowly. "But not until you're fully recovered."

She sighed in consternation. She really did feel fine. She wasn't sure how much recovery time William thought was needed.

"By the way, the annual Coolabah picnic horse races are this Saturday. Would you like to attend?"

Another outing with William! She very much wanted to step out with him again and the races sounded like glorious fun.

She smiled. "I'd very much like to go."

"Good. After the races, in the evening, we have the Picnic Race Day Ball. It's a big day and probably one of the biggest events of the year. People come from miles around to attend."

Her pulse pumped in excitement when she thought about the anticipated race day frivolities and the prospect of spending an entire day and evening in William's company.

Chapter Fifteen

Lillian looked at her wardrobe with despair. She had four days until the picnic races and absolutely nothing to wear. Before she'd left England, she'd sold her more glamorous party and luncheon dresses and, apart from the one evening gown, had only kept a handful of her sturdier, conservative outfits. Dresses, blouses and skirts that were neat and practical for a governess serving duties on an outback sheep station, but were not nearly impressive enough for a day like the annual picnic races. She understood that a country race day would bear no resemblance to a similar event in the city—however, it was still one of the largest local social events and she knew that the ladies would take great delight in dressing up for the occasion.

Lillian needed to seek Mrs. Thompson's assistance. Perhaps she'd know where ladies' attire could be purchased in one of the bigger towns. William was away, sheep mustering, and wasn't due to return until late on the Friday before race day, so she had time to arrange transportation to and from wherever she would need to go.

She found Mrs. Thompson dusting in the drawing room and immediately explained her clothing predicament.

The housekeeper stopped what she was doing and looked thoughtfully at Lillian, eyeing her up and down.

"I have an idea," the older woman announced. "Come with me."

Lillian followed her to a bedroom on the second level. A large bed stood in the middle, covered with a colorful patchwork counterpane. Side tables with decorative porcelain kerosene lamps stood either side of the bed. In the corner of the room sat a table with a pitcher and basin, and the opposite corner held a black Singer treadle sewing machine.

"What a lovely room," Lillian exclaimed. "So vibrant."

"Yes, it is pretty. This was Ruth Cartwright's bedroom," Mrs. Thompson explained. "Toward the end, when she was so sick that it was better that she slept alone. She needed almost constant care. We had a live-in nurse for a while and the doctor was a weekly visitor." She glanced around the room. "William had it wallpapered especially for her. He'd hoped that the bright flowers would provide comfort and cheer."

Tears pricked the backs of Lillian's eyes, as she thought of the young mother lying so sick in bed but drawing consolation from the cheery décor provided by her husband.

"Here we are," Mrs. Thompson muttered and opened a large trunk at the foot of the bed.

Lillian crouched next to her and watched the older woman pull various items of folded clothing from the trunk.

"Ruth had some lovely dresses. They'll be too big for you and a little outdated, but between the two of us, we should be able to fashion something appropriate for the picnic race day and something for the ball afterwards," the housekeeper said, laying items of clothing out on the bed.

Lillian admired the luxurious chiffon, silk and lace garments spread out before her. She ran a hand reverently across a stunning dress of pale green silk with a delicate lace overlay in darker green and a draped sash to be tied at the side of the waist.

"These are very lovely," she murmured. "However, I do have money and I just need to get to the nearest city where I can purchase something. Besides, I'm not sure that it would be appropriate for us to destroy Ruth's beautiful dresses."

"Nonsense," Mrs. Thompson declared. "For one, getting you to the city is easier said than done and we wouldn't be 'destroying' Ruth's dresses—we would be reusing them—and in turn, they will be re-loved. Ruth sewed most of these dresses—she was an excellent seamstress. She would send away to Sydney for the fabric and patterns. She also sewed most of the children's clothes, reusing anything that she had at hand. It was the only thing to be done during the war years when getting hold of fabric was often difficult and expensive. Ruth disliked waste. She would re-fashion many of her clothes by just a change of ribbons or lace. She would give a hat a new look by adding some feathers or some beading." Mrs. Thompson smiled wistfully. "I remember when she fashioned a new hat for a church picnic out of lace doilies and chicken feathers, which she'd painted blue. It was a real hit and in war times, who needs doilies when a new accessory can make you feel a little bit special and soften your worries for a day?" The older woman looked Lillian in the eye. "Now, if there's one thing that I'm absolutely certain of, she would abhor the fact that her beautiful creations are gathering dust, unused and unloved, sitting in a trunk!"

Lillian smiled at the image that Mrs. Thompson was creating in her mind of Ruth Cartwright.

"She must have been a very talented and resourceful woman," Lillian said in admiration.

"She was," Mrs. Thompson agreed. "But she was not sentimental or romantic, nor was she selfish. She was practical. She knew she was dying and she accepted that, but her one worry was William and the children. She told me one day, not long before she passed, that her dearest wish was that William would find someone else to share his life with. A woman who would love him and the children. She didn't want the little ones to be without a mother figure. I believe she told William the same thing. So please, Lillian, don't distress yourself over this. I knew Ruth well and I know that she'd be beyond pleased that her clothes will once more see the light of day."

Lillian wondered at the housekeeper's imparting to her Ruth's wish that William would find someone else. *Is she suspicious about William and me?* Lillian studied her face but saw nothing other than an honest and straightforward expression.

"Now, let's have a look at some of these dresses. We shall try the green one first," Mrs. Thompson stated.

Within moments, Lillian found herself undressed and standing in front of a beveled mirror, wearing the pale green silk and lace.

Ruth must have been significantly taller than Lillian—the dress pooled around Lillian's feet and the arms were too long—but she could tell that it would only take some minor adjustments and taking in at the waist and hips to make the dress fit appropriately.

"It is lovely." Lillian twirled around. "Ruth really was very talented."

"I think we can work with this one for the picnic race day and this deep red velvet dress will look lovely for the ball," Mrs. Thompson said, as she held the dress up in front of Lillian to study it in the mirror. "It brings out the natural mahogany color of your hair."

The dresses decided upon, the women got to work with the alterations. Lillian felt much more comfortable about the day and evening ahead, knowing that she'd be dressed appropriately and wouldn't embarrass William. She still worried about his reaction to her altering and wearing his wife's clothes but she'd find out soon enough what William's response would be.

* * * *

The Saturday of the picnic races dawned bright and sunny. William was looking forward to spending the day with Lillian and was hoping that some enjoyment and time spent in each other's company would serve to relax her a little. He also had another agenda—he wanted to be seen together and not just as property owner and governess, but also as potential companions, while observing the protocols of propriety. It was a fine line to walk, he knew.

He'd given their situation much thought, and although their current relationship was not ideal, he'd have done anything to have experienced half as much with Lillian ten years ago. Since she'd set sail for England and subsequently out of his life, he'd never allowed himself to hope that he would see her again and had delegated her memory to a locked compartment within his heart as he'd conscientiously moved on with his life.

He'd never spoken to his wife about Lillian but he knew that Ruth had been aware there had been someone before her, whom he'd loved and cherished, and her awareness of that pained him. Before she died, she'd told him that she hoped he would find someone who would love him and the children as much as she did. He was sure that she'd have approved of Lillian and that she'd be happy for him.

Now, he had to focus on the way ahead for himself and Lillian. He didn't want to rush things with her. Albeit that he'd taken her virginity and introduced her to equally enjoyable sexual activities, he also wanted to solidify their emotional relationship and for that, he needed to move slowly and surely. There was one fact that he was completely confident about and that fact was that Lillian was his—indisputably, undeniably his. He wouldn't let her go a second time and he needed to prove to her that they belonged together. He knew *his* feelings, but he was still unsure about hers.

The intimacy that they'd shared was new to her—unfamiliar sensations and a new sexual awareness that he wanted her to grow into, embrace and feel comfortable with. He knew that he'd rushed the sexual side of things but he wouldn't rush the relationship. To start with, he didn't want to marry her immediately. People would talk and Lilly deserved more than a quick, thrown-together wedding where all the guests would be questioning the reason behind such a hurried affair. *He* didn't care what people thought, but he wouldn't put Lilly through any uncomfortable, less than ideal situations *and* he had to be sure that she was ready to spend the rest of her life with him.

Of course, he'd already admitted to himself that he wouldn't let her go and in truth, he couldn't ever see himself doing so easily, but she required time to adjust, to make her own decision, because he couldn't bear for her to tie herself to him just for reasons of expectation and security. For too long she'd been living a life decreed by others and he knew that for Lilly to be truly happy, she'd have to make a decision based on her terms and above all, he needed to be sure that she still loved him.

Chapter Sixteen

Lillian had finished dressing. The green dress had turned out pleasingly and she was happy with the alterations they'd made. Ruth's taller stature meant that the gown midriff hung lower on Lillian, giving the dress the fashionable dropped waistline. She and Mrs. Thompson had removed much of the lace, so the bodice now had a simple V of lace overlay in the front and back. The skirt of the dress flowed loosely to swirl around her calves. It was fashionable and appropriate for a picnic race day and she hoped that if Ruth was looking down on them, she'd be proud of what they'd achieved and happy with how well her dress looked.

She donned a dark green hat, which she'd brought with her from London. It was adorned with a large satin bow and she fixed it to her hair with two hatpins. The hat was the height of current fashion and she'd been unable to part with it before she'd left England. It was one of the few luxury concessions she'd allowed herself.

She left her room and went to meet William in the drawing room. Taking a deep breath, she opened the door, entered and closed it quietly behind her.

William was standing with his back to her. When he turned to face her, his eyes grew wide and his jaw hardened, a muscle twitching erratically in his cheek. He was angry.

"I'm s-sorry. I shouldn't have presumed... I didn't have anything appropriate... Mrs. Thompson thought..."

Lillian didn't know what to say—how to explain. She knew it had been a bad idea to alter his wife's dress. She and Mrs. Thompson had discussed the fact that Ruth wouldn't have minded, but she'd just realized horribly that they hadn't taken William's reaction or feelings on the matter into consideration.

She needed to get back to her room, to get out of the dress that had obviously caused William so much offense and distress.

"Excuse me," she whispered, turning to flee.

"Lillian!"

Her name, spoken in such a commanding tone, stopped her in her tracks.

"You look beautiful," William said softly.

Slowly, Lillian turned to face him. "I'm sorry. I should have asked your permission before I altered Ruth's dress. It was just that you were away mustering and Mrs. Thompson insisted that Ruth would not have minded, that she would have hated the fact that her lovely garments are being unused and unloved."

William smiled. "Millie is correct, of course. Ruth hated waste, of any type—particularly given things were so difficult during the war. She most definitely would abhor the fact that her clothes are sitting unremembered and idle in a trunk. I meant to give them to charity, but I never got around to it. Ruth has been gone for some time now, Lillian. It was just a shock to see that dress again—it was a favorite of hers and mine. I wouldn't have recognized it but for the striking color."

"So you're not mad?" Lillian asked, hope and relief tingeing her voice.

"No. I most definitely am not mad. Now, come here."

Lillian hesitated then moved toward him. When she drew closer, he grasped her to him and wrapped her in a warm embrace. She circled her arms about his waist and pressed her head against his chest, reveling in the hard strength of him and his masculine scent. It was a place where she felt protected and comforted.

He pulled back a little, cupped her chin and lifted her face so she could meet his eyes. "I'm sorry. I should have asked you if you had appropriate attire. I didn't think," he said quietly. "I could have arranged for a shopping expedition or for some fabric to be delivered."

"I sold most of my good dresses before I left England. I needed the money more than I needed pretty clothes."

He tensed against her and closed his eyes momentarily, as if in pain. "I'm sorry that you were ever in that position. You must have been terrified, not knowing what awaited you in Australia and having to endure that long voyage alone."

She shrugged. "I managed. I just had to have faith that everything would work out."

"Well, I'm beyond relieved that you made it here, to me, safely," he stated and dropped his mouth to hers.

Lillian's knees grew weak and her heart rate doubled as William swept his tongue into her mouth to tangle and dance with hers. He banded an arm tightly around her waist, held her to him and deepened their kiss, slanting his lips across hers. Everything flew from her mind and all sense of reality left her as she lost herself in William's arms, in the feel of him possessing her with his kiss. She snaked her arms up around his neck, gripped the hair at his nape and sank further into his embrace, succumbing to his mouth as he drank from her.

All too soon, he pulled away, steadying her with two hands on her shoulders while she caught her breath.

He dropped his forehead to hers. "That should keep me going for the day. We should go. Are you ready?"

"Yes," she breathed. "I'm very excited."

"Good. It should be a fun day." He smiled and led her from the room.

* * * *

Colorful picnic blankets were spread far and wide. Ladies were strolling with parasols and children were playing and running through the throng. Men stood in groups, chatting about horse form and history while bookies cried out the latest odds. It was a hive of activity — a typical day at the country races — and Lillian felt a wave of exhilaration sweep through her. She had a small amount of money she'd brought with her from her savings that she would use to place some little bets later.

They located a good position to set up their picnic blanket and Mrs. Thompson and Lillian set to work unpacking the food. They'd assembled a delicious array of cold roast lamb, potato salad, bread and cheese, and had packed some homemade blackberry wine. The children ran off to meet up with their friends and William went to speak with some of the locals to discuss horses, farming and wool prices. When he returned, he was carrying two fold-up wooden chairs, which he set up next to their picnic blanket for her and Mrs. Thompson.

They located the children and sat to eat lunch. There was something about eating a meal in the sunshine and among such frivolity that made the food even more delicious. Lillian drank a few glasses of Mrs. Thompson's fruity wine and was feeling decidedly tipsy, heightening her mood for enjoyment. They chatted to neighbors, who stopped by to say hello, and William introduced her to those whom she didn't know. She was having a lovely time, relaxing and enjoying the beautiful, sunny day. At one o'clock, William announced that the races would soon start.

"Oh good," Lillian exclaimed in excitement. "I'm going to place a few little bets."

William grinned. "Would you like me to give you some tips? I've had some interesting discussions with some of the locals."

"Yes, thank you."

"Remember, these are not the races you will be accustomed to in the city," William explained. "It really is more about the social occasion and it's one of the few opportunities when we get together as a community. The horses are predominantly owned and ridden by locals, but we do have fun predicting the winners."

He went on to outline the horses and jockeys and those who he expected to do well, explaining the odds against each.

"Do you have enough money?" he enquired mildly.

Lillian gave him a sharp look. "Yes, thank you. I have some money put away. I can definitely manage to make a few small bets."

William regarded her coolly. "I'm merely looking out for you, Lilly. I would hate for you to feel obligated to spend money that you don't have."

"Well, I've managed quite well on my own thus far, thank you. I'm going to take a stroll around, then place a few bets for fun." She stood and stretched. "I need to exercise my legs after sitting for so long."

Lillian marveled at all the brightly colored stands selling lemonade, jams and cakes. There were people playing games of horseshoes and children running sack races.

Childhood memories of similar race day picnics flooded her consciousness and left her feeling pleasantly nostalgic for the carefree, happy days of her youth.

She turned a corner, one eye trained on the game of horseshoe in front of her when a figure to her right caught her attention.

"Well, if it isn't the little governess," a voice sneered.

Lillian turned to find Mary Simpson at her side. The woman appeared less than pleased to see her and made a show of looking her up and down, an expression of contempt crossing her features.

Lillian thought quickly and opted to be civil to the woman. After all, it was too nice a day to spoil it with petty nastiness from the likes of her.

"Good day, Mrs. Simpson," Lillian returned politely. "I hope you're enjoying the festivities."

"*You* obviously are," the woman rejoined sarcastically. "After all, you do have the handsome and highly sought after William Cartwright by your side. Just where you're angling to be permanently, no doubt."

"I'm sure I don't know what you mean," Lillian responded mildly. "I'm not certain if you're aware, but William and I are childhood friends. As such, is it very surprising that I've become the children's governess?"

She was pleased to see the look of surprise cross the woman's features. Obviously Mrs. Simpson was not aware of the history that she and William shared.

She recovered quickly. "I don't think that *you* are aware that William and I share some history ourselves."

Lillian had had enough. The woman clearly felt slighted, and while she couldn't really blame her, by the way William had explained things, there was nothing serious to their relationship. She decided that the time for playing nice was over.

"As it happens, Mrs. Simpson, William did explain to me your relationship — such as it *was*. He also mentioned to me that it was a casual affair and one which he has no wish to continue."

The other woman paled beneath her heavily rouged cheeks. "You think that your youth and beauty will win him over. But William needs a real woman, a woman who is experienced in the arts of taking care of a man. A woman who can make him a good wife," she spat hatefully.

So this is the crux of it. Mary Simpson obviously has designs on William that journey beyond the bedroom. She looked the woman over and knew that William would never have pursued more than a casual affair with her. She was brash and brassy and from what Lillian had learned thus far, she could also be quite spiteful — all qualities, she knew, that William would despise in a serious partner. No, while it was clear to Lillian that Mary Simpson had perhaps harbored a wish to become the next Mrs. Cartwright, it was also clear to her that William would never have encouraged the woman to think thus.

"Mrs. Simpson," Lillian said quietly. "Despite what you might think, I'm just the governess. Now, if you'll excuse me." She turned away from the bitter woman and walked quickly in the opposite direction.

Lillian seethed quietly as she returned to their picnic blanket. The nerve of the woman to suggest that she was angling to marry William! What William had ever seen in her, Lillian could only guess at, but she assumed that it had rested on her willingness to share her bed so readily.

As their picnic blanket came into view, so, too, did two newcomers who'd obviously made themselves quite comfortable. Lillian recognized Mr. George Dawson and his daughter Margaret, who had taken the seat vacated by Lillian earlier. Mr. Dawson was lounging casually on the picnic blanket, sipping on a glass of blackberry wine and chatting amiably.

What enflamed Lillian, however, was the blatantly flirtatious attention of the young Miss Dawson toward William. She was giggling shamelessly at something that William had obviously said and had placed a small gloved hand on William's shoulder as she tittered prettily into her other. Even more vexing to Lillian was the fact that William appeared to be enjoying the attentions of the young woman. He reclined on the blanket in a very masculine manner — one leg hooked underneath him while the other was bent at the knee, his arm resting across it at the elbow. His right shoulder relaxed against the chair in which Miss Dawson was seated.

From an outsider's perspective, the little party of picnickers made a lovely tableau and could easily be assumed to be a comfortable, happy family enjoying the day of festivities.

Suddenly and inexplicably, Lillian felt like an interloper and as though joining the group would be a rude intrusion. She was frozen to the spot for a long moment, racked with indecision and an overwhelming feeling of loneliness. Then, quickly, her wits once more restored, she spun on her heel and strode in the opposite direction, desperate to make an escape before her presence was detected.

Chapter Seventeen

"So, Cartwright, how is your new governess working out?"

William looked at the other man in surprise. "Fine, thank you for asking. The children adore her and Miss Hamilton is very good with them."

"So how is she coping with life in the outback? It can't be an easy transition for her, coming from London as she has."

"Miss Hamilton is not new to the area or the outback lifestyle," William remarked. "We grew up together. That's how I knew she'd be the perfect person to teach the children what they need to know. I see her time spent in England as an advantage, actually. I imagine that she has a great many experiences that the children will benefit from."

George Dawson narrowed his eyes thoughtfully. "I didn't realize that the two of you share a history."

"Just the history of childhood friends, Dawson," William responded mildly. "And the mutual respect that situation often engenders."

He was not about to discuss his private life with the likes of George Dawson. While he had nothing against the man, he didn't class him as a close friend and he had a feeling that Dawson wouldn't like the fact that he considered Lillian to be much more than just his governess. Thinking of Lillian made him glance around for her. *What is taking her so long?*

He hadn't missed all the admiring looks that she'd been receiving since they'd arrived. He wasn't surprised — she looked breathtaking. She was fresh and vibrant and she easily surpassed in loveliness all the women at the gathering. He looked up to where Miss Dawson sat by his side, dressed in pale pink. She looked very pretty and could be quite charming, but in his eyes, she lacked the exquisite beauty and clever wit of Lillian.

Miss Dawson, seeing his eyes on her, grinned coquettishly and fluttered her fan as he smiled at her absently.

"Cartwright," George Dawson interrupted his reverie.

William looked in the man's direction to see him smile smugly.

"Sorry to interfere with your perusal of my daughter's lovely countenance, but we would like to invite you to lunch next week. It's been too long since we have spent some time together. We need to catch up."

William nodded noncommittally. "Yes, it's been a while. Lunch next week would be very nice, but I have to check my calendar. I expect a busy week on the property."

Margaret Dawson giggled and slapped him on the arm playfully with her fan. "Oh, William. You have a manager and station hands who can run things for an afternoon."

He nodded absently, not wanting to commit to anything specific. He was now quite concerned with Lillian's continued absence and decided that it was time to go in search of her.

* * * *

Lillian found herself at the stables. The smell of hay and the rich scent of horses assaulted her senses and calmed her instantly. She'd always loved horses. She found them to be soothing and reassuring creatures that had the ability to tap into a person's emotions and provide comfort when needed. As if to prove her philosophy, a mare pushed her head over a stable door into Lillian's shoulder and snorted softly against her skin. Lillian smiled and reached up to stroke the animal's nose.

She was enjoying the peace of the moment. She couldn't quite believe how a perfect day had turned into a less than perfect one so quickly. She understood that she'd overreacted just now when she had seen that the Dawsons had joined their picnic, but she hadn't been able to help herself. The feelings of isolation and loneliness had been overwhelming and had taken her straight back to her dark days in England. She needed to distance herself from the situation and gain some rational perspective. She had no right to act jealously or be irritated by William's associations and she was appalled at her own behavior, but things had been moving so quickly between them that she was confused by their relationship and her own feelings. Seeing William again after so many years had thrown her into turmoil and resurrected all her feelings for him that for so long and so hard she'd tried to bury. Now she was not only faced with William and all the wondrous sensations he aroused in her, but also the women with whom he associated, who seemed to have hidden expectations and agendas. The whole situation was stirring her into a turbulent mass of emotions and she had to take a step back to evaluate. She was no longer the sixteen-year-old girl who had fallen head over heels in love with her childhood sweetheart. She'd experienced a lot since that time, much of which was difficult, but all of which had served to make her a stronger person. She needed to take that strength now and use it to defend herself against any additional, potentially hurtful situations.

Lillian had continued to stroke the mare's soft nose, taking comfort in the gentle creature's nearness. A waft of tobacco smoke swirled toward her and alerted her to the fact that she was no longer alone. Startled, she turned to see John Steele leaning casually against a nearby post, quietly watching her while he sucked on a pipe.

"Mr. Steele," she greeted him cordially with a slight nod of her head.

"Hello again, Miss Hamilton. May I say that you're looking particularly lovely today? In fact, I would go so far as to say that you are the loveliest lady at this gathering."

Lillian blushed. "Thank you. That is very kind of you to say. Although I would have to disagree."

He shook his head in admonishment and walked toward her. "You are too modest, my lady."

She smiled slightly and stepped away from the mare, giving her silky coat one last, soothing caress.

"To what do I owe this unexpected meeting?" she asked with a raised eyebrow.

"It's just coincidence, I can assure you, but I'm glad that I ran into you. Please accept my apologies for my behavior at the dinner dance. I acted appallingly. I very regrettably misconstrued your desire for a walk."

Lillian nodded in acknowledgment and watched as he tamped down his pipe before slipping it into an inner pocket of his waistcoat.

He offered her his arm. "Will you allow me to make it up to you? Will you walk with me? You look like you're in need of some pleasant conversation and diversion. I love horses but they are not great conversationalists."

Lillian smiled and linked her arm with his. "That is true, but they *are* very good listeners and providers of comfort. Horses have always soothed me."

"And what has you in need of comfort, may I ask?"

Lillian studied him while they strolled. She knew that William harbored a dislike for John Steele, but as he hadn't bothered to enlighten her about it, she could see no harm in taking an innocent walk with the man in broad daylight. Besides, Mr. Steele had happened along at a time when she could use a distraction and some light conversation.

"Nothing specific," she finally answered.

"It wouldn't have anything to do with Mary Simpson, would it?"

Lillian threw him a sharp look. "Why do you ask?"

"I saw you with her earlier. I was placing a bet when I saw you walk past and I'd planned to follow you to offer my apologies for my behavior the night we met. When I looked up next, you were engaged in conversation with Mary and it looked to be quite heated."

Lillian gave him a level stare. "She's under the impression that I'm more than a governess and she believes that I'm harboring some idea of acquiring William for myself."

He looked shocked. "I can't believe that she would approach you like that. Everyone knows that she has designs on William Cartwright, but to accuse *you* of such a thing is totally inappropriate."

"I was a little taken aback but I understand it for what it is. I won't let her jealousy get to me."

She supposed that she *was* more than a governess. What her actual status was in William's life, she was unsure about, and she definitely wouldn't be elaborating on it to virtual strangers.

John tightened his hand on her elbow. "Well, I admire your fortitude. I don't think that I would be quite so understanding, given the circumstances."

She smiled in gratitude. "Thank you."

They rounded a corner and Lillian caught sight of a tall, impressive figure striding in their direction. It wasn't hard to miss William's formidable and intimidating physique, particularly when anger emanated from him in waves. He came to an abrupt halt in front of them and wrenched her away from John Steele's hold.

"I've been looking everywhere for you," he growled. "I was worried!"

"I went for a walk," Lillian responded coolly. "I didn't want to disturb you and your neighbors."

He narrowed his eyes on her before turning his arctic glare on her companion. "It didn't take you long to seek out the company of Miss Hamilton, Steele."

"I didn't realize that you were required to vet her strolling companions, Cartwright. Miss Hamilton looked to be in need of some pleasant diversion and I offered my services."

"Of course you did. You just happened to be in the right place at the right time."

"That is exactly the case," Lillian retorted sharply. "We were doing nothing more than enjoying a stroll together. Now if you'll excuse me, I will see you back at our picnic."

After being harassed by William's jealous paramour and confronted by the cozy spectacle of him with his very eligible neighbor, she was in no mood to indulge his jealous flights of fancy. She spun on her heel and started quickly for their picnic area. She'd not ventured far, however, when William caught her up.

Grasping her by the arm, he halted her. "What were you doing with him, Lillian?" he asked, his voice ominously low. "You know my feelings about that man."

"I don't know *why* you feel the way you do," she responded. "In any case, it was just an innocent walk. I'd grown tired of being confronted by the ladies of your acquaintance."

His jaw hardened. "What's that supposed to mean?"

"Your Mary Simpson is unhappy that you've called a halt to your liaison and she wasted no time in telling me her opinion on the matter."

"She is not 'mine'," he snarled. "*You* are mine and I will not have you liaising with gentlemen that I see as unfit!"

Lillian was dumbfounded. "I don't believe that you've any say in the matter," she said coolly.

"That's where you're wrong, my sweet, and don't test me on the subject. I'll speak to Mary. She had no right to confront you."

Lillian studied him, his fierce expression brooking no room for further argument, and she decided that she'd let the discussion rest for the moment.

"Fine." She shook her arm free of his grasp and started once more to walk in the direction of their picnic.

William again caught her within two strides and, taking hold of her elbow, he tugged her close to his side. He leaned down to speak in her ear, his voice dripping with ominous promise, "Just wait until we get home, Lilly. I'll show you who you belong to."

Chapter Eighteen

Mrs. Thompson and the children were not joining them for the ball that evening. They'd all enjoyed an early dinner of salad and cold meat before the children were bathed and put to bed and Lillian had left Mrs. Thompson in the kitchen making a cup of tea that she planned to take to her room when she retired for the evening.

Instead, it would be just William and Lillian. The idea of attending with William, as if they were stepping out together, had Lillian a little nervous. William, however, had no such qualms and had insisted that he would want no other woman on his arm. This stance of his was proving more than a little confusing. Did it mean that he wanted to show everyone that she was more than an employee, more than just the governess? Of course, there was his continued references to her as *his*, which she found to be at once irritating and strangely exciting. Apart from that, William hadn't said anything to her in regards to their relationship status, so she'd decided just to follow his lead.

The velvet maroon dress had turned out beautifully. It was cut lower than she would have initially liked, but Mrs. Thompson had declared that she should show off her best assets, as long as it was done tastefully. The V neckline flaunted a decorous display of cleavage. From there, the dress fell straight to below her waist where a wide satin sash tied at the side, providing the adornment and a break between fabrics. The dress ended just above her ankles in a swirl of maroon chiffon.

She'd just finished styling her hair when there was a light rap on her door and William strode briskly into the room.

The man really has no boundaries. As he paced toward her, she smiled slightly and her stomach fluttered at the sight of him dressed in his black tuxedo and looking strikingly handsome.

He stopped behind her so that their reflections were repeated in the beveled mirror through which she'd watched him enter.

He bent his head to her ear and spoke in a low, seductive voice, "You look stunning, Lilly." He breathed in deeply, scenting her. "Hmm, apples, my favorite smell in the world."

Their gazes met in the glass as he brought one hand up from behind her to caress her cleavage, gripping her hip with his other. "But I'm not sure I approve of you showing so much of this delectable skin. If I let you out looking like this, I'm going to have to beat the men off you with my fists."

Lillian's head spun as his breath tickled her ear and his proprietary words stamped themselves on her brain.

"I'm going to have to show you who you belong to, like I promised you earlier today." He dropped his hand from her hip to inch her dress up her thighs until he had the fabric bunched around her waist. He groaned low in his throat when her silk pantyhose and lace undergarments were revealed and displayed decadently in the mirror.

"Hold your dress up," he commanded, his hungry gaze meeting hers in the reflection.

She grasped her dress, holding it in place above her waist as William slowly drew her lace undergarments down her legs. Her breathing grew shallow and her heart rate beat a mad tattoo against her ribcage.

He pressed himself against her buttocks and ground his hips, intensifying the sensation of his solid erection. She whimpered and arched her back, inviting him closer.

"It's been five days since I've had you," he rasped. "Do you feel how hard I am? How badly I need you?"

"Yes," she gasped. "Please, William."

He snaked a hand across her lower abdomen, caressing the inside of her thigh with his other hand, circling the sensitive skin in a slow motion just above her pantyhose. She started to grow wet with desire, the dampness seeping out of her sex, the feeling familiar now and oh so welcome. She moaned in appreciation and thrust her hips back against his heavy, throbbing length. She tried to bob lower, tried desperately to make his caressing fingers reach that sweet spot between her thighs.

He was having none of it, however, and seemed determined to move at his own pace. He stilled and growled a warning in her ear. She whimpered and stopped her movements as her eyes met his once more.

He cupped her chin, manipulated her head to the side and nibbled on her neck while he continued to caress torturous circles on her inner thigh with his other hand.

Lillian's senses were on overload. Her nipples pebbled painfully, warmth pooled low in her belly and her insides clenched in anticipation of his touch to her sex.

She watched their reflection with bated breath as he slowly slipped a hand beneath the lace of her undergarments to slide a finger along her moist folds. His touch sent her nerve endings sizzling and her heart rate skyrocketing. She jolted at the impact. He kept one hand clamped tightly on her chin and continued to devour her neck, running two fingers of his other hand up and down the outer lips of her aching sex. Relentlessly he massaged her, using his fingers to swirl her juices up through her center and lightly over her clitoris.

His touch was so light it was torturous and she needed more. "Please," she begged.

"You are so wet, sweetheart. So moist for me," he purred against her skin.

His eyes blazed fiercely in the glass as she writhed against him, her need overcoming his demands to keep still.

Finally, he slipped a finger inside her, then another and pressed up deeply. She moaned and closed her eyes as he filled and stretched her with his strong, callused fingers.

"So tight," he hissed. "God, I want my cock inside you."

"Yes, yes," she cried, desperate for more.

He bent at the knees to accommodate their height difference and ran his hand from her chin, down her side, to her hip until he reached the back of her knee, where he cupped it, swept her leg up and opened her wide.

She gasped at the sight of her sex, spread so open and exposed in the mirror. She could see the moisture glistening between her legs and William's fingers probing in and out of her slick channel. She pressed her back into his chest and used his body to stabilize herself.

She was panting now — her breath coming in soft little puffs that matched the rhythm of his thrusting fingers. Her legs began trembling and pressure built in her core, a gradual gathering of roiling sensations that had her bucking her hips in a shameless attempt to drive William's fingers deeper.

Then abruptly he withdrew, slowly and inexorably until he circled the tips of his fingers over the outer lips of her sex lightly. The building pressure in her loins started to abate, her budding orgasm began drifting away from her and she whimpered. She *needed* more. She was so close and she couldn't understand why that sensation she wanted so desperately still eluded her.

She tore her eyes away from the erotic display between her thighs and sought William's gaze. She met his intense stare — dark and hooded with lust.

"Please," she whispered desperately.

He dropped his mouth to her ear. "What do you want, sweetheart?"

"I want *that* feeling."

He chuckled and dipped his fingers in once more and thrust them high and deep. She moaned and threw her head back, resting it on his shoulder.

"Yes," she hissed.

William tightened his hold on her waist and straightened so that she was suspended in front of him, his chest and upper arms bulging magnificently as he took her entire weight. He tugged her leg wider to allow him greater access and she gasped.

That was it—the gathering pressure inside her started to gain momentum and she writhed her hips, desperately bucking against his thrusting hand. Then he placed his thumb on her clitoris, massaging the tight little bud of nerves until the sensations inside her grew overwhelming—like a cresting wave—and with one final tug on that sensitive button, she tumbled over a blissful edge. She cried out as her inner muscles clenched and throbbed around William's fingers and he brought her down from her orgasm gradually, softening the thrust of his fingers and nipping the shell of her ear while she relaxed against him in a panting heap.

He lowered her gently to the floor. "That should ensure you think about me all evening, even when I am not at your side."

"Hmm," she hummed lazily and dropped her dress. The realization of what she'd just done hit her and mortification took hold. She blushed fiercely, looking anywhere but at William's reflection.

"Hey," he said sternly, cupping her chin and angling her head so that she was forced to look into his eyes. "Don't be embarrassed, sweetheart. Don't shy away from your feelings—embrace them." He dropped a kiss to the top of her head. "Now, finish getting ready and meet me downstairs," he instructed before leaving her alone.

"William's right. I need to get over my silliness." She fixed her hair, re-pinning a loose tendril. The things they did were so intimate and still so new to her that she couldn't help but feel self-conscious. But she determined to lose her embarrassment. After all, she loved him and the things they did together felt so right and so special that it could be nothing but *good*.

She finished adjusting her hair and makeup, straightened her dress then proceeded downstairs to meet William.

Chapter Nineteen

The Coolabah town hall was beautifully decorated for the occasion of the Picnic Race Day Ball. Garlands of eucalyptus leaves and wattle hung from the eaves and adorned tables, filling the hall with an appealingly fresh aroma. A band was set up on the central stage playing popular dance tunes and adding to the general air of festivity, and along the walls long tables were laden with roast meat, salads and cakes. A bar had been erected on one side of the room, offering punch, beer and goblets of wine.

William kept his hand on Lillian's lower back as he steered her into the ballroom. She looked lovely. Her mahogany hair was piled on top of her head with tendrils curling delicately around her face. Her emerald eyes sparkled and her cheeks were flushed with excitement and, he suspected, with the after-effects of the orgasm he'd recently given her. He wasn't happy about the amount of her creamy plump cleavage that was exposed but apparently it was fashion—or so he was told—so he'd quickly fallen silent on the subject.

He constantly marveled at the changes he saw in Lillian. She was still his Lilly but she was also so much more mature and womanly, and if he'd thought at sixteen that she was the prettiest girl he'd ever seen, then at twenty-six, she was stunningly beautiful. In those ten years, she'd developed curves in all the right places, her face had grown more refined and she'd acquired an agreeable maturity and worldliness. Even her more somber, reflective attitude appealed to him. She was magnificent, and every time he looked at her, his breath hitched in awe and a cold fear would grip him—fear that he would lose her again. He was trying to tread very carefully with her. He wanted to make it so that she couldn't be without him, so that she wouldn't even be tempted to look at another man—he wanted her to need him, as he needed her. Only then could he be confident in taking their relationship to the next level.

He leaned down to speak in her ear. "Would you care for a glass of wine?"

She smiled and nodded as she cast her gaze about the great room.

"I'll be a moment. Wait here," he instructed and turned toward the bar.

He ordered a beer for himself and a wine for Lillian. As he walked back to where he'd left her, George and Margaret Dawson waylaid him.

"Cartwright!" the man cried, slapping him on the back jovially.

"Dawson," William nodded. "You are looking lovely this evening, Margaret."

The young lady blushed, tittered then smiled brightly and placed her hand on his arm. "Thank you, William."

He looked down at the drinks in his hands. "If you'll excuse me, I was just on my way over to Miss Hamilton." He gestured in the direction he'd left Lillian waiting.

"Of course, but make sure you hurry back. Margaret is saving the first dance for you," Dawson said with a wink and a shoulder nudge.

William made his way toward Lillian and noted that two young men had joined her. "Fucking randy vultures," he cursed under his breath as he strode to her side.

"Here," he said briskly, handing Lillian her glass of wine and eyeing her companions.

"Thank you." She gave him a slight smile and continued to listen to one of the young men recounting his horseracing exploits earlier that day.

William didn't miss the fact that the two men couldn't keep their eyes on her face, but kept dropping their gazes to skim across her breasts.

He grasped Lillian's elbow and tugged her closer to his side. He knew it was a proprietary gesture but he couldn't help himself. He wanted these two little pricks to back off and he was about to suggest that Lillian dance with him when George and Margaret Dawson descended on him once again.

"Cartwright, I believe you promised the first dance to my lovely daughter." George pushed Margaret in William's direction.

William cast his gaze down to Lillian to gauge her reaction and was met with an impassive stare.

"Of course," William replied stiffly and held his arm out to the young Miss Dawson. He was seething with frustration as he swept her onto the dance floor. He knew that his absence would give one of those little pricks the perfect opportunity to ask Lillian to join them and sure enough, a moment later, he saw her sweep by in the arms of Mr. Horseracer.

William clenched his jaw and tried to focus on the dance and the young woman in his arms. He was nothing if not a gentleman. It wouldn't be fair to let his frustration flow through to Margaret Dawson.

"So you will come to lunch on Thursday," she was saying decisively.

He shook himself out of his reverie and looked down at her in surprise. *Did I just unwittingly agree to something?* Obviously he had, if her happy smile and continued chatter about the expected lunch were anything to go by.

He smiled vaguely as she started to discuss the other ladies at the ball, what they were wearing and whether their dresses were suitably fashionable. He couldn't for the life of him understand why she'd think for a minute that he'd find the topic of conversation interesting — that was until she mentioned Lillian and her intention became clear.

"Miss Hamilton looks quite well this evening. Her dress is very pretty," she commented mildly.

It was immediately obvious that her talk of women's fashion was a way for her to lead the conversation to Lillian. She was clearly fishing for information.

"Yes," he agreed. "She looks lovely."

A frown marred her pretty features.

He gazed down at her as he turned her around the dance floor and noticed when her eyes alighted on something over his right shoulder. She bit her bottom lip and tore her gaze away from what was interesting her then looked up at him.

"*You* are obviously not the only man who finds Miss Hamilton *lovely*," she said slyly, her gaze returning to the same spot over his shoulder.

He immediately swung them around to see what she was referring to and caught sight of Lillian and the young man across the dance floor. He was holding her far too closely for William's liking. Infuriating him further, the man leaned down to speak in Lillian's ear. Whatever he said had her tipping her head back and laughing gaily.

William's vision hazed over with red as he worked to steady his breathing and stop himself from racing across the floor to yank Lillian from the man's arms. He envisioned his fist smacking into the guy's jaw and he started to shake with the ferocity of his thoughts.

Margaret's voice cut through the fog, drawing him back to the present.

"Miss Hamilton appears to be enjoying herself. That *is* nice. It would be good for her to meet some eligible men in the area."

William glared down at her. "She's not here to meet eligible men."

She shrugged daintily and stepped a little closer to him. "Even so, it appears that she's found some agreeable male company."

He prayed for the dance number to be over quickly so that he could take his leave of Margaret gracefully and go in search of Lillian. Watching her dance with another man and seeing that man make her laugh so freely made him feel murderous. He knew it was unreasonable but he was powerless to stop the feeling. He kept an eye on them and when he saw the man wrap his arm tighter about her waist, he clenched his jaw so tightly that he feared he would break a tooth.

The irony of the song that the band was playing was not lost on him and served only to deepen his black mood. Finally, the last strains of *When I Lost You* faded away and he was able to take his leave politely of Margaret.

"Thank you for the dance." He bowed curtly and kissed her hand before stepping off the floor to go in search of Lillian. He didn't miss Margaret's little huff of irritation but he had no time for indulging her temper. He was suddenly desperate to ensure that Lillian was safe and well and back by his side.

* * * *

Lillian watched the couples dancing and marveled at how different this country ball was from the balls she'd attended back in England. In England, people enjoyed learning popular new dance styles that had obviously not reached the Australian outback yet. Watching the couples on the dance floor now comforted her. There was something reassuring in seeing that the traditional dances were not lost.

She was enjoying the company of Mr. Stratham. He was charming and made her laugh but he didn't have the dizzying effect on her that William did. He didn't make her breath hitch nor did her stomach bottom out whenever she looked at him. But he was very pleasing to talk to and served to help her forget that William had spent so little time by her side and more time in the company of Margaret Dawson. To add to her distress, she couldn't help thinking that William and Miss Dawson made a handsome couple, and she'd make a very good match for him. The young woman obviously had feelings for William and George Dawson seemed to like and respect him.

She was sipping on a glass of punch and listening with half an ear to the gentleman by her side when she spotted William striding toward her. He didn't look happy and she couldn't understand what he'd have to be annoyed about. She suspected it was because she was in the company of a strange gentleman but William was hardly in a position to cast aspersions.

She sighed and readied herself for a repeat of the behavior that he had displayed at the picnic earlier that day.

He drew level with her. "Where have you been?" he demanded.

"I've been dancing, like you, and Mr. Stratham here has been keeping me company," she responded mildly.

A loud clearing of a throat drew her attention back to Mr. Stratham, who had drawn himself taller and squared his shoulders. If she weren't so worried about how his actions would be perceived by William, she'd have smiled at his bid to appear more foreboding.

William's glare swung from her face to settle menacingly on Mr. Stratham. "Can I help you?" he snarled at the man who quailed slightly under his intense gaze.

"Not at all. I was merely keeping Miss Hamilton company after she did the honor of dancing with me," Mr. Stratham explained coolly. "And you are?"

"Responsible for her," William snapped.

Lillian gaped and struggled to swallow a sip of punch. *What is he thinking?* Of course, he'd been spouting about her belonging to him and she knew that he disagreed with her associating with strange gentlemen, but this took the cake! As far as she was concerned, William's responsibility toward her started and ended with her position as his children's governess. He'd never given her any indication to think otherwise and William throwing his weight around at social functions was exasperating and tedious.

She was just about to rebut his absurd declaration, when, like a vulture sensing an easy meal, Mary Simpson swooped in.

"William," she purred. "You must dance with me."

Lillian looked the woman over and noted that her cheeks had been re-rouged and her lips were coated in an alarming shade of bright red lipstick. The woman really was a brazen hussy. As if to prove her assessment, the woman boldly brushed her substantial breasts against William's arm and cast a sly look in Lillian's direction.

Yes, Mary Simpson knew exactly what she was doing and had chosen her moment to interrupt them perfectly.

Lillian cast her gaze toward William and didn't miss the slight grimace of distaste that crossed his features at Mary's blatant attention, but Lillian had had enough. She'd endured too much from William's want-to-be paramours and she was determined not to let anything else interfere with her sensibilities that evening. She was feeling decidedly delicate and she wanted nothing more than to be away from William and his lady friends.

"Yes, go and dance, William," Lillian encouraged sweetly, holding her arm out to Mr. Stratham. "I'm sure Mr. Stratham won't mind joining me for a stroll. It's quite warm in here and I'm in need of some air."

"I'd be delighted," the young man responded, politely taking her elbow and steering her toward the balcony doors.

She knew William would be furious with her, but she was in no mood to indulge his petty issues.

She'd made it halfway across the room when she felt an iron-like grip on her wrist before she was yanked from her position beside Mr. Stratham, spun around and pulled into a solid chest. She looked up into the cold, hard eyes of William as he towered over her — a seething mass of angry male.

He lowered his head to hers. "You will *not* be taking a stroll with anyone but me," he said coolly, wrapping an arm around her waist and tugging her forcefully onto the dance floor.

Lillian had no opportunity to register a complaint as she was swept into William's arms and whirled into a fast-paced waltz. She didn't miss the surprised looks on the faces of the people close by at William's dominant, somewhat aggressive, manner.

He tightened his hold and turned her expertly on the dance floor. When Lillian looked up into his face, she could still see the anger glinting in his hazel eyes.

"What did you say to your Mary Simpson? She can't have been too happy at being so unceremoniously disregarded," Lillian commented mildly.

William scowled down at her. "For the last time, she's not mine and I didn't say anything. I was in too much of a hurry stopping *you* from taking *another* stroll with a strange man."

Lillian laughed. "I'm sure that my virtue is no longer an issue, William. You took care of that."

"Don't say things like that," he snapped. "Do you know how happy and relieved I am that no man has had you before me?" His voice softened and he lowered his head to hers. "To me, you are everything that is virtuous and good. And you're all *mine* — in every way."

Lillian flushed and her heart rate stuttered at his possessive words. When he said things like that, she could almost believe that he wanted more from their relationship, but she also worried that too much had changed in ten years. A deep anger for her father burned within her and if she took hold of it too tightly, she knew she'd be in danger of becoming bitter and twisted. No, she needed to move on and try to rectify the wrongs perpetrated by her father all those years ago.

She relaxed and let William lead her around the floor. It felt good to be in his arms. He was an excellent dancer—smooth and confident—and he'd make anyone he danced with look proficient and graceful.

She was feeling marginally better when the final strains of the music died away and William led her from the dance floor.

Chapter Twenty

Lillian awoke slowly. She was being jostled from side to side, her cheek resting against a hard chest. William's spicy aftershave enveloped her and she breathed deeply, inhaling his familiar scent.

She wasn't sure what was going on. She recalled arriving home, where she had stumbled wearily to her room, washed quickly, changed into her nightgown and collapsed into bed.

"William?" she muttered sleepily, lifting her head to look around.

"Hush, sweetheart." He cupped her head and pushed gently so her cheek rested back against his chest. "I'm taking you to my room. I can't be without you for one more night."

At his words, her insides clenched in anticipation and her weariness fled. She should oppose him and, in fact, she'd done just that when they'd arrived home. Lillian had deliberately wished William a curt goodnight before she'd retired to her room. She'd still been angry with him over the events that had transpired at the ball. But it now appeared that he'd decided to take matters into his own hands and she knew that she wouldn't stop him—his power over her body was too great for her to resist.

William strode through his open bedroom door, kicking it closed then locking it behind him. She marveled at the ease with which he managed it while still keeping her clutched in his arms. He walked to the bed and deposited her gently on the covers.

"I know you're upset with me, Lilly, and I hate that." William sat next to her. He caressed her cheek and gazed down into her face, the soft light from the bedside lantern casting his features in shadows. "I can't sleep knowing that I've distressed you. I need to make things right between us. I know that I'm being selfish, but I can't help it. I'm going crazy with my need to be inside you again."

Lillian shuddered and her mouth went dry. She couldn't believe how much she wanted and needed that herself. At the mere thought of it, her sex grew wet and swollen and she locked her legs together, squirming, trying to relieve the sensation.

Then something else he'd said to her earlier sprang into her mind. "You said that we couldn't do that again."

He sighed and scrubbed a hand over his face. "Yes, I did say that, but I also just admitted that I'm selfish where you're concerned."

He leaned down and brushed his lips over hers. "I can't think straight through my need for you. We'll be careful."

Lillian studied him. "Can't have me getting pregnant," she said. "What would you do then?"

He glared at her. "Don't be sarcastic, it doesn't suit you. Anyway, of course I'd look after you. What do you take me for? I've already made it quite clear that I feel responsible for you."

She raised her eyebrows at his last remark but decided not to pursue it. She'd be lying if she said that she didn't want him and anyway, she suspected he was very aware of how he affected her. She put her churlish attitude down to her arduous day dealing with William's forward lady friends.

"I'd love to see you growing round and lush with my baby," he said quietly as he caressed her face. "But I would hate to see it out of wedlock."

Lillian melted at his words then went cold and sulky at his last statement. *He could rectify the wedlock issue in a moment.*

William stood then stooped to remove his shoes and socks. Straightening, he locked eyes with hers and she watched him untie his bow tie then unbutton his dress shirt. She relished the chiseled muscles of his chest and abdomen as he slowly revealed them to her. He shrugged his shirt off his shoulders, undid his trousers then pushed them and his briefs down his firm thighs. She gasped as his huge erection sprang free and bobbed in front of him, the tip reaching to his navel. She'd forgotten how big he was and a shiver of unease ran through her.

She ran her gaze up his body and met his amused expression.

"You stretch to fit me, my love. Remember?"

She nodded and scooted to a sitting position. She couldn't resist—she had to touch him. She swept her hands across his sculpted chest before brushing them down his sides and tracing the defined V on his abdomen.

He hissed and sucked in a breath at her touch, his stomach muscles rippling deliciously at the movement.

"How do you get muscles like these?" she whispered in awe, sweeping her hands across his tanned skin.

"All the work I do on the property. Shearing sheep, riding, mustering, manual labor." He shrugged and smiled. "I also box." He looked down to watch her stroking his stomach and groaned.

"I need you naked. Arms up," he demanded.

She raised her arms above her head. William stepped toward her and grasped the hem of her nightgown then pulled it over her head in one smooth movement.

As her nude form was revealed, she rushed to cross her arms over her breasts.

"Don't," he said softly. "I want to see you."

Slowly, she lowered her arms. He stepped back to study her.

He gazed hungrily at her bare flesh. "You have the prettiest breasts, so full and pert. Do you see what I see, Lilly? Look at how small and pink your nipples are, just begging me to suck them."

She gasped and colored at his language but didn't turn her head away. She was mesmerized by his reverent gaze and the longing in his eyes.

"Feel how they pucker and pebble at my words?" He arched an eyebrow and brushed a thumb over one then the other.

She moaned and thrust her breasts toward him.

"Lie down," he instructed and climbed onto the bed next to her.

She shuffled back and lay down, anticipation heating her blood and making her breathing erratic.

He settled his body between her legs. "Just relax, sweetheart," he mumbled against her skin as he swept his lips across her cleavage, then his hot mouth found a nipple and he sucked, hard. With one hand, he found her other nipple and rolled the taut bud between his thumb and finger.

Lillian groaned and arched her back, inviting to him to take more. He bit down on her nipple then soothed it with the flat of his tongue. The sharp sensation sent a hot current searing from her breast to the sweet spot between her thighs, making her cry out and tremble beneath him.

"William," she gasped, fisting his hair.

"I know, sweetheart," he crooned and leaned back, staring in fascination at her extended nipples.

His erection, hot and throbbing, was pressed against her thigh and she wriggled underneath him. Longing coiled tighter in her belly. She was wet and swollen with need, the thumping beat between her legs growing insistent.

Finally, he started to move south, trailing kisses down her ribcage, across her abdomen until he reached her mons where he inhaled deeply. "You smell so delicious." He nuzzled her with his nose and swiped a finger through her center. "Fuck, you're so wet. I need to taste you."

Her belly somersaulted at his erotic words, then his mouth was on her. He swept his tongue from her anus to her clitoris, licking through her folds. Her inner muscles clenched and her legs stiffened as he worked his tongue through her cleft over and over again.

"You taste so good." He pushed her legs wider then backed away a little to study her.

She struggled up on her elbows. "What are you doing?" she asked breathlessly.

"Looking at how plump and pink you are." He buried his head between her legs once more, licked her fluidly and sucked her labia into his mouth.

"Ooh," she cried out, flopping back and gyrating her hips. Perfect sensations rolled through her, making her insides throb in rhythm with his probing tongue.

"Please, William," she begged, gripping his hair and yanking him against her.

He thrust one finger then another into her channel and swirled his tongue around her clitoris, circling lazily before sucking the tight little bundle of nerves into his mouth.

Her internal throbbing intensified as the pressure built.

"I can tell that you're close, Lilly. Let go and give it to me," he demanded. He thrust his fingers into her harder, pumping in and out of her slickness easily before he clamped his mouth over her center and sucked.

Sensation overtook her and she let go. Her insides convulsed and she held her breath, trying desperately to ride out the overwhelming waves of pleasure rocketing through her trembling body.

William brought her down gently, sucking the pulses out of her core as she floated back to earth.

She lay limp and boneless, trying to regulate her breathing. The mattress dipped when William crawled up the bed.

He worked his way between her legs and hovered over her. "Open your eyes," he demanded softly.

She fluttered her eyelids open and gazed up at him suspended above her, his elbows resting either side of her head.

"There are those beautiful green eyes," he said huskily. He brushed his lips over hers and licked the seam of her mouth. "Can you taste yourself on me? See how good you taste?"

She blushed then returned his kiss, opening her lips to invite his tongue to tangle with hers. She *could* taste herself on him—tangy, erotic and not at all unpleasant. His hot erection pressed against her thigh and she wriggled beneath him as he deepened their kiss, claiming her mouth with a ferocity that took her breath away.

He swept one hand down her side to her hip then between her thighs where he brushed his fingers lightly through her cleft.

"So slick and swollen," he whispered reverently against her lips, still teasing her folds. "Always so responsive."

She squirmed beneath him and yanked his hair, desperate to feel him inside her.

He chuckled softly and swept his lips from her mouth to the soft spot below her ear where he sucked before nibbling on the lobe.

She moaned, goosebumps erupting all over her body, and her nipples hardened to tight points.

"I'm going to take you now." He reared back and positioned his thick erection between her thighs. Then he thrust into her, seating himself to the hilt.

She yelped at his ferocious penetration. He stilled, supporting his body on his elbows as he gazed down at her, waiting for her to adjust to his size.

"Jesus, you're so tight." He breathed deeply and brushed the hair from her face before he started to move.

She felt so full and stretched to capacity. She moaned as he drew his thick length slowly out of her then pushed back in. On each outward draw, he dragged the broad head of his shaft across her clitoris, the stimulation sending electrical currents spiraling outward from her core.

She gripped his muscular biceps and bowed her body, desperate to feel more of him, but he continued with his slow, steady strokes, leisurely pulling out and pushing forward.

"Please," she whimpered.

"You want it harder, Lilly?" He groaned and thrust in deeply, circling his hips to rub his pelvis against her clit before slowly withdrawing. His hair lay damp with perspiration and the veins in his neck corded as he continued his measured pace.

"Yes," she cried, propelling her hips up in an attempt to spur him into action. Her stomach clenched and a dull throb developed in her womb, but that pleasurable release still remained elusively out of reach.

"My darling wants it harder," he grated through clenched teeth. "Like this?" he asked on a hard, soul-jarring thrust.

She groaned, feeling his thick length penetrating her, and pumped her hips to meet his ferocity.

He picked up the pace of his strokes until he was thrusting fiercely, the force pushing her up the bed so she had to grasp his shoulders and hold onto him tightly.

The pulsing sensation in her insides turned into a full-blown tempest as his rhythm increased and his breathing grew choppy and erratic.

"I can feel that you're close," he said, plunging deeply. He slid his hand between their sweat-slicked bodies and found the sensitive bundle of nerves between her thighs. "Come for me. *Now*." His gaze bored into hers. He massaged her clitoris with deft fingers and reared back to pound her faster.

Suddenly her orgasm gripped her, sending her insides into a quivering, throbbing frenzy. She stiffened and cried out in pleasure.

William growled triumphantly and closed his mouth over hers, swallowing her cries and kissing her passionately.

She felt weak and boneless and wrapped her arms around his neck, allowing him to control the kiss. He took her mouth possessively and forced his tongue between her lips to tangle with hers. His breathing quickened and his thrusts grew rougher as he worked toward his own release.

He broke their kiss, supported his body on his hands and pumped his hips, gyrating his pelvis.

She watched, mesmerized by his abdominal muscles rippling and quaking with his lunging movements. He clenched his jaw and met her gaze as he withdrew and took hold of his thick erection, wrapping his palm around the base to fist himself to completion. He growled low in his throat, pumped semen over her stomach and breasts, and used one hand to rub the evidence of his release into her skin.

"Christ." He flopped onto his back at her side. "That was incredible."

Lillian couldn't open her eyes and a calm drowsiness had descended on her. "Hmm."

William's chest bucked against her on a silent chuckle.

"I've worn you out, my darling," he said, caressing her face.

The mattress dipped next to her, then she heard the sound of water. Quickly, he returned to kneel beside the bed, sweeping a cool washcloth over her breasts and abdomen before tenderly swiping it between her legs.

She opened her heavy lids to watch him.

"Are you sore?" He gave her an appraising look as he tended her. "I shouldn't have been so rough with you."

She wriggled, testing her limbs and inner muscles, and winced when she felt a twinge deep inside.

"A little. Although it's not unbearable, I'm just not used to it."

He set the washcloth aside and cupped her face in one hand. "Do you realize how happy I am that you *are* so unfamiliar with the sensation? It means that I'm the only man who's been here." He ran a finger gently between her folds.

Her eyelids fluttered closed and she arched into his hand, relishing the feel of William's fingers as he delicately sifted through her damp sex.

"Hmm, you are an insatiable little thing," he murmured appreciatively. "You're tired and you need to sleep. Let's get you back into your nightgown."

Stooping, he retrieved her nightgown from the floor and, with one hand, pulled Lillian into a sitting position. "Arms up."

She raised her arms and William swiftly dropped the garment over her head, tugging her arms through the sleeves.

She slumped back onto the mattress and lifted her hips so William could drag her nightdress down her legs. She was so tired that she could barely keep her eyes open. William climbed onto the bed next to her.

"Lie on your side, facing away from me," he instructed.

She did as he asked and he pulled her back against his chest then wrapped his arm around her waist. "Sleep now, sweetheart."

She barely registered his words as her eyelids closed and she fell into a peaceful slumber.

Chapter Twenty-One

William awoke slowly, relishing the feel of Lillian in his bed and in his arms. It was so comforting having her compact and curvaceous body pressed against him. He dipped his head to her hair and deeply inhaled the familiar scent of apples — and a slight hint of coconut. *Hmm, delicious.*

His morning erection throbbed insistently and he couldn't help but grind his hips against the soft pillows of her backside. Her nightgown had ridden up in her sleep and she lay gloriously naked from the waist down, providing silky smooth flesh to slide against his hard length.

He looked over Lillian's shoulder at the bedside clock — it was still early and he figured he had an hour until the rest of the household started to stir.

He groaned low in his throat and gently rocked against her, snaking an arm underneath her nightgown to cup her right breast. He squeezed the globe gently and brushed his palm across her nipple until he felt the peak stiffen and tighten.

She moaned in her sleep and instinctively pressed back against him. Fuck, she was amazing—so sexually receptive that she took his breath away. No other woman had ever made him feel the way that she did. The triumph that he felt when she orgasmed so unreservedly and so spectacularly was heady and powerful. To have such a beautiful and sensual creature writhing beneath him in ecstasy was exhilaration exemplified.

He should carry her back to her room and her own bed, but the feel of her in his arms was too good to cut short and his cock was rock hard and in need of attention.

She whimpered and settled her backside tighter into his pelvis. He hissed a breath and swept his hand from her breast down to her pubic hair where he caressed her softly, probing her folds with two fingers. Even in sleep, she was moist and ready for him. He had to have her and every intention of delivering her back to her room vanished instantly.

He nuzzled the soft skin below her ear and kissed a trail down her neck, the scent of her overwhelming his senses. Always he'd associated the aroma of apples with Lillian and a sense of *déjà vu* hit him, so strong that it sent a sharp pang through his chest.

He snaked his other arm underneath her, reached for her left breast and pulled her tighter against him. He enveloped her, one hand at her breast and the other, probing her slick heat, anchoring her body to his as he continued to kiss her neck.

She moaned deep in her throat and moved her neck to the side, allowing him better access to her delicate skin. Her hips rocked against his hand, enticing his fingers to plunge deeper.

"Are you awake, sweetheart?" he asked softly.

"Hmm."

He chuckled. "Still sleepy?"

"Yes." Her voice was low and husky, stiffening his cock further.

"Just relax, my darling. I'll do all the work." He swept his hand from between her thighs to cup the back of her knee then lifted her leg and opened her wider.

"I want you to grasp my cock and position it at your entry," he instructed, his voice tight with need.

He heard her sharp intake of breath before he felt her small hand grasp his erection, sending his abdominals into spasms and tightening his balls.

"Quickly, Lilly. I need inside you. Now."

She guided him gently until he felt the tip of his cock brush her warm, wet entrance and he could hold back no longer. He thrust into her hard and fast, seating himself, balls deep.

She shuddered around him, her sex clenching his cock and gripping him like a fist.

"Fuck," he groaned. "You feel so good, sweetheart."

He held still for a moment, relishing her tight, slick heat before he started to move, slowly pulling out then plunging deeply and gyrating his hips. He gripped her waist with both hands and manipulated her body, pushing her forward and withdrawing then pulling her back hard against him to bury himself inside her once more.

She covered his hands with her own and hung on as he fucked her, allowing him total control of her body's movements, giving herself over to him completely.

He thrust faster and harder and tightened his grip on her hips to piston her more forcefully up and down his thick length. His balls pulled up and lust coiled hot and tight at the base of his spine. He brushed one hand down her stomach to reach her clit and massaged the little bud with his thumb, pressing down as he pumped into her.

She arched her back and cried out. He felt her internal muscles start to flutter and he knew that she was close.

"Come on, Lilly. Give it up," he bit out. Then he felt it. Her inner walls contracted and pulsed around his cock, her whimpers and shudders spurring him toward his own climax.

He stiffened as she milked him and his orgasm raged through him in a glorious, boiling eruption. He pulled out quickly, gripped the base of his erection and fisted himself to completion.

He struggled to regain his breath and clutched her closely, panting into her hair and nuzzling her neck, enjoying the afterglow and slow ebb of his orgasm.

Finally, he looked across at the clock and groaned. "I have to get you back to your room." He kissed her hair, climbed out of bed then stooped to retrieve his trousers from the floor and pulled them on.

He gazed down at her for a moment and marveled at her beauty. Her hair lay tousled from sleep and sex and her cheeks were flushed. Her generous cleavage, so plump and creamy, begged to be caressed and kissed. She was the epitome of every man's fantasy and she was in *his* bed and she was *his*. The thought exhilarated him and terrified him in equal measure. Exhilarated him, because at this point in time she was his, but terrified him, because he felt that at any moment she could be taken away from him, or she could leave. If that happened, he didn't know how he'd survive.

He shook his head, stepped toward the bed and lifted her so that she was cradled against his chest.

"I can walk, William," she said, wriggling to free herself.

"I know, but I want to carry you. I like you being in my arms. Stop squirming."

She sighed and rested her head on his shoulder as he started walking toward her bedroom.

The house was still silent but he knew Mrs. Thompson would be up and about very soon. He wouldn't risk Lillian being seen gallivanting about in her nightclothes.

When he reached her room, he entered it and placed her on the bed.

"Try to get some more sleep," he advised, kissing her chastely on the lips. He brushed her tousled curls from her forehead and ran his finger down her cheek. "Have a good day, beautiful girl."

He gave her one long, last look then turned and left the room.

* * * *

Lillian stood writing sums on the chalkboard for the children to solve. She'd made a game of it and each correct answer brought them closer to revealing the giraffe that she'd arranged in a dot-to-dot configuration. They'd worked steadily throughout the morning and Lillian was pleased with their progress. She planned to let them leave early and enjoy some of the sunshine before it was time for their dinner.

It was a lovely day and she intended to spend the remainder of the afternoon assisting Mrs. Thompson in the vegetable garden. She needed some fresh air and exercise and she was looking forward to getting her hands dirty. Her aunt had never approved of her love of gardening and had thought it a pastime strictly reserved for the lower classes and discouraged Lillian at every opportunity. It was one thing about her aunt that Lillian didn't miss—her tendency toward snobbery.

Finally, the children finished their sums and Lillian could release them to play.

She hurried to her room, changed into an old blouse and skirt and tied a scarf around her hair before making her way downstairs and out into the garden.

Mrs. Thompson was already there on her hands and knees, weeding a section of the vegetable bed. Lillian knelt opposite her and started to assist, turning the soil as she went. They worked in companionable silence for a while, Lillian enjoying the feel of the cool earth between her fingers. It was relaxing and pleasing work. She'd always loved nature and the outdoors, and gardening had always provided an outlet for her as well as a quiet time of contemplation.

She thought about William. He'd mentioned something called a prophylactic, which he'd explained were rubber sleeves that fit over the penis to prevent disease and pregnancy. They'd issued them during the war. She didn't ask if he'd had cause to use them while he was abroad—she didn't want to know. He'd discussed the option of using one but he hadn't sounded particularly enthusiastic, and to be honest, it had sounded rather strange to Lillian. Not having any sphere of reference, she'd let William do as he thought necessary.

Her thoughts drifted to how much she'd changed in the relatively short period she'd been back in Australia. She was worldlier now, more experienced, which was incongruous, given that she'd moved from a bustling city to the Australian outback. She understood that it was her newfound sexuality and all the associated feelings and experiences that went with it. She suddenly felt like a woman—more sophisticated and knowing. She smiled to herself. It had been two days since she'd last been with William but if she concentrated hard enough when she was lying in bed at night, she could almost feel him moving on top of her. She imagined his unique, masculine scent and the feel of his rough hands on her breasts and thighs. She shivered, feeling the familiar tightening in her belly and the warm, accompanying glow.

She noticed that Mrs. Thompson had stopped her weeding and she looked up to find the older woman studying her thoughtfully.

"Are you not well, Lillian? You look a little flushed."

She nodded quickly. "Quite well. Just a little warm, thank you."

She regarded the other woman carefully across the vegetable garden and speculated, not for the first time, about whether Mrs. Thompson suspected something was different between her and William. The woman had gone back to weeding, however, and showed no outward indication that she was in any way suspicious.

I'm paranoid. She knew what they were doing was not proper, but stealing about in the house made it seem that much more immoral.

She sighed and dug into the soil with a trowel to extract a rather stubborn weed. The sound of horses and men's voices made her look up toward one of the outer paddocks. The men had obviously finished working for the day and were returning to the homestead and their quarters. They were dusty and patches of perspiration dotted their work shirts. Lillian scanned the men until she identified William, and as was fast becoming habit, her heart stuttered at the sight of him. He sat tall and formidable in the saddle and his muscular thighs gripped his horse's flanks expertly as he maneuvered the animal around the stockyard between groups of sheep and the working dogs.

"Handsome, isn't he?"

Lillian looked across at Mrs. Thompson. "Yes, he is," she agreed, shading her eyes with a hand to watch the men while they worked.

"Well, I'd better go and wash up and check on dinner. We're having lamb stew this evening," she informed Lillian. She struggled up from her kneeling position and dusted off her skirt.

"Can I help?"

"You can collect some potatoes and zucchini for me. That would be marvelous. I need to feed that man before he collapses from exhaustion."

Lillian smiled and got to her feet. "Potatoes and zucchini coming up."

She'd collected some potatoes and was picking zucchini when the familiar scent of horses, leather and a unique earthiness wafted to her and alerted her instantly to the presence of William. She straightened and turned to see him leaning casually against the nearby fence, his booted feet crossed at the ankles.

"How are you, Lilly?"

"I'm well, thank you. How was work on the station today?"

"Good. The shearers sheared about six hundred sheep. It's a great start."

"You don't shear the sheep?"

"Not generally. I muster them. I employ shearers to shear them."

Lillian looked him over. He was covered in red outback dust and he looked tired. "You look exhausted and you're in need of a bath."

He laughed. "Yes, to both. But I'm guessing Mrs. Thompson will be wanting to feed me first."

Lillian grinned. "She does. She's just gone inside to finish dinner. Why don't you clean up? I'll finish collecting the vegetables and meet you in the kitchen."

She looked down at her hands, which were encrusted with dirt. Trickles of perspiration worked down her spine. She would need to take a scrubbing brush to her nails and a bath seemed like a wonderful idea but that would have to wait until later.

She finished collecting the vegetables and took the basket to the kitchen. She then scrubbed her hands and nails with soap. She was still dressed in her old clothes and felt rather scruffy to be sitting at dinner, but life on a sheep station was far less formal than the life she'd been accustomed to in England. Work came first and time was not wasted on dressing for dinner unless one had visitors. Meals were invariably taken in the kitchen and while faces and hands were scrubbed, no special effort was made with dressing and formal table settings. They also had to be careful with their water consumption. Water was a precious commodity and anything that required excessive use of water, such as washing of unnecessary clothes, was frowned upon and avoided where possible.

Lillian rounded up the children and ensured that they washed before they sat to eat. She made her way to the kitchen and assisted Mrs. Thompson with serving the lamb stew and laying the table with condiments and thick slices of bread.

Dinner was always a joyous affair and the children were happy to spend time with their father, particularly as he'd been so busy during the last few days. William recounted some amusing stories from the shearing shed, which had them all in fits of laughter, and the children brought him up to date on their schoolwork.

It was relaxing and familial and Lillian found that she enjoyed this part of the day the most. She felt like she was part of something special, as if she belonged with the family, and it always warmed her heart to share such an innocuous event, such as eating with those she loved.

She was fast becoming attached to the children and knew that she could love them as her own. She worried about the prospect of having to leave eventually, but pushed the thought to the back of her mind. She was here for now, with the ones she loved, and that was all she would focus on.

Chapter Twenty-Two

Lillian readied the children for bed and left William to read them a story. She returned to the kitchen to wish Mrs. Thompson goodnight and put some water on to boil for tea as she contemplated taking a bath herself. It wasn't an easy task, boiling enough water to take a decent bath then lugging the cold bathwater outside to use on the garden. Bathing the children was relatively simple. They only required a little water to soap them up and wash them off sufficiently. Which is what Lillian generally did to wash. She would soap herself all over then sponge herself off. Washing her hair was always accomplished by standing under the garden water pump, or, when the weather was cold, over the big copper in the washroom.

She was waiting for the water to boil for her tea when William strode into the kitchen, the bathtub suspended over his head as if it weighed nothing at all.

"I was contemplating a bath, but I think you need it more than me," she remarked.

He grinned roguishly. "*We* are taking a bath."

Lillian widened her eyes, her gaze darting to the kitchen door. Surely he wouldn't risk bathing together?

He chuckled at her scandalized expression. "Mrs. Thompson knows that I will be bathing and she definitely won't risk entering the kitchen to find me in the midst of my ablutions."

Lillian smiled. She imagined that the sight of William naked would send Mrs. Thompson into a swoon that she'd never recover from.

The idea of a bath—and a bath with William at that—was an opportunity too good to refuse. Before she talked herself out of it, she slipped upstairs to her bedroom to collect her bathing accouterments, a clip for her hair and a nightgown then returned to the kitchen.

When she entered, William was pouring water into the tub. She stood, fidgeting as he went to and from the copper collecting bucketfuls until the water level was sufficient.

"That's perfect." He stuck his hand in to test the temperature. He stood and threw her an assessing look as he walked toward the kitchen door and closed it with a soft thud. "You need to undress now, sweetheart."

Slowly, Lillian removed her shoes and stockings then untied the scarf from her hair. She turned her back and started unbuttoning her blouse. Behind her, she heard the muffled sounds of clothing being discarded. Undressing so blatantly in front of William made her feel awkward. She'd started to unfasten her lower garments when William pressed his bare chest against her back, wrapping his arms around her waist. He stilled her fumbling fingers with his hands over hers and helped her to unhook her skirt before slipping it down her hips. She stepped out of it unsteadily and William turned her to face him.

He fingered the lace on her brassiere and his eyes darkened. "You're so lovely."

Her breath hitched as she met his intense gaze, her body breaking out in goosebumps, her nipples straining against their silk confines.

"Let's get you out of this," he said, reaching behind her to unclasp her brassiere and tugging the garment down her shoulders.

Her breasts bounced as their restraints were removed.

His eyes glazed over. "Fuck," he whispered, bending his head to suck a taut nipple into his mouth.

A pleasurable current zapped through her and stopped to pulse between her thighs.

He released her nipple with a loud popping sound then knelt before her and started unhooking her girdle. She stiffened and blushed as he went to work, deftly releasing the hooks and eyes. He stopped and gazed up at her with a smirk.

"This isn't the first time that I've removed a lady's undergarments, Lilly. Don't be embarrassed."

She looked down at him and a small smile touched her lips. She ran her fingers through his hair. It was so soft, even covered in a fine coat of outback dust. The action soothed her nerves a little. She knew it was silly to feel awkward at this juncture, after all of the other things that they'd done, but it was an automatic reaction. The act of physically undressing had always been so personal and intimate so the awkwardness was difficult to switch off.

He smiled up at her, then slowly leaned forward and planted a kiss on her belly. "Just relax, sweetheart,' he coaxed softly, working swiftly to remove the remainder of her underclothes.

Soon she stood naked. She tugged on William's hair to urge him to rise but he just chuckled then bent his head to the apex between her thighs and inhaled deeply. She stiffened for the second time, mortified that she hadn't washed since that morning and to make matters worse, her monthly course was imminent.

"William, please. I'm going to start bleeding at any moment," she whispered, embarrassment tingeing her cheeks pink.

He looked up at her. "Are you sure?"

She huffed an exasperated breath. "Yes, I started cramping earlier today, if you must know."

"Good, then a bath will help and it means that you're not at your most fertile," he waggled his eyebrows mischievously. "And you smell amazing, Lilly. Like apples and…coconut."

She giggled at his outrageous proclamation and he smirked, rising to his feet. His eyes were dark and hungry, drinking her in.

"Your body is beautiful." He cupped her cheek.

Abruptly, he swooped her up, cradling her to his chest. He stepped into the tub and lowered them both into the warm water. He settled himself against the back of the basin and maneuvered her so that she sat between his legs.

She sighed in contentment as the water engulfed her and leaned her head back to rest against William's chest. He scooped water into his palms and splashed it over her shoulders and breasts before grabbing a bar of soap and lathering it between his hands. He bent his head to sniff the bubbles. "Hmm, apples," he said appreciatively. "This smell has always reminded me of you."

When he gripped her around the neck and started massaging her with his large, calloused hands, she moaned in pleasure.

"Move your hair, sweetheart," he said against her ear.

She swept her hair up and fastened it with a clip, shivering as William's breath whispered across her dampened skin. Slowly and rhythmically, he massaged her neck then moved to her shoulders and kneaded her taut muscles like an expert. Her body responded instantly and she melted against him, a warm, mellow feeling overwhelming her limbs.

"You know, I should be doing this for you," she mumbled. "You're the one who's been riding hard and mustering sheep for the past few days."

He chuckled. "I'm used to it and besides, I much prefer to have my hands on your beautiful, satiny skin."

She whimpered as he let his hands drift lower. He cupped her breasts, circling each nipple with his thumbs and elongating them to hard points.

"You have gorgeous breasts. They fit into my hands perfectly, like you were made just for me. Are they tender?"

"A little."

"They feel heavier, like lush, ripe melons." He breathed against her ear and massaged the mounds gently, sending a shiver rippling through her.

She moaned and thrust her breasts up and into his palms, silently inviting him to take more, to grasp harder. She felt his smile against her neck as he plucked each of her nipples and rolled the taut buds between his thumb and index fingers. The sensation sent a sharp quiver directly to her groin.

He stopped abruptly, the absence of his touch leaving her bereft and wanting.

"Shuffle down and tip your head back. I want to wash your hair."

She unclipped her hair and did as he asked so that William could scoop water over her. When her hair was wet, she sat up and glanced behind her to find him studying her array of bathing products quizzically.

"Which one is for hair?"

She smiled and handed him the bottle of coconut oil shampoo she'd brought with her from England.

He unscrewed the top and poured a generous amount onto her head, then gathered up her hair and worked the shampoo into a lather, massaging her scalp with strong, deft fingers. She groaned softly, the incredible, relaxing sensation radiating from her head outward to her limbs, leaving her boneless.

She lolled her head forward in sleepy relaxation. "Have you done this before?"

She felt his chest buck on a silent chuckle. "No. Ruth was far too..." He paused. "Conservative and...practical to ever take a bath together. She wasn't at all romantic and she would've felt that we shouldn't be wasting time bathing each other."

"Perhaps she was right," Lillian commented, suddenly disconcerted by what they were doing.

He sighed heavily as he bent his head to hers, his breath flowing whisper soft against her ear. "No, that was Ruth. This is *us* and I love bathing with you. Now, tilt your head back so I can rinse the shampoo out."

She shuffled forward once more so William could ladle water over her head. She wondered what rinsing in their bathwater would do to her hair, but she didn't care—it felt so good to be cared for and nurtured that she'd do it every day if he wanted to.

She sat up, her back once more to his front, and he twisted her hair up and secured it with her clip. "I love your hair," he remarked. "I love that you've kept it long."

He rested his legs on top of hers, his feet hooked under her ankles so he could spread her legs with his, opening her to him.

He bit her earlobe, the sensation sending a shiver through her. He swept his hand up her side to her breast and cupped it, tweaking a nipple between his thumb and forefinger.

She gasped and thrust her breast into his hand, desire flaring hot and strong in her belly. He continued rolling the taut bud and nuzzling her neck. "Hmm, you smell delicious. Good enough to eat," he rasped against her throat and lapped the residual moisture from her skin.

She squirmed in his hold, desperate to close her legs and provide some relief to her aching core, but he held her fast, prolonging her torture.

He swept his other hand down her side and across her abdomen. "I know what you want, sweetheart," he said softly, sliding his hand between her thighs.

She arched her back, splashing water over the side of the tub. "William, *please*."

She tried once again to close her legs but he kept his firmly against hers and plunged one finger then two into her. Next, he pushed up, stroking that tender spot on the wall of her vagina.

"Just here," he whispered, curling his fingers in a come-hither motion and pressing his thumb against her swollen clitoris.

"Oh Lord," she cried, writhing against him as sparks of pleasure zapped through her.

"Fuck, you're so tight. I can feel your muscles clenching around me."

She stiffened, moaned and tried desperately to reach that pleasurable pinnacle. Vaguely she registered his other hand still rolling and tugging on her tender nipple until the sensations collided at the pulsing beat between her thighs.

His thick erection throbbed insistently against her backside as he plunged a third finger inside her and pumped them slickly while he circled her clit with his thumb. "Come. Now, Lilly."

His demand was all she needed. She arched her back and held her breath, a surge of euphoria rolling through her and tightening her insides. Her muscles pulsed and quivered—her orgasm intense and protracted by her spread legs—sending delicious palpitations deep to her core.

"That's it, my darling." He softened the thrust of his fingers to bring her down slowly. "You're so beautiful when you're in the throes of passion."

She whimpered and slumped back against him, struggling to regain her breath and regulate her thudding heart rate. Her vision cleared and she was immediately aware of the incessant solidity of his erection pressing against her back and pulsating a demand for relief.

She sat up and turned around so that she was straddling his hips and his shaft was nestled between her thighs. His eyes were hooded and dark with lust as he gazed at her from beneath black-fringed lids.

She gave him a coy smile. "I think you're in need of something."

He smirked and thrust his hips up lazily, causing another wash of water to lap over the rim of the tub.

She giggled. "Mrs. Thompson is going to wonder what you were doing in here to cause such a mess."

He clasped her hips and lifted her so that she hovered over his length. He gave her an intense look, pulled her down hard, impaling her and filling her completely.

She gulped and gazed at him with wide eyes as she accustomed herself to the depth and stretch the unfamiliar position induced.

"It's deep this way," he commented and stilled, allowing her to adjust. "You have control, sweetheart. You set the pace."

At her curious look, he grasped her waist and lifted her, then pulled her back down and thrust up with his hips. "Ride me, like you ride a horse."

She gasped and arched an eyebrow at his wicked grin. She gripped his thighs between her knees and pumped up and down, resting her hands on his muscular shoulders to steady herself. She knew she was doing something right when his mouth dropped open and he groaned low in his throat.

"That's it. Just like that," he whispered, clutching her around the waist and guiding her body forcefully along his length.

He leaned forward, sucked her bottom lip into his mouth and took her in a punishing kiss, his tongue sliding and slipping against hers as he growled into her mouth.

She found a rhythm, drawing her body all the way up his erection until the tip brushed her folds, then plunging down to impale herself fully.

"Fuck," he choked and pumped his hips up to meet hers.

The cords in his neck strained with his effort to retain control.

He sat up straighter, bracing himself on the back of the tub and clamping his mouth onto the soft skin where her shoulder met her neck.

She moaned as she felt his cock swell and fill her lower belly, stretching her to capacity — the feeling was extraordinary and it had never felt so deep.

Their movements grew choppy and rough and more water sloshed over the side of the tub.

"I'm close," he ground out between gritted teeth. "I need you to get there."

He slid his hand between their slick bodies and found her clit. Circling it with his thumb, he sent sparks of pleasure spiraling outwards. He held her close with one arm banded around her waist, thrusting up hard, sucking on her neck and massaging her tight little nub.

Sensation built then coalesced in an internal pulsing heat. She cried out, her orgasm ripping through her and propelling her insides into quaking, undulating contortions.

William followed, rearing up with his hips, clutching her body tightly against his and growling low in his throat as he came in long hot spurts inside her.

They lay silent, relaxing together until the water started to grow cold. William dunked his head and washed his hair quickly then stood and stepped out of the tub. After grabbing a towel, he wrapped it around his waist before picking up another one and opening it in invitation to Lillian.

She stood then stepped into his waiting arms.

"Thank you for the bath, my lady," he said, dropping a soft kiss on her nose. "How are you feeling?"

Her limbs felt warm and loose but a dull ache had taken root in her belly, no doubt spurred to action by her vigorous sexual activity.

"Good."

William gave her an appraising look. "Are you sure?"

She nodded and clutched the bath sheet tighter around her. He cocked his head to one side, studying her for a moment, then stooped to pick up her nightgown.

"Arms up," he ordered, raising the garment above her head.

Lillian dropped the towel and stretched her arms up so William could slip her nightgown over her head. He quickly gathered her belongings then shrugged into a robe.

He glanced around the kitchen. "I'll clean up here in the morning. It's late and we should get to bed." He took her hand and led her to the door.

Chapter Twenty-Three

William left Mulga Creek early to ride to the Dawsons' property for dinner. The local roads leading to the properties were not designed for automobiles and he preferred to avoid driving when possible. Besides, he loved riding and he wanted to use the opportunity to check the dam levels and his outer property fence lines. He expected to be at the Dawsons' just after mid-afternoon. He planned to stay overnight and leave at dawn the following morning. It was a long ride — four hours at a trot with an additional half hour to rest his horse.

He could have done without the disruption to his schedule, particularly at such a busy time on the property. He'd left his station manager in charge and expected things would run smoothly in his absence, albeit a little slower now that they were down his horse and mustering skills.

He supposed he should be looking forward to sharing the company of George and Margaret Dawson over a relaxed dinner, and a month ago, he would have. But things had changed since Lillian had re-entered his life. Where once he'd looked at Margaret in a potentially romantic sense, he was no longer harboring the same feelings. He liked her. She was sweet, charming and certainly pretty, but she didn't make his pulse gallop and his cock hard just by looking at her. *No, Lillian is the only woman ever to have that distinction.*

Then again, it would be good to get his mind off things and take some time to regain perspective. He couldn't think straight when Lillian was around and when he was working, he was too busy and involved to think about anything other than the job at hand. Perhaps dinner with Margaret and George Dawson would give him time for some self-reflection and an opportunity to examine his feelings a little more closely. Also, if he was to be brutally honest with himself, he wanted the opportunity to spend some time around Margaret, without the distraction of Lillian. He knew it was unfair, but he hoped that some time in the presence of an attractive woman would help him define his feelings. He needed to be sure that what he was feeling for Lillian was real and not merely the residual emotions of a childhood love.

He reached the Dawson property by mid-afternoon as he'd planned and, after securing Victory in the stables, he made his way to the house.

The Dawsons were sitting on the front verandah drinking lemonade. When they saw him approach, George jumped up and hurried to greet him.

"Cartwright. Good to see you, man. I trust the ride over was uneventful?"

"It was, thank you." William smiled and returned the older man's enthusiastic handshake.

He turned his attention to Margaret, who was attired in a pale blue lace dress that fell to just below her knees. Her cap of sleek blonde hair was secured behind one ear with a delicate blue flower. She looked pretty and fresh and served to remind William just how dusty he was after the long ride.

"Margaret," he greeted her with a slight bow. "Excuse me, but I'm in no condition to take a lady's hand." He spread his arms to indicate his general state of disarray.

She smiled and tittered prettily. "Of course. I'll show you to your room, where you can freshen up before we have dinner."

William followed gratefully with his saddlebag as she led him to a room upstairs then down a long hallway. It was a different room from the one he'd stayed in previously and was farther removed from the rest of the household.

Margaret left him on the threshold of his chamber with instructions to join them on the verandah where they would take dinner.

He quickly removed his shirt, walked over to the washbasin and dunked his head gratefully into the cool, lavender-scented water. Immediately the inexorable ocher-colored dust, trapped within his hair, tinged the water a dull brown. He scrubbed his face, arms and torso then toweled dry with a cotton cloth provided for the purpose before retrieving a clean shirt and trousers from his bag. He instantly felt better and far more civilized. He combed his hair, splashed aftershave tonic onto his neck then gazed into the mirror. He was in need of a shave, his jaw stubbled with two days' growth, but it couldn't be helped. He hadn't had time to shave and he figured the Dawsons wouldn't mind. At least he'd rid himself of most of the dirt and he no longer smelled like horseflesh and sweat.

He made his way to the verandah and sank gratefully into one of the comfortable wicker chairs. Margaret handed him a tall glass of lemonade, which he drank in a few long gulps, easing the dryness in his throat. She laughed and refilled his glass before taking a seat next to him.

A table covered with a white linen cloth and set with crystal and silver had been established at the far end of the verandah.

"I'll serve dinner soon. We're having egg salad to start, followed by lamb pie and for dessert, we have strawberry sponge cake," Margaret informed him proudly.

He studied her curiously and wondered if she knew that lamb pie was his favorite dish.

"Lamb pie, one of my favorites."

She smiled shyly and dropped her gaze to her lap. "Yes, I know."

He didn't have an opportunity to ask how she knew, as George Dawson joined them. Not that it mattered. It just left him with an odd feeling that people had been talking about him without his knowledge. *What else does Margaret Dawson know about me?*

* * * *

"Will we be expecting William today for lunch?" Lillian asked Mrs. Thompson, as she measured out flour for the bread dough.

"No. He left for the Dawson property this morning for a dinner engagement. He'll stay there overnight," she replied, packing more wood into the slow-combustion stove. "I expect him back by noon tomorrow."

Lillian stilled, a fierce jealousy gripping her. The feeling was so unfamiliar and so intense that it physically hurt her chest.

Why didn't William mention anything? Why would he feel the need to hide his plans from me and why stay overnight?

Mrs. Thompson slammed the oven door closed and continued with her explanation, as if Lillian had spoken her thoughts aloud. "It's a long ride—four hours—so Mr. Cartwright stays overnight."

"How often does William visit the Dawson property?" Lillian asked in a voice that she hoped imparted casual inquiry.

"Oh, not very often, perhaps once a month. There was a time when I thought that Mr. Cartwright was interested in the young Miss Dawson."

A searing pain cut through her as the housekeeper voiced Lillian's own fears. She glared down at the table pummeling the bread dough in hurt frustration and tried desperately to appear unaffected. She blinked her eyes rapidly in an attempt to halt the tears that threatened to overflow at any moment.

"Lillian, you are kneading the dough, dear, not killing it," the woman commented good-naturedly.

She looked down to see that the dough was flattened against the table top, where she'd pounded it into pancake-like submission. She took a deep breath, ran her hand through her hair to regain her composure and worked to stop herself from fleeing the kitchen in a sobbing mess.

"Look at that. I was miles away, thinking about the children's lesson this afternoon," she lied smoothly.

Mrs. Thompson was no longer paying attention. She busily ticked tasks off a to-do list.

Lillian quickly gathered the dough into a ball and put it into a greased bowl, then she covered everything with a cloth and placed it next to the slow-combustion stove to prove.

"Well, then," she declared with forced cheerfulness, dusting off her hands. "I'd better see to the children's lessons."

She needed to escape the kitchen and Mrs. Thompson's presence. She needed to be alone to mull over this information, and giving the housekeeper no chance to delay her, she quickly exited the kitchen.

When she reached the sanctuary of her room, she closed her door and leaned against it, letting out a deep sigh of relief at being alone with her thoughts and fears.

She paced to the window, stared out of the glass and contemplated what she'd just learned. It was nothing, she assured herself. William was just attending an innocent dinner at the neighboring property. There was no reason for her to be feeling insecure and jealous. *Why then did William not tell me? Does he have something to hide?*

She thought back to all the times that she'd seen William and Margaret Dawson together. She recalled them dancing closely at the Dawsons' dinner dance where she'd also come across them outside and alone. Then at the picnic races, she'd seen them looking so comfortable together — like the perfect couple. And later at the ball, where they'd danced again and when William had saved the first dance for Margaret.

A cold dread settled in her chest as she mentally reviewed William's and Margaret's behavior toward each other. She suspected that Margaret had feelings for William. In fact the young lady made it very obvious, but she wasn't sure of William's feelings toward Margaret. He'd never mentioned anything to Lillian, but then, given their circumstances, William would hardly discuss his feelings about someone else. She wondered with a sinking feeling whether William had another agenda. Although what that could be, she had no idea. The fact that William had yet to discuss with her what he wanted, if anything, out of their relationship made her nervous.

Her heart had always belonged to William and she'd given herself physically to him, without restraint or fear, because truthfully, he'd been the only man that she'd ever wanted, even after all these years. She couldn't imagine being with anyone else and she had hoped William felt the same way. Now she wasn't so sure. She prayed she was overreacting and that there was no justification to her fears, but the fact remained that William had not told her of his plans and, while she was not his keeper, she had to wonder *why* he hadn't told her what he was doing. In her experience, acts of omission generally meant that there was something to hide. In this case, she hoped desperately that he would prove her incorrect.

She knew she could have been more forthcoming about her own feelings, that perhaps her shyness and occasional awkwardness did not communicate fully what she felt for him. But she was unused to such intimate situations and, apart from William when they were younger, the only other person she'd been very close to was her aunt and she had definitely never discussed intimate things with her. No, Lillian had been conditioned to abide by conservative values and proper manners and behavior. She was taught that ladies did not express themselves in anything other than polite and correct language and definitely did not wax lyrical about sexual activities and personal feelings. She couldn't quite resolve why, then, the act of being physically intimate with William was so much easier than discussing her feelings with him. She guessed it was her body's natural reaction to him. When he was close and when he was making her body feel those delicious sensations, all other considerations fled her mind.

She sighed heavily as her thoughts brought her full circle to her current distress and she resolved that she could do nothing but cast her fears aside for the present and focus on things to keep her mind busy. With that resolution, she tidied her hair and washed her hands and face before she went to find the children to ready them for their lessons.

Chapter Twenty-Four

William sat relaxing after dinner with a whiskey and a cigar while George Dawson outlined his latest plans for his property.

Dinner had been a pleasant affair that had given William the chance to examine any residual attraction that he might have felt for Margaret and he was beyond relieved when all he felt was a friendly attachment. She'd flirted with him, outrageously at times throughout dinner, to the point where William had grown concerned, but when he'd cast a glance at her father, he'd either not observed it or was studiously ignoring it. It was clear to William, however, that Margaret Dawson was throwing all her feminine wiles in his direction and he would have to tread with caution where she was concerned. He felt confident that his behavior thus far toward her had been nothing but courteous and polite, but after her performance earlier that evening, he could no longer ignore the fact that her feelings were obviously stronger. He then decided to take a step back and distance himself from any further unnecessary association with the Dawsons. It was true that he respected George Dawson and valued his acquaintance, but he didn't want to be responsible for any feelings of ill will that an unrequited attachment might engender.

William took a sip of his whiskey and nodded in agreement while George continued discussing his plans but only listened with half an ear as he resumed his internal musings.

Margaret was young, probably a year or two younger than Lillian, and she would find a nice young man to attach herself to, so he just needed to be clear with her that it wouldn't be him. He understood that, isolated as they were, it would be easy to fasten one's affections to someone nearby and available, and he had no doubt that what Margaret felt for him was in the league of a harmless infatuation. Nevertheless, he'd have to nip it in the bud before Margaret got carried away.

George Dawson leaned forward and topped off William's whiskey before his conversation took a different turn.

"Well, Cartwright, what did you think of dinner? My Margaret is an accomplished cook. Wouldn't you agree?"

"It was a delicious meal and I complimented her on it."

"She would make someone a good wife, eh?"

William narrowed his eyes and observed the other man over the rim of his glass. "Yes, I have no doubt she would."

George grinned widely and took a large swallow of whiskey. "No doubt you must have thought about taking another wife. It must be lonely, a young, virile man like yourself."

William coughed and tried not to choke on his drink, not fooled for a moment by Dawson's deceptively casual tone. *Fuck, the man has no shame.* "I have *not* thought about it," he said irritably and took a long, fortifying mouthful of liquor.

"Ah now, Cartwright, don't be coy. There must be some young thing who has caught your eye?"

William studied George as he refilled his glass, wondering idly if the man was trying to get him drunk and, coming to the quick conclusion that he was, figured it was an obvious attempt to loosen his tongue.

"You know me, Dawson. Coy is not an adjective that I would ever use to describe myself."

"Keeping your powder dry, eh?" Dawson said, tapping his nose conspiratorially.

"Not at all. I have no plans to take a wife in the near future." He wasn't about to divulge his personal life to George Dawson, even with the considerable amount of whiskey currently floating around in his system. He looked at his watch, conscious that he had an early start and not relishing the prospect of a four-hour ride on little sleep.

"Well, I should turn in," William announced. "Thank you for your hospitality, Dawson."

"Not at all. Any time," he replied jovially. "It's been good to catch up and I know that Margaret enjoyed the company."

William nodded politely, shook the man's hand then made his exit. The whiskey had started to catch up with him and his head was swimming as he made his way upstairs to his room. He undressed quickly and gratefully fell into bed and a deep slumber.

* * * *

He wasn't sure what woke him. He struggled to sit up and was momentarily dazed by the unfamiliar environment. He peered around the dark room groggily and scratched his head, trying to determine what had disturbed his sleep. The room was in deep shadow, the curtain fluttering from the breeze through the open window. Perhaps it was a noise from outside. He sat, his back resting against the headboard, and shoved a hand through his hair, exhaling deeply. He hated being awoken suddenly. It always left him feeling twitchy and off kilter. He knew it was the after-effects of the war. Ever since then, it only took a slight noise or movement to have him rearing up in bed in readiness for quick action. It was getting better, though. At least now he didn't automatically reach for his rifle and prepare to take cover.

He cursed quietly and lay back down, hoping he'd return to sleep quickly. It was then that a movement by the door caught his eye. He sat up again and shoved the covers aside before leaping out of bed.

"Who's there?" he demanded. He reached toward where his rifle rested against the wall.

"It's just me, William," replied a feminine voice, breathless and hesitant.

"What the fu—?" He recognized the dulcet tones of Margaret Dawson. "Margaret? What the hell are you doing in my room? I could have killed you!"

"I'm sorry. I didn't mean to startle you."

"Well, that's what happens when you sneak into people's rooms in the middle of the night. What do you want?"

He crossed his arms over his chest and waited for her explanation. He was very conscious of the fact that he was naked and cursed himself for not having had the foresight to at least sleep in his underclothes. He hoped to God that the room provided enough shadow to conceal his nudity. The last thing he needed was for her to fall into a fit of hysterics. That thought fled his brain rapidly, however, when he heard the strike of a match and saw the following flare as she touched the tip of it to a candlewick.

He sucked in a sharp breath as the room was brightened by a faint glow. *What the fuck is she doing?* He could see her clearly now, dressed in a sheer white gown that left nothing to the imagination, the candlelight illuminating her body through the gossamer fabric. Her full curves swayed voluptuously when she took a tentative step forward.

Christ, he had to work to keep his body's natural reaction from rearing up at full attention and embarrassing the crap out of him. He shook his head, trying to clear his whiskey and sleep-addled brain, but even through his confused state, he couldn't help but compare Margaret to Lillian. Lillian's curves were delicately voluptuous and fit perfectly in his hands. He loved her long, silky hair, which he would weave through his fingers to grasp her head closer to his, and he adored her perfect rosebud lips that he ached to kiss every time he looked at her.

Margaret was certainly pretty and her figure, outlined enticingly as it was at that moment, was curvy and pleasingly plump, but the sight of her didn't make his blood heat and his pulse roar in his ears. She was simply an attractive woman with a reasonable body, who was obviously trying her damnedest to seduce him.

He narrowed his eyes at her as she stared blatantly at his naked body and licked her lips, her gaze lingering too long on his cock.

"You have a magnificent body," she said. "So much better than I imagined. You're so hard and muscular." Her voice had taken on a sultry note.

What the fuck? William's mind raced while he worked out how to extricate her from his room without causing a disturbance.

"Margaret, you shouldn't be here." He spoke quietly and surely, hoping to telegraph through his tone that he wasn't interested.

She walked slowly toward him, swaying her hips seductively. He would have taken a step back but the wall was behind him so he held his ground, his arms crossed defensively across his chest when it was clear she wasn't going to leave easily.

"Remember those times we danced together, the walks we've shared? Think of all the times you've visited here. I know you were looking at me as more than an acquaintance, William."

Shit, he'd at one time thought about perhaps taking things with her to another level but he'd always kept those feelings strictly to himself and had never been anything other than polite, if not even slightly reserved with her. How had she concluded that he might want her?

"I'm sorry if I've given you the wrong impression." He kept his voice low and soothing. "But nothing can happen between us."

She stopped in her tracks and fixed him with a malevolent glare, made even more hostile by the play of candlelight across her features. "Is it because of *her*? The bland little governess?"

William hardened his jaw and tensed. "Lillian is anything *but* bland. And this has *nothing* to do with her and everything to do with *you* misinterpreting my feelings toward you. I believe I've only ever acted in a friendly and courteous manner."

"But everything changed when she came along. Before she arrived, you were attentive toward me. I thought you really liked me and wanted me." Her voice had taken on a whiny quality and her lips trembled.

William sighed and ran a hand through his hair in exasperation. In truth, he hadn't spent that much time in the company of Margaret and her father—such was the way of the outback—but he supposed that it would have been easy for her to have romanticized the time that he'd spent with her and have taken it to mean something it wasn't.

Margaret placed the candle on the bedside table and, taking advantage of his brief silence, she stepped toward him, closing the distance between them until she was flush against his chest. The feel of her full breasts pillowed against his front had his cock rearing up automatically and he fought his body's reaction before she took it to mean that he wanted to take things further.

He grasped her upper arms and pushed her back gently. "Margaret, please."

"I can see that you want me, William. I want you too."

Her blue eyes shimmered with lust as she reached down and gripped his cock firmly, pumping her fist up and down his length until he was once more rock hard. *Christ*, getting rid of her was going to be more difficult than he'd initially anticipated.

He grabbed her wrist. "Stop, Margaret. It isn't going to happen."

She smirked at him, waving her free hand over his crotch. "You're aroused and you want me. You know I can make you feel good."

He eyed her suspiciously and gripped her other wrist to deter her from touching him. This was not the behavior of an innocent virgin. It appeared that Margaret Dawson was accustomed to the arts of seduction and the realization startled him. It also made his rejection a little easier to do, knowing that she was not as naïve and vulnerable as he'd first thought.

"Margaret, let me be clear. I. Am. Not. Interested."

He didn't give her a chance to respond but released one of her wrists and, keeping hold of the other, he started tugging her toward the door.

She struggled to get out of his hold. "What is wrong with you?" she jeered. "I'm practically throwing myself at you and you reject me?" She laughed coldly. "Are you not interested in women?"

William finally reached the doorway with the seductress still in tow. "I'm very much interested in women. I'm just not interested in you." He grasped her upper arms and lifted her so that she was no longer in his room but standing on the other side of the threshold.

"Goodnight, Margaret." He quirked his lips in amusement. "It has been…interesting."

He didn't wait for her angry response but closed the door firmly in her face. Leaning against it, he breathed a deep sigh of relief and silently congratulated himself on diverting certain disaster.

Chapter Twenty-Five

Lillian gazed out of the window of the upstairs classroom. She'd been looking out for William's return. She glanced at her watch. He should have been back over two hours ago. She supposed that something *or someone* could have detained him but Mrs. Thompson had been adamant that he'd planned to return early. It was a busy shearing time on the property and William hadn't intended to leave for long.

She was worried about him.

She decided to call a halt to the day's lessons. The hot, stuffy air in the little upstairs room was making the children fractious and grumpy. She could no longer hold their attention and her own attention level was little better.

She dismissed the children to play and went in search of Mrs. Thompson. She found her in the washroom and immediately voiced her concerns.

"What time did William plan to return? I'm starting to become worried."

Mrs. Thompson frowned and glanced at her watch. "Twelve o'clock or thereabouts. Two hours ago." She looked out of the window and worried her bottom lip. "It's unlike him to change his plans. He knows we'd be concerned."

"Where are the men?" Lillian inquired.

"At the northern end of the property. Too far away to get to them quickly and they move around quite a bit."

Lillian gave the housekeeper a long look.

"I'm going in search of him," she finally announced. "I'll take one of the horses and start for the Dawson property."

Mrs. Thompson wrung her hands. "Are you sure that's a good idea? It's been a long time since you've ridden. I don't want to be worrying about you too."

"There's nothing else for it. The men are too far away and something could have happened to William on his way back here." She patted the other woman on the shoulder. "I'll be fine. Please don't fret."

The housekeeper didn't look convinced but set off to the kitchen to pack some provisions as Lillian rushed upstairs to change into suitable riding attire.

In less than an hour, Lillian had saddled a horse and was ready to go. The readying of the horse had taken her longer than it should have. It had been a long while since she'd ridden, and she had only saddled a horse herself a few times. The heavy stockman's saddle had been unwieldy but she'd eventually managed and she was confident that she'd fixed it correctly. The animal was an older mare and Lillian felt happy that she could handle her with ease.

Mrs. Thompson had packed her water, sandwiches and a Thermos of coffee. Lillian had also strapped a blanket to her saddle and included a basic medical kit with her provisions. She hoped fervently that their concern turned out to be baseless, but she wanted to be prepared.

She set out, following the fence line in the direction of the Dawson homestead. She told herself that she'd see William at any moment galloping toward her. But when an hour had passed then another, her hopes of seeing William safe and well had started to diminish. He could still be with George and Margaret Dawson but she knew that if he'd extended his stay, he'd have sent word. It would have been easy enough to send a message through one of Dawson's men.

She stretched her arms and back. The unaccustomed position in the saddle was tiring and she could feel her muscles starting to seize. She'd just decided to stop for a break when up ahead she spotted Victory, William's horse — without William in the saddle.

"Oh my God," she breathed. Her heart rate jolted and cold fear gripped her. She kicked her horse into a gallop and raced toward Victory, praying that William was not badly hurt. He was an expert horseman and that fact worried her more than anything. It meant that something serious must have happened for Victory to be wandering around without his master astride him.

She bent low over her horse's head and urged the animal into a faster gallop. Her pulse thundered in her ears and her breathing was heavy with dread as she neared William's horse. Not far away, lying unmoving on the ground, she saw William. She skidded her horse to a halt, leaped from the saddle and ran toward him.

"William!"

He lay pale and still, a gash on his temple seeping blood. Her heart stuttered and she emitted an involuntary cry. Kneeling next to him, she checked his pulse and nearly swooned with relief when she felt it beating firmly beneath her fingers. She lifted each of his closed lids and checked his eye movements then shook him gently. When he didn't respond, she rose and hurried to her horse to retrieve her water bottle and the medical kit. She returned to William and, wetting a cloth, she pressed it to the wound on his temple. She poured more water onto another cloth and wiped William's face and neck, hoping the cool fluid might revive him.

It was still hot and she had no idea how long William had been lying in the open under the fierce sun. She undid the buttons of his shirt and splashed water onto his chest.

When she removed the cloth from his temple, she was relieved to see that the gash had stopped bleeding and didn't appear to be too deep. The medical kit held a small bottle of alcohol, which she used to douse his head wound. When the alcohol splashed across his temple, he groaned.

Lillian shook his shoulder gently. "William. William, it's Lilly. Wake up."

When he didn't respond, she splashed more alcohol onto his wound and he hissed.

She peered down into his face and grinned happily when he opened his eyes. They looked a little glassy but at least he was conscious.

"What the fuck? Lilly?"

She pressed his shoulders down to ensure that he stayed still. "Yes, William. When you were so late returning home, I came looking for you. You must stay still until we check that you haven't broken anything."

He narrowed his eyes on her. "You came looking for me? Alone?"

"Well, what else could I do? All the men are on the other side of the property, mustering sheep."

She stared down into his handsome face and breathed a sigh of relief at his awareness. He hadn't shaved and the stubble on his jaw gave him a rakish edge. She shouldn't be thinking about how attractive he was, but she couldn't help it. Even lying on the ground with a head wound, he was the handsomest man she'd ever seen.

She shook herself into action. They needed to get moving before the day grew any later. "Have you broken anything? I don't want you to move until we can be satisfied that you won't do any more damage to yourself."

William lifted himself to rest on his elbows. "The only injury I seem to have sustained is this head wound. I'm sure I'll be a little stiff from the fall but everything feels to be in working order."

Lillian lifted her water bottle to his lips. "Here. You need some fluids."

He took the bottle from her and tipped his head back, taking a long drink.

"Are you all right to stand?" She didn't want to push him but they needed to get moving.

He handed her the water bottle. "I'm fine. I think I'll have a splitting headache, but I'll be able to ride."

She crouched behind him and helped him to his feet. He swayed for a moment and she wrapped her arms around his waist to steady him.

Lillian gazed up at him in concern. "You're not feeling unwell, are you?"

"No. I just need a minute."

She held him steady while he took three deep breaths, in through his nose and out through his mouth. When he could stand unassisted, she led him to where Victory waited patiently, a short distance away.

"Hey, boy," William greeted his horse affectionately and patted his nose.

Lillian helped him into the saddle and ensured that his feet were securely in the stirrups.

William grinned down at her. "I've ridden horses since before I could walk, Lilly. I'll be fine."

She gave him a mock glare. "You've just been knocked unconscious! You need to be careful."

He laughed and saluted her. "Yes, ma'am."

"And anyway," she continued, swinging herself up into her saddle. "If you're such a fabulous horseman, how did you manage to come off?"

William scowled at her. "Accidents *do* happen, even to the most experienced riders. As it happened, we came across a snake and Victory panicked then reared. I wasn't paying attention and I came out of the saddle. Now, can we please head home?"

Lillian smiled and took up her reins. The relief she felt that William was alive and acting belligerent was palpable. "Well, we can thank the Lord that you don't seem to be hurt too badly. Let's get you home." She turned her horse's head in the direction of Mulga Creek and kicked her into a canter.

Chapter Twenty-Six

William grunted and struggled to sit up in bed. He felt a bit woozy and a little stiff but other than that, he didn't feel as bad as he'd expected. He tried to gauge the time. The dark sky outlined by his window told him that it was late evening or early morning.

He tentatively touched a hand to his temple and felt the bandage wrapped around his head. His headache had passed, thankfully. He grinned wryly when he thought about Lillian's and Mrs. Thompson's fussing over him. He'd started to get a little irritated with their mother-hen act, but he had to concede that he did feel better. The cold compress they'd applied to his head and the pain medication definitely seemed to have worked. He'd drawn the line at calling the doctor, however. The property was too far out to bother the doctor unnecessarily and he'd felt no ill effects such as nausea or loss of memory — just a thumping headache.

He couldn't believe that Lilly had ridden out to find him. She'd saddled a horse, no less, and boldly embarked on a rescue expedition. He couldn't forget how well she used to handle a horse, but that was years ago and he doubted she'd done much riding in England. His initial reaction to her riding out alone to find him had been anger. But she'd been right when she'd pointed out that the men were working too far away to have offered any assistance. If his injury had been serious, it would have taken them too long to reach him. Add to that the fact that Lilly hadn't even been sure he'd been injured and might have just extended his stay with the Dawsons. He could accept her rationalization at attempting to find him.

A noise from the other side of the room made him start and he peered into the dim recesses.

"William?" a soft voice inquired.

"Lilly. What are you doing in here so late?"

He made out her shadowed form as she rose from a chair and made her way over to the bed.

"We were worried about you. I told Mrs. Thompson that I'd sit with you through the night. We thought it best that you not be alone."

She sat on the bed next to him and her wonderful scent invaded his nostrils. God, she was beautiful, dressed in a white muslin nightdress and matching gown, her hair—loosely plaited—hung over one shoulder. He couldn't see her face clearly but he knew that if he could, he would see rosy cheeks and lovely, large emerald eyes. His mind went back to the previous evening when Margaret Dawson had crept into his room and he couldn't help but draw comparisons yet again. His Lilly was pure, gentle and sweet, while Margaret Dawson had proven to be brash and pushy. And while his body had responded naturally to the sight of hers, he hadn't desired her in the least. Seeing Lilly again looking so lovely and wholesome had his heart literally bursting with emotion.

He caressed Lillian's cheek. "You shouldn't have worried. You'll be exhausted tomorrow," he chided gently.

"Nonsense, I'll be fine. How do you feel?"

He grinned. "Actually, all things considered, I'm feeling good. My headache is gone."

"I'm glad. I'm going to light the oil lamp so I can take a look at your head wound."

She struck a match and a soft glow lit the room. She placed the lamp on a side table and picked up a medical box.

William studied her as she searched through the contents. The soft light illuminated her body under the gauzy fabric of her gown and her lush curves were presented enticingly to him. Once again, a flashback of the previous evening shot through his brain, when another young lady had displayed herself provocatively to him. The difference being that Lilly was unaware of the transparent effect of her gown.

He watched as she bit her lip and rummaged through the medical contents to extract a clean bandage and some antiseptic. Her breasts swayed alluringly with her movements and when she stood, he could make out her rosy-tipped nipples perfectly. His gaze wandered down her torso, across her flat stomach and rounded hips then zeroed in on the dark triangle of hair between her thighs. He groaned low in his throat and his cock hardened instantly.

Lilly startled. Obviously misinterpreting his groan for one of pain, she immediately felt his forehead.

He smirked at her concerned expression.

She narrowed her eyes on him. "Care to tell me what you're finding so amusing?"

He remained silent for a moment, enjoying the feel of her cool hand on his skin. He let his attention drift down the delectable contours of her body and he shifted, his erection swelling to painful proportions. "I'm just enjoying the view."

She followed his gaze, looked down her body and gasped. "Goodness! I had no idea." She wrapped her gown tighter around her body and glared at him. "William, now is *not* the time to be thinking lascivious thoughts! You're ill!"

He chuckled. "Lilly, my sweet, lascivious thoughts are never far from a man's mind, particularly when a beautiful woman's assets are so temptingly displayed."

He reached out and tugged her gown open so that he could again admire her curves. "Please, humor a sick man."

She gave him an appraising look. "Well, you're obviously recovering." Her attention settled on the tented sheet at his lap. "And it appears that a particular part of your anatomy is definitely functioning."

He grinned and allowed her to unwrap the bandage from around his head. She palpated his wound with delicate fingers, making him wince. "It looks good," she announced. "It doesn't appear infection has set in." She applied antiseptic and rewrapped his head with clean gauze.

She packed everything back into the medical box and set it aside. "Do you need anything else for the pain?"

"No. My headache is gone. I just want you, lying next to me."

"William, we can't do anything. You sustained a head wound today," she admonished.

"I know. I just want to hold you." He wanted that desperately. He needed to lie with her in his arms and wake up with her warm, luscious body pressed against his.

She gave him a long look then stood and removed her outer gown. She walked to the other side of the bed, drew the covers back and slid in next to him.

Immediately, he wrapped an arm around her waist and tugged her to him, burying his face against her neck and inhaling deeply. "You smell so good," he mumbled against her skin. "Good enough to eat."

She giggled then abruptly grew silent. William couldn't miss the sudden tension in her body.

He drew back from her and rested his head on the pillow, looking at her profile. "What's wrong?"

She chewed her bottom lip and turned her face toward his. "Why didn't you tell me that you were going to the Dawson property and spending the night?"

He turned onto his back and threw one arm behind his head as he stared at the ceiling. "It wasn't important. George Dawson wanted to catch up with me and discuss his plans for his property. He wanted my opinion on some matters."

He could hardly add that he had wanted to see Margaret Dawson when he wasn't in the company of Lillian so he could assess whether he was attracted to the other woman and test his feelings for Lilly.

"I know that I don't have any right to question your movements. I just wondered why you would tell Mrs. Thompson but not me."

He hated to hear the hurt in her voice. He didn't really know why he hadn't told her about his visit to George Dawson. Perhaps there was a part of him that had felt guilty about his double agenda and he hadn't wanted Lillian to become suspicious. He also wasn't used to telling too many people his arrangements. He was accustomed to doing what he wanted, when he wanted to.

He turned to face her once more. "I'm sorry, I didn't think. You have to remember that I'm used to telling Millie and my head stockman my plans. I just did what I always do." She was still chewing that plump bottom lip of hers, which was distracting the hell out of him and not helping his aching cock. "I usually *do* spend the night there. The property is a long ride from Mulga Creek and I've stayed there quite a few times."

He suspected her problem was with Margaret Dawson and the fact that he'd been under the same roof as her on more than a few occasions. He couldn't blame her, he supposed. If he thought back over the times he'd run into Margaret while in the company of Lillian, he could see why she would be suspicious. Margaret hadn't exactly been guarded in displaying her affections toward him.

"I have no romantic feelings whatsoever toward Margaret," he said quietly. "She is merely the daughter of a neighbor and someone with whom I'm friendly."

He reached over and extinguished the oil lamp, then turned on his side and pulled Lillian toward him, spooning her, so her soft, round buttocks pillowed his cock. At the feel of her curves, his flagging erection instantly revived and he couldn't help but grind his hips into her. She wriggled against him and he didn't miss her small intake of breath. He smiled against her neck and kissed the delicate skin under her ear.

"Sleep now, darling." He tucked her tighter against him.

Chapter Twenty-Seven

Lillian awoke with a solid body crushed against her back and something even harder pressed insistently against her buttocks. She tried to wriggle out of the muscular arms banded around her middle but she was stuck fast.

"Good morning, beautiful." William's voice, husky from sleep, caressed her ear. His warm breath tickled her sensitive skin and made her nipples pebble. Unable to resist the pull of his masculine voice and body, she relaxed into him.

"Good morning," she murmured, pushing back against him to feel his rigid length lodge between the cheeks of her buttocks. "How is it that...?" She tried to find the right word. "That it's still hard?"

He chuckled, the vibrations sending delicious tingles through her.

"It's a common thing for a man in the morning," he explained, thrusting his hips to demonstrate.

"You mean that you always wake up *that* way?"

William's hot breath against her ear had her trembling. "Only when I have the most beautiful woman that I know in my bed."

He moved his hand from where it rested on her hip and grasped her left breast and squeezed. Palming her breast, he caressed her hard nipple with the flat of his hand. She gasped, a jolt of desire rocketing through her to pool low in her belly.

"William," she breathed. "I don't think that you're well enough."

"Oh, I'm fine," he contradicted. "In fact, I think that this is exactly what the doctor would order."

She shivered as his hands wandered down her torso, then pulled up the hem of her nightdress, exposing her breasts.

"These are so beautiful, so full and round," he whispered against her neck. "Are you still bleeding?"

"No. I finished yesterday."

"Good." He massaged her breasts and tweaked her nipples. She moaned and ground her backside into his pelvis, relishing the feel of his thick length as it slid between her legs. She opened her thighs in silent invitation, needing to feel him inside her.

He chuckled. "I've created a very greedy girl. Are you wet for me?"

"Yes," she gasped.

He released her breasts and ran his hand down her side as he sucked on the skin of her neck. "Let me check." He plunged two fingers into her core and groaned. "So moist and tight. Fuck."

He teased her, slowly thrusting his fingers in and out then stroking over her swollen folds.

She cried out and pumped her hips against his hand. "Please, William."

He was provoking her, getting so close but not making contact with her clit. Circling around it then pushing deep into her channel. She groaned and pivoted her hips in a desperate attempt to manipulate the direction of his fingers.

Still suckling her throat, she felt him smile against her skin. "What do you want, my sweet?" he mumbled into her neck. "Is this what you want?" He found her clitoris with his thumb and he massaged the little bundle of nerves while he thrust deeply with his fingers. She was on such a knife-edge that she came almost immediately, trembling and shaking as her insides pulsed in release.

He hissed a breath. "God, I love how fast I can make you lose control. Now I want to feel your tight, slick heat contracting around my cock," he rasped, pushing his rigid length into her from behind.

He filled her to capacity and she moaned as he stretched her with his shaft and stroked the swollen walls of her channel.

He grasped her waist and pumped his pelvis, slapping his hips against her backside with each thrust. He grunted his satisfaction in time with his plunges, his warm breath at her ear sending goosebumps flaring across her flesh.

The pressure started to build deep inside her, the sensations swirling and coalescing at her core.

"Touch yourself," he demanded, lifting her left leg and splaying her thighs wider. He gripped her wrist and coaxed her hand down, his fingers covering hers to guide her to where he wanted them.

"That's it. Feel how wet, plump and swollen with arousal you are?"

She felt the slickness between her thighs and whimpered, brushing her fingers across her clit. She pressed the little nub harder and rubbed while he drew his hips back until the tip of his cock caressed her folds, then he plunged again deeply.

Her breathing quickened and the tightness in her belly told her that she was close.

William's breathing became labored and choppy, his voice rough. "Come on, Lilly." He screwed his pelvis into her and the internal dam burst. Her muscles spasmed and waves of ecstasy washed over her, her body shaking with the force of her orgasm.

Lillian could tell that he was near to his own climax. He gripped her waist, his movements growing aggressive as he strove to reach his peak. He plunged twice then withdrew. "Fuck, Lilly." He groaned and shuddered, pumping his release all over her arse.

* * * *

William pulled Lilly tightly against his chest. He adored waking up with her in his bed, loved the feel of her lush curves as they molded to him. Softness pillowed against steel. She was so feminine, so beguiling that every time he looked at her, his heart rate increased and he got a strange, light feeling in the pit of his stomach. He caressed her hair and planted a kiss on her temple, not wanting to let her go, wishing that they could stay there together forever.

"We should get out of bed," Lilly murmured. "Mrs. Thompson will wonder how you are and any moment she's going to come knocking on your door."

He blew out a frustrated breath. Yes, he had no doubt that his intrepid housekeeper would come seeking him out very soon.

He climbed out of bed and strode to the basin for a washcloth. Returning, he pulled the covers back and grasped the hem of Lillian's nightdress. "Lift your hips," he requested.

She sighed and lifted her backside. He took his time drawing the fabric up to her waist and marveled at her supple legs as they were revealed to him.

"You have beautiful skin," he whispered and bent to plant a soft kiss on the inside of her thigh. He swiped the washcloth between her legs and diligently cleaned her. It surprised him that she didn't blush as she usually did when he performed such intimate acts on her body. The fact pleased him. It meant that she was becoming comfortable with him and her nudity.

He returned to the basin and refreshed the cloth. "Turn over, Lilly."

She rolled onto her stomach and he swept the washcloth over her back and in the crevice of her lush backside. The sight of her smooth, round curves, displayed so temptingly to him, had him growing solid again within seconds. He quickly finished cleaning her up and pulled her nightdress down, cursing inwardly that he couldn't afford to risk diving onto the bed and ravaging her a second time.

He collected her gown and held it open for her in invitation. Just as she'd slipped her arms into the sleeves and was fastening the front ties, a knock on the door startled them both.

William quickly grabbed his nightshirt and shrugged into it. Satisfied that he was decent, he called out for his housekeeper to enter. Lillian had taken up her previous position in a nearby chair.

Mrs. Thompson bustled into the room with a breakfast tray. "How is the patient this morning?"

"I'm fine, Millie. Lillian just checked my bandages. I have no headache. In fact, I feel as good as new."

His housekeeper appraised him shrewdly before depositing the tray on a side table. "You shouldn't overdo things, William. You had a bad fall," she admonished.

Out of the corner of his eye, he noticed Lillian stand and walk toward the open door.

"Well, I shall leave you to your breakfast," she said quietly, before slipping out of the room.

He endured the attentions of his housekeeper for a few minutes until he managed to convince her that he felt fine and was suffering no ill effects from his fall.

When he had his room to himself once more, he finished his breakfast and performed his morning ablutions.

He thought about Lillian and pondered about taking their relationship to the next level. The truth was that he was terrified of losing her. She belonged to him. After all the years of separation, he finally had her in his grasp and in his bed. He didn't want to let her go — he couldn't. Of course, the rational part of his brain knew that it wasn't just up to him. Lilly, of course, had to be in agreement. He just couldn't be sure what he'd do if it looked like she was going to run. Could he stop himself from detaining her? He didn't know.

Unfortunately, even though it hurt to admit it, he wasn't yet certain of Lilly's feelings toward him. He was positive that she cared for him. She wouldn't have ridden after him yesterday if there was no fondness on her part, but he couldn't discern the *depth* of her feelings for him. Hitherto she hadn't expressed any particular sentiments of affection toward him but he hoped that it was just her attempt to protect herself. He could appreciate that feeling. He still suffered from the suspicions caused by the pain from their years of separation. He *also* found it difficult to voice his feelings, as his mind continued to whisper for him to be careful, that he had to armor himself against the risk of heartbreak. Then his heart spoke to him and told him to go for it, to throw caution to the wind and embrace the passion he felt for Lillian with both arms.

He sighed heavily. He wouldn't think about it now. He didn't have time. He'd missed two days of work. Even though he employed good men, they were one man down with his absence and they would need to make up some lost ground.

He dressed quickly, anxious to get going, and had just grabbed his bush hat when a knock sounded on his door. He turned to find Lillian standing on the threshold. The sight of her made his chest ache. She was attired in a sensible blouse and skirt and she'd pulled her beautiful hair into a tight chignon. Her emerald eyes were clear and her cheeks rosy. His eyes drifted to her plump, red lips — lips that just begged to be kissed. Quite simply, she was the loveliest woman he'd ever seen, even dressed as she was in her conservative governess attire.

"I thought that we could do away with the head bandage and I'll replace it with a sticking plaster. I daresay you'll be more comfortable."

He grinned and moved toward a chair. "I would much prefer that. I don't think that I can wear my hat with this gauze wrapped around my head."

She walked toward him and set the medical kit on a nearby table. "Are you sure you're up to working?"

He smiled at her worried tone and the concern clouding her eyes. "I'm really quite well, Lilly. I wish everyone would stop worrying."

She deftly unwrapped his bandage, checked his wound and hummed in approval. "It still looks good.

It's closing nicely." She applied antiseptic ointment and sticking plaster to his temple.

"I'm going to be gone for one, perhaps two, days." He grinned. "I'm telling you of my plans. I don't want you to worry. I won't have you racing around the countryside on horseback alone again."

She smiled sweetly at him, then lifted her hand and grazed his jaw with her knuckles. "You've shaved. I quite liked that roguish, stubbled look on you."

His breath stuttered at the scorching look she offered him.

"Thank you for telling me, William. I'll miss you when you're gone."

He stood swiftly, shoving his chair back at the same time, and reached for her. Grasping her uppers arms, he pulled her against his chest. "I'll miss you too, Lilly, my sweet." He lowered his mouth to hers, barely grazing her lips with his own. "More than you'll know."

Her body was so soft, so compliant against his harder, muscular form that he couldn't help but tug her closer. Sweeping his hands down her back, he found her round buttocks and squeezed the lush cheeks in his palms. She moaned low in her throat as he took her mouth in a deep, passionate kiss. He couldn't get enough of her taste — so sweet, like marmalade and tea. He cupped her backside harder and ground his pelvis into hers, demonstrating to her how much she affected him. He took their kiss deeper, drinking from her as if she were an oasis in the desert. Finally, he pulled away so they could catch their breath. Panting, she looked at him, her lips red and puffy from his harsh treatment of them. He rubbed his thumb across her mouth, gently caressing and soothing.

"You look so beautiful right now. All flushed, your lips swollen from our kiss. Remember this moment when I'm away and know that I'll be thinking of you."

He cupped her cheeks in his hands and bent his forehead to hers. "I'll see you in two days, my sweet Lilly. Take care and *no* riding around the countryside on your own."

"I promise." She smiled, pecked him on the cheek and left him, closing the door softly behind her.

He stood staring after her for a few seconds. He was worried. He wasn't superstitious, but something sinister at the back of his mind told him that this could be the last time he'd see her, and that possibility scared the life out of him.

Chapter Twenty-Eight

It was midday, the day after William had left, when Lillian noticed the telltale dust cloud that alerted her to the fact that someone was approaching the property.

She set her trowel aside and stood from where she'd been kneeling in the garden bed planting seeds. Shading her eyes from the fierce sun, she peered into the distance and tried to determine who the visitors were. The red haze surrounding the vehicle made it difficult to identify anything, but she thought she detected just one occupant in the automobile. She tried to remember if William had mentioned that he was expecting company. She couldn't recall anything, but evidently someone was on his or her way and Lillian needed to hasten inside to freshen up.

She made her way into the washroom where she scrubbed her hands and face free of dirt then she hurried to her room to remove her scarf and fix her hair. The clothes she was wearing were reserved solely for gardening but she had neither the time nor the inclination to change. She had no idea who the visitor was, but she doubted that they were coming to see her. It would be enough that she looked tidy and presentable.

She was descending the stairs when Mrs. Thompson was making her way up. "Lilly, Mr. Dawson is here to see you."

Lillian frowned. "I don't know what he could possibly want with *me*."

"He came by one of those infernal automobiles. Perhaps he's just giving it a run and has popped in to say hello," the housekeeper suggested.

"Perhaps," Lillian muttered distractedly as she continued down the stairs.

Taking a deep breath, she entered the drawing room. "Mr. Dawson." She dipped her head in greeting. "Please allow me to apologize for my attire, I wasn't expecting company."

"Good afternoon, Miss Hamilton. Please don't distress yourself, you are looking lovely as usual." He took her hand and placed a kiss on the back. "Shall we sit?"

Lillian nodded and took a seat opposite. "I'm not sure why you want to see me." She needed to get to the bottom of his mysterious visit.

He smiled congenially. "Cartwright mentioned that you and he grew up together."

"Yes, our fathers were friends." She wasn't going to divulge any more information. As far as Lillian was concerned, her and William's history was no business of George Dawson's.

"I think it was quite evident to everyone who attended the Picnic Race Day Ball that you and he are quite close. In fact, William's attentions toward you drew a lot of comments."

Lillian flushed when she thought about William's high-handed behavior that evening. At the same time, she determined that she wouldn't be drawn into whatever game George Dawson was currently playing. "I'm sorry, Mr. Dawson, but you still haven't told me why you're here. Is there something that you wish to discuss with me?"

He smiled, although it didn't reach his eyes, and Lillian immediately felt uneasy. A sudden and disturbing sense of foreboding washed over her, turning her blood to ice water.

"Let me get straight to the point, then," he sneered. "Your Mr. Cartwright, pillar of the community and decorated war hero, has impregnated my daughter!"

Lillian gasped in shock, her hand shooting to cover her mouth, an involuntary moan erupting from low in her throat. Cold, hard dread settled like a stone in her stomach. She couldn't believe what she'd just heard — it *couldn't* be true. She knew William, knew him to be a gentleman of integrity and honor. But even as those thoughts raced through her brain, so too did a sinister subconscious whisper. *"He was intimate with you. You gave yourself to him with no promise of something more."* He'd shown, too, concern for the possibility that she'd become pregnant — was that because he'd suspected that the same had happened with Margaret?

A fierce nausea slammed into her. She doubled over where she sat and wretched pitifully, wrapping her arms around her stomach in a futile attempt at self-comfort. She breathed deeply in through her nose and out through her mouth, her vision focused blurrily on the floral carpet as she fought the sick feeling sweeping through her. She had to regain control. Nothing could be achieved by her turning into a weak, blubbering mess, particularly in front of the likes of

George Dawson. She peered up at him through lowered lashes to find him gazing dispassionately at her, his expression almost one of disdain. Like she was an irritating inconsequence, a technicality to be dealt with swiftly and with no fuss.

Pain speared through her and settled on her chest like a heavy weight. Then one thought worked its way through the morass of her mind and took root above all others. If what George Dawson said was correct—and she had no reason to believe that he would lie about such a serious matter—then William needed to support Margaret and their unborn baby. He had to make an honest woman of Margaret Dawson and take her as his wife immediately.

Lillian drew herself upright in her chair and faced the man sitting opposite. She fixed her facial features into an impassive mask. "I daresay that you have a plan," she probed, gazing steadily at him.

He gave her a crocodile grin that turned her stomach. "I do, indeed, and there is no time to waste."

Chapter Twenty-Nine

"Fuck!" William roared, kicking a chair viciously and sending it splintering against the wall. He whirled around and, spying a large glass vase, he snatched it up and sent it flying into the wall after the chair, where it shattered into hundreds of crystalline pieces.

He braced both hands on the mantelpiece and hung his head between his arms, trying to rein in his rampant temper. He took a couple of deep breaths and speared a hand through his hair in anger and frustration. He couldn't believe that she'd do this to him. He refused to believe that she'd take his heart, rip it out and fucking shred it—*again*—just like she had ten years ago!

The evidence, though, was bloody irrefutable! He stalked to the letter, which he'd crushed into a ball and flung against the wall after he'd read the bullshit written in it. He stooped and retrieved the missive, smoothing it out so he could once again torture himself with the words that were sure to finish him. *Her* words, which had obviously been designed to cut him deeply, to crush all sentiment and leave him heartbroken—and they would. He knew that he wouldn't get over losing her a second time.

Throwing the letter on his desk, he poured himself a large whiskey, needing something to calm his nerves and temper. He downed the liquor in one swallow, relishing the burn down his throat and welcoming the warmth when it hit his gut, grounding him. He poured a second, smaller glass and settled behind his desk. He stared at the flattened piece of paper, at the cursive written in her hand, but in words that he'd yet to fully comprehend.

Dearest William,

When you read this, I will be gone and all I can say is that I'm sorry.

I have come to realize that this life on the land is not what I remembered. It is a hard, sometimes brutal existence and one I fear that I'm not suited for.

I have thought long and hard about my decision to leave and believe that it's for the best. I will miss you and the children desperately, but I can only think that my position as governess was of a temporary nature and that perhaps it's best to leave before the children become too attached to me.

"Goddamn!" William cursed and swallowed the rest of his whiskey. The children were already attached. Fuck knows how he was going to explain Lillian's sudden absence to them. *And what about me? Couldn't she see that I'm attached to her and have been for over ten fucking years!*

He looked at the dreaded letter and continued to read.

Please tell them that I love them. Perhaps you can make up a suitable story to explain my departure, one that will make my leaving easier for them to understand.

Thank you, William, for taking me into your home and for your kindness. You've made a fortunate life for yourself and your family. You are held in much regard in the community and I know that you will find someone who will make you and the children happy. Please know, that is all I have ever wanted for you — your happiness.

Yours with affection,
Lillian

William chuckled coldly. Lillian hadn't even been able to bring herself to sign off her letter 'with love' — that should tell him everything he needed to know. What he couldn't understand was her sudden aversion to the outback lifestyle. At no time since she'd arrived had she indicated that she hated it. In fact, it had been the exact opposite.

He leaned back in his chair and stared unseeingly into the fireplace. He wondered if he could catch her. He wasn't going to allow her to waltz back into his life then simply waltz back out with no reasonable explanation—at least no explanation that he was prepared to accept. According to Mrs. Thompson, Lillian had slipped out, unnoticed, in the middle of the previous night. He'd spoken to some of the men and ascertained that the docile mare that Lillian had ridden to his rescue was missing from the stables. He didn't care about the loss of the horse. If anything, he was relieved that she was not on foot and had a decent animal at her disposal. The fact that she was alone and in unfamiliar countryside riddled him with anxiety. Anything could happen to a woman traveling unaccompanied, particularly a woman as beautiful and alluring as Lillian.

Even through his hurt and fury, he was terrified for her safety. Where she planned to go, he had no idea. Insofar as he was aware, she had no connections in Australia beyond the ones that she'd made since her return. Then again, she could have met someone in her travels to whom she'd reached out for help—a man perhaps, willing to assist a damsel in distress.

He cursed again, shot up from his chair and started pacing his study. She was *his*, damn it, and the thought of another man taking her and touching her made his blood boil with rage. The only problem was she'd been straightforward in her explanation for leaving. She hadn't allowed much room for conjecture.

Pain tightened his chest and he slumped his shoulders. Perhaps he shouldn't go after her. He recognized that he was being self-serving in his need to reclaim her. Lillian had made her decision and obviously, her future plans didn't include him. He'd set himself up for this moment, risked his heart, his soul and his very sanity just for the chance of having her in his life again—for the chance of *keeping* her!

He set his mouth into a grim line when he recalled the last words of her letter. She actually thought that someone else could make him happy and she *hoped* for it? How could she be so fucking cold-hearted? Did she not see that she was the *only* woman for him?

He leaned his elbows on the desk and grasped his hair in both hands, desperation gripping him with iron-like tenacity. Never could he remember feeling so impotent and out of control. The sensation terrified him.

Chapter Thirty

Lillian had been riding a long time, with a stop for three hours in the early morning to water her horse and attempt a fitful sleep. Not far into her swift departure she'd realized that she didn't even know her horse's name, so she'd taken to calling her Whinny, after the soft whinnying sounds the animal made.

Lillian stretched and twisted in the saddle. She was stiff and sore and knew that she would have to stop soon to rest again. She frowned and checked her watch. It was imperative that she put as much distance between herself and Mulga Creek as she could. She was worried that William would come after her and she had to avoid that at all costs. Common sense told her that William would have a very difficult time catching up with her, considering that she had at least a ten-hour head start on him and he had no idea in which direction she was traveling. The fear still nagged at her, however, and had her looking over her shoulder every five minutes.

Scanning the horizon, she checked her watch again and decided that she'd continue for another hour then rest. Whinny was walking sedately now. She hadn't wanted to tire the mare too much so she'd slowed to a trot half an hour after they'd left the property and, taking into consideration the break they'd had in the early morning, she was confident that the horse was not overtaxed.

Her mind wandered to George Dawson's shocking and life-changing revelation. She was still finding it difficult to believe that William could be so callous and indiscreet with his affections. And lying to her about it was the ultimate betrayal. She'd asked him not three nights ago about his relationship with Margaret Dawson and he'd sworn that they were just acquaintances. Tears blurred her vision and she swiped angrily at them. She'd cried far too much. She was surprised she had any tears left to spill. The pain and hurt were so raw and so deep that she doubted she would ever recover. It was a physical ache in her chest that sharpened and drilled deeper whenever she thought about William. Her only distraction was to focus on her immediate situation and find her way to a safe haven — wherever that may be.

George Dawson had been oddly well prepared and had planned for Lillian's departure with care. It had been a relief, yet also disturbing, knowing that the man had been scheming to have Lillian removed in order to make way for his pregnant daughter. She couldn't blame him, she supposed. His priority would obviously be Margaret and ensuring that she was not disrespected or dishonored any further, but it was still unsettling. When Lillian had asked George Dawson how far along Margaret was in her pregnancy, he had proclaimed that it was unimportant — either unable or unwilling to tell her. It *was* important to Lillian, however, for it would tell her *exactly* when William had been intimate with the other woman. There was, of course, the possibility that George Dawson had been lying to her, but she couldn't believe that a father would risk the reputation of his daughter and for what gain? Lillian had racked her brains and couldn't come up with any reason as to why the man would lie about something so serious. And her own observations of William and Margaret Dawson and William's own admission regarding his relationship with Mary Simpson did nothing but lend credence to the situation. William was obviously very...liberal with his favors and she and Margaret Dawson were just two in what was quite probably a very long list. She just prayed to God that she herself had not fallen pregnant. *That* possibility was too terrifying to consider and she pushed the thought to the back of her mind.

William would have returned and found her letter by now. She had worded the missive carefully, not wanting to give anything away as to the true reason for her leaving. She'd hoped to give the impression that she was leaving because she wanted to, with the underlying message that she didn't love him, for she'd not been sure that William would have accepted anything less. Lillian would not be the reason that Margaret Dawson became an unwed mother and besides, she knew that William would act honorably. Lillian just wanted to make the situation easier for him by eliminating herself from the equation and thereby limiting William's assured guilt. She had no doubt that when he was told about the baby, William would marry Margaret immediately. Even after discovering, as she had, his indiscretion, she knew deep down that he was a good man who would do the right thing.

She checked her watch, scanned her surroundings and decided that she would stop to rest. She dismounted and collected her belongings from the saddlebags. She'd packed food and water for herself and her horse. The rest of her possessions were meager. She'd only taken what she could pack into her carpetbag, which was a change of clothing, some warmer articles for the cool nights and her personal items. She'd put her money into a purse, which was hidden in a pocket of her skirt. She dearly wished that she had trousers to wear. It would make horse riding so much more comfortable. As it was, she'd chosen a loose skirt with enough fabric to allow freedom for movement.

She organized a food bag for Whinny and stood for a moment stroking the mare's nose and taking comfort from her soft snuffling. She'd initially balked when George Dawson had suggested that she take a horse. She definitely hadn't wanted to steal from William, but George had been insistent. He had wanted to ensure that she made enough headway before William discovered her departure and George had promised to have the horse returned. It hadn't taken her long to agree. She understood that it would be dangerous and stupid to attempt to leave on foot and taking a horse was her only other option.

As part of Dawson's plan, she was due to meet John Steele in one hour, at three o'clock. Hopefully he'd be waiting for her at the fork in the road, as George Dawson had informed her. The whole scheme had seemed ludicrous at first, but she'd seen no other option and she'd been particularly concerned about traveling with a relatively unfamiliar gentleman.

However, Dawson had quite rightly pointed out, it was preferable than her traveling unaccompanied. After so many hours of riding alone and in unfamiliar territory, she was immensely relieved that she had agreed. At least John Steele was not a complete stranger and she felt that she knew him, if only a little. She had wondered at George's decision to involve him, but she assumed they were friends and hadn't questioned it. She was relieved to have assistance from any source.

She took George Dawson's hand-drawn map out of her pocket and the accompanying compass then checked her bearings. She was confident that she was heading in the correct direction and she gauged that her timing was on track, give or take some minutes either side of three o'clock. Their ultimate destination was Byrock, which was some distance from her current location. George had worried that William would seek her out at Coolabah train station and possibly intercept her. Whereas he wouldn't expect that she would travel all the way to Byrock, particularly unaccompanied, as he assumed her to be.

She repacked the saddlebags and mounted Whinny, wincing when her sore muscles settled into the curve of the horse's back. She checked her compass once again, turned Whinny's head in a northeasterly direction and kicked her into a trot.

Chapter Thirty-One

William was convinced that he was slowly going insane. He was pacing his study relentlessly, not allowing anyone in, speaking to no one, as powerful emotions erupted and warred within him. He vacillated between feelings of hatred, love, betrayal and despair, until he was left feeling dazed and disoriented. He'd tried, but he couldn't reconcile Lillian's actions with what he was sure were her true feelings. He was convinced that she still loved him. He'd recalled every moment that they'd spent together since her return. Every word spoken and every gesture made. He'd tortured himself with visions of her underneath him, moaning and crying out in ecstasy while he'd thrust into her or pleasured her with his fingers and tongue. He remembered vividly when she'd taken his cock into her mouth, how she'd opened her lips and sucked him in, hesitant with her tongue as she had tasted him for the first time. Her innocence and sweetness had been disarming, as had her willingness and enthusiasm to please him. And when she'd told him that she wanted to taste him, to swallow his essence, it had been his undoing.

He propped both hands on the mantelpiece and stared into the dying embers of the fire, thinking furiously. *What happened between when I left three days ago and now? Did something occur to prompt Lillian to leave, other than what she states in her letter?* He just couldn't fathom her one-hundred-and-eighty degree turn around. Perhaps Mrs. Thompson could tell him something. He'd only spoken to her briefly, had just barked a couple of questions regarding what she knew about Lillian leaving and had scarcely given the woman time to tell him anything else.

He had to find Mrs. Thompson and question her further. He raced to the door, nearly tearing it off its hinges in his haste to open it.

He found his housekeeper sitting at the kitchen table, her head cradled in her hands. Guilt assailed him. He hadn't considered how much she cared for Lillian and how she would also feel her loss. He entered quietly and placed a hand on the older woman's shoulder. She startled and looked up at him with watery eyes.

"William." She struggled to stand but he stayed her, keeping his hand on her shoulder and pressing her gently back into her chair. He took a seat opposite and tried to control his impatience.

"Millie," he spoke softly. "Can you think of anything that happened to Lillian while I was away mustering? Anything that would precipitate her leaving?"

She sighed heavily and wiped her eyes. "I can't understand it. She seemed so happy here and she loved the children. She enjoyed gardening. Did you know that?"

He curled his lips into a tight smile. "Yes, I know." Talking about Lillian in the past tense disturbed to him. "Is there anything unusual that occurred?" he pressed.

She stared over his shoulder, her gaze unfocused. "The only thing out of the ordinary was the visit from Mr. Dawson."

William froze. Dread coiled and tightened the base of his spine. "What?"

Mrs. Thompson shrank away from his intense stare. "I didn't think anything of it," she whispered. "I assumed he was taking his automobile for a run and just stopped in to say hello."

William shot up from his chair and started pacing. "How long was he here and what happened after he left?"

"He visited for an hour and a half, approximately." Mrs. Thompson wrung her hands in agitation. "When he left, Lillian went straight to her room claiming a headache." She looked up from the table, her face pale. "I didn't see her for the rest of the evening." Her eyes widened as the import of her words sank in. "Do you think Mr. Dawson is somehow responsible for Lillian leaving?"

William scowled, fury emanating from his every pore. *Why didn't Mrs. Thompson mention this before? How often does George Dawson stop by the property, for Christ's sake?* He was suddenly and overwhelmingly certain that something George Dawson had said or done was the reason for Lilly leaving them. Nothing else made sense. He thought back to his odd conversation with Dawson a few nights previously and grew even more agitated. The man had an agenda. What exactly it was, he couldn't be sure. But Dawson's questions regarding his relationship with

Lillian and his insinuations about his daughter and William taking another wife had been peculiar.

"I'm *certain* George Dawson is responsible," William snarled.

He had no time to waste. He needed to speak to Dawson before it was too late. Before something happened to Lilly and he lost her forever.

* * * *

Lillian had been relieved to find John Steele waiting patiently at the arranged meeting spot. It had taken her longer than she'd anticipated to arrive and she'd worried that he would grow tired of waiting and leave.

"Miss Hamilton," he greeted her warmly and helped her from her horse. "Do you need to rest for a moment? You look tired."

Lillian smiled and tried in vain to stem the tears that threatened, but she couldn't. And, she realized with horror, her bottom lip was trembling uncontrollably and her eyes were overflowing. Fat teardrops ran unchecked down her cheeks.

She was mortified that a kind word could overwhelm her so. "I'm s-s-sorry. Everything has just been so sudden and a little shocking."

He frowned and drew her into his arms. "Hush now," he crooned. "It's understandable. You are overcome."

He stroked her back soothingly and Lillian melted into his warm embrace, taking comfort from his caring ministrations. She'd never felt so alone and so frightened — even the long trip from England to Australia hadn't been so nerve racking. At least at that time she had employment and accommodation to look forward to. Now she was homeless and utterly heartbroken and once again facing a future without William in it. She shivered and pulled away from John Steele. "Please forgive my outburst. I don't want to make you uncomfortable."

He smiled and caressed her cheek. "Please don't apologize, I'm here to help. I'd like to think that we're friends."

Lillian returned his smile tremulously. "Yes. Thank you for meeting me."

"Think nothing of it. There is nowhere else I'd rather be." He turned to his horse and retrieved a blanket and a small hamper from his belongings. "Let's rest for a moment and take some refreshment."

Lillian took his outstretched hand and followed him to the shade of a nearby tree where he spread the blanket out and helped her to sit.

"Mr. Steele—"

"Please, call me John. As we'll be traveling companions, I think that we can dispense with the formalities. May I call you Lillian?"

She smiled. "Of course."

"You were going to say?" he prompted.

"I just wanted to thank you again for your kindness. I don't think that I would be capable of finding my way to Byrock without assistance."

He scowled. "Nor should you. Gallivanting around the countryside alone is no position for a young lady to be in." He reached out and grasped both of her hands in his larger ones. "Do you have a plan once we reach Byrock?"

She looked away. "No. I'm taking one day at a time."

"Hmm." He ran his thumbs in circles over the backs of her hands. "I won't allow anything to happen to you, Lillian. I'm here to take care of you."

Lillian turned back to him in surprise. "I have money, John, and I'm independent. I'm not a weak girl in need of assistance. I can take care of myself..." She faltered for a moment and looked around the unfamiliar and harsh environment. "However, I do appreciate your help now."

She couldn't miss the devilish smile and the roguish glint in his eye. She shivered as an inexplicable chill worked its way down her spine.

Chapter Thirty-Two

William jogged up the stairs of the Dawson property and flung the front door wide, rattling it on its hinges and sending a young maid scuttling for cover. *"Dawson!"*

He'd driven like the devil possessed him to get to the property as quickly as possible. Now he would wait no longer. He *needed* an explanation. It was too much of a coincidence that Lillian's departure had occurred not long after Dawson's visit.

William stalked down the hallway and entered the drawing room where George Dawson was rising from his seated position at a writing desk.

"Cartwright," Dawson greeted William mildly. "Why all the fuss?"

William advanced on him menacingly, his eyes glinting with suppressed fury. "Don't play the innocent with me. You know very well why I'm here."

Dawson raised his eyebrows.

"Let me make it simple for you. Where the fuck is Lillian?"

Out of the corner of his eye, William saw Margaret Dawson enter the room. "What on earth is all the commotion about?" she questioned, her gaze landing on William.

"Apparently, Cartwright's little governess has run off and he has some notion that I know where she's hiding," Dawson smirked delightedly at his daughter then looked back at William. "I assure you I have no idea."

"Then it's just a coincidence that Lillian left not long after you visited her?" William asked, his voice dripping with sarcasm.

Dawson shrugged. "I don't profess to know what goes on in the heads of young ladies."

William cast a sidelong look at Margaret. She had her head cocked to the side studying him quizzically, a soft smile curling her lips. He looked back at Dawson. The man had retaken his seat and was leaning back in his chair, a look of calculated nonchalance composing his features.

William's tenuous hold on his temper snapped. He stalked to where Dawson sat. "*Enough!*" He slammed both fists on the desk. The older man jumped in alarm and tried to back away but he was caged between the wall and William's heaving body. William grinned wickedly, enjoying the fact that Dawson had misjudged his own actions. By trying for aloof indifference, he'd literally backed himself into a corner.

William leaned forward, bracing his body on his arms. "I'm not going to ask you again, old man. You tell me what you know, or be prepared to face the consequences." He watched as a myriad of emotions crossed the other man's face—fear, calculation then anger.

"I'll tell you what I know," Dawson snarled. "You have the audacity to stride into my home and throw your weight around, after impregnating my daughter!"

Whatever William had expected to hear, it definitely hadn't been that. The air left his lungs as the implication of what Dawson had just said hit him full in the chest. "What the fuck are you talking about?" he whispered, incredulous.

The other man turned smug. "Just what I said. I don't think that I have to *explain* it to you, do I?"

William stepped back a pace, confusion crossing his features. This couldn't be happening. No wonder Lillian had left. If she thought that Margaret was pregnant with his child, it would be the ultimate betrayal to her. Fury boiled in his veins. He clenched his fists and he felt the tendons in his neck bulging with the effort to refrain from lashing out and punching the man. He took three deep breaths, trying to calm his raging temper. He needed to get his priorities in order. First and foremost, he had to determine the direction in which Lillian was heading.

William straightened and spun around to face Margaret, his eyes glinting dangerously. "You told your father these lies?"

She smiled slyly and walked toward him, her hips swaying provocatively. "I'm sorry, William, I had to tell him."

What the fuck is she talking about? Is she insane? William looked at her in disbelief and held his arms in front of him to halt her advancement. "Stop!" he ordered roughly.

"And you *are* going to marry Margaret, Cartwright. I demand that you make an honest woman out of my daughter!"

William whirled back to face George Dawson and laughed coldly. "You're insane, man! Your daughter *tried* to seduce me under this very roof three nights ago. I've never known your daughter intimately. I have no doubt that some man has been there, but it definitely wasn't me."

Margaret gasped as George's face turned purple in his outrage. "How *dare* you!" her father ground between clenched teeth.

"No!" Once more bracing his arms on the desk, William leaned toward George. "How dare *you*! I don't have time to deal with your delusions or those of your daughter. You're going to tell me where Lillian is right now or, so help me God, I'm going to pummel the information out of you!"

Dawson's face paled and his eyes grew wide. "C-C-Cartwright, you have to do the right thing. *And* we can combine our two properties. Think of what we could do together."

William gaped at him. "Is this your agenda? To get your slimy, greedy hands on my land?"

"No, that's just a side benefit for both of us." Dawson's tone turned cajoling. "This is for the best, William. Even Miss Hamilton is in agreement. That's why she left. She understands that her continued presence would make matters difficult for you and Margaret. She didn't want to stand in the way of you marrying my daughter."

"Lillian is mine!" William bellowed, making Dawson jump in alarm. "How fucking dare you interfere with me and what's mine!" William shook his head, trying to dispel the madness. "Let's get one thing straight," he said, his voice ominously low. "Not now or *ever* will I marry your daughter!"

Dawson started to protest but William slammed his palm on the desk with a look of warning. "I can't believe that you prompted and encouraged a young, innocent woman to leave my protection. You are despicable! Now tell me where she is," he thundered the last.

Dawson cowered under William's furious glare. "She's headed for Byrock," he whispered.

"Byrock?" William asked, incredulous. "How the fuck is she going to make it to Byrock alone, you bastard?" He straightened and shoved a hand through his hair in anxiety. He started toward the door, his mind already working to formulate his subsequent plan of action, when Dawson's next words stopped him dead in his tracks.

"She's not alone."

William turned and stabbed the other man with an intense stare.

"John Steele is with her," Dawson explained.

A red haze of fury engulfed William, narrowing his vision to a pinprick as feelings of dread, possessiveness and jealousy conflicted and coiled in his gut. "Dawson, you start praying now that nothing happens to Lillian." William's voice turned into a turbulent rumble. "If Steele touches one hair on her head, he's a dead man—as you will be. Now, you start fucking talking and tell me *everything* that I need to know."

Chapter Thirty-Three

"We should stop soon. It's getting dark."

Lillian turned to where John was looking westward, toward the sinking sun. "I agree," she replied, despondent. All day, she'd been dreading the point when they would stop for the evening. The thought of spending hours in the dark and in the middle of nowhere with John Steele made her uncomfortable. Granted, he'd acted like a consummate gentleman, but she couldn't help but feel awkward at the prospect of passing so much time alone with him, yet she needed to rest. The unfamiliar position in the saddle for such a long time had her muscles aching and screaming for relief, and she was exhausted. The last twenty-four hours had drained her physically and emotionally. She'd been on horseback, give or take some resting time, for fifteen hours of those twenty-four. She was also dreading the enforced contemplation time, time in which she knew she would think about William. The heartache and betrayal she'd been pushing to the back of her mind would invade her thoughts and haunt her dreams. And the pain in her chest that she had been steadily keeping at bay would assault her at full force. No, the silent, uninterrupted evening hours were an anathema to her, even if they offered some physical relief.

John, dismounting from his horse and tying the reins to a nearby tree, roused Lillian from her thoughts. Her mare had been following John's stallion and sidled up next to his steed to wait patiently.

"Lillian, we need to rest." John reached up to help her dismount.

She accepted his assistance, too tired to do anything else. When he wrapped a strong arm around her waist and another under her knees, she sank against him.

"I'm sorry, John, I'm just a little weary." She gave a small laugh. "I'm not accustomed to spending so much time astride a horse."

He settled her on her feet, ensuring that she was steady, and grasped her shoulders as he gazed at her intently. "You look pale." He moved his hands to cup her cheeks in his palms, brushing the sensitive skin under her eyes with his thumbs. "And you have dark circles here. You need to sleep."

She smiled. "Hopefully, all this fresh air and riding about in the countryside will ensure that I have a few hours of blissful slumber."

"Good. I'll build us a fire then we can eat." John turned back to his stallion and started to unpack supplies. "You get comfortable and I'll settle the animals."

As John started to unsaddle the horses and organize food bags, Lillian retrieved a small satchel and blanket from her saddlebags and made a makeshift bed. She wet a handkerchief with water from her canteen and wiped her face and hands, grimacing when the cloth turned a dull brown from the outback earth caked on her skin. What she wouldn't give for some warm, soapy water at that moment. She sighed and hung the cloth from a tree branch to dry. She couldn't use any more water than absolutely necessary, particularly for personal hygiene.

She stood and dusted off her skirt, sending a red cloud billowing around her. She turned to where John was unbuckling his saddle. "I'll collect some kindling for the fire," she announced and strode from their makeshift camp.

Lillian used her skirt to hold the wood that she collected. The branches were dry and brittle, some bleached to bone color from the severe Australian sun. It would make effective kindling for their fire but she couldn't help but ponder the arid conditions and harsh environment the outback presented. Still, she mused, she loved it. There was something beautiful and unique about the untamed and unforgiving countryside. It was a land of extremes. The line *'Of droughts and flooding rains'*, from Dorothea Mackellar's poem, danced through her mind. She straightened and looked west toward the sinking sun where the orange orb was staining the sky a brilliant red and turning the landscape beneath to a coal black. She sighed gratefully as a feeling of peacefulness swept through her at the lovely sight. As if to thank her for her warm thoughts, Mother Nature chose that moment to send three kangaroos hopping across the skyline. They were pitch-black shapes backdropped by a golden sphere. She gasped at the beautiful display and stood mesmerized until the kangaroos vanished over the horizon.

"There you are."

John's voice startled Lillian out of her reverie. She jumped and spun around to face him, completely forgetting about the fact that her skirt was hiked up to her thighs. John's gaze slid from her face down her torso to rest unabashedly on her legs. He licked his lips. Even in the dying daylight, she could make out the lust darkening his eyes. She shivered in apprehension before quickly composing herself.

"I have the kindling," she said briskly, moving past him and walking back to their camp. She willed her heart rate to slow. John's obvious desire had made her feel uneasy and she needed to put some distance between them.

She dropped the branches next to a circle of rocks that John had arranged.

"Put the kindling down first." John instructed, having followed her back. "With some tinder stacked loosely on top." He scattered bark and dry grass across the small pile.

Lillian watched as he slowly built the fire, starting with kindling and tinder, which he lit, then he blew on the bundle until it was steadily aflame. When the fire strengthened, he added some of the larger branches then he arranged some thicker pieces in a tepee shape over the flames. The process fascinated her and she paid close attention, committing the method to memory.

Soon they had a roaring fire and were boiling a billy of water. Lillian unpacked some cheese and bread that they toasted over the flames and washed down with sweet black tea. It was basic fare but Lillian couldn't recall anything ever tasting so good. She was hungrier than she'd realized and the sugary brew had given her some much needed sustenance. She felt the color return to her cheeks and the food, combined with the warmth of the fire, made her drowsy. She started to doze but was startled when John laid a blanket on the ground next to hers. She looked at him uneasily but he just smiled mildly.

"It will be warmer, Lillian. You know how cool the nights can be."

"Yes, of course," she concurred.

Earlier, she'd retrieved her coat and a woolen scarf from her belongings and these she wrapped tighter around her before lying down and trying to make herself comfortable. She felt John sidle closer to her and she willed herself to relax, telling herself that his nearness was just to keep them both warm through the cold evening hours.

She listened to the crackling of the fire and the hooting of an owl, allowing the twilight sounds to soothe her. It wasn't long before exhaustion wore her down and she succumbed to sleep.

Chapter Thirty-Four

William had never moved so fast in his life. When he returned to Mulga Creek, he quickly packed some supplies before saddling Victory and riding fast in the direction that George Dawson had said Lillian was heading in to meet Steele.

He knew they were both on horseback, which meant they wouldn't necessarily follow the road. He would bet money that Steele would avoid the road at all costs. The only way he had a chance of catching them was on horseback also. He wasn't supposed to know they were heading to Byrock, so he had to assume that they wouldn't be expecting him to follow. Also, he imagined they'd be traveling at a slower rate. Lillian wasn't used to long periods in the saddle and they would need to rest often.

William decided to ride into the evening to gain some distance. He didn't usually ride at night but Victory was a sure-footed horse accustomed to harsh terrain, so he'd decided to risk it. It would be worth it to gain some additional ground.

It took him five hours to reach the fork in the road where Dawson had said Lillian was meeting Steele earlier that day. He hoped to God that she'd been able to make her way there. Just the thought of her being lost and alone was enough to undo him. George Dawson had assured him that he'd given her detailed directions, but until William had her in his arms again, his raging fears would not be stilled. He decided to break for a rest and leave at first light. He'd ridden Victory hard and his horse needed to recuperate.

He unpacked a blanket from his saddlebags and made a makeshift bed, not bothering with a fire, confident that his oilskin coat would keep him warm enough. He'd dreaded the act of stopping, knowing he'd be unable to think about anything else but the fact that Lillian was with Steele, alone and in the outback. A deep fear gripped him and a jealous possessiveness coiled and tightened his gut. He'd spent time with Steele in the war, and what he knew of the man didn't ease his mind at all. No, John Steele was a womanizer and, to make matters worse, his treatment of women in the past had been appalling and anything but gentlemanly. It was obvious that he wanted Lillian, which burned a rage through William like nothing he'd ever experienced. Never had William felt so impotent. He just had to pray that Steele would treat Lillian like the lady she was. Anything less was inconceivable to him.

* * * *

John woke Lillian early and it took her a moment to get her bearings. She was surprised she'd slept so well but, given the arduous events of the previous days, her body had obviously needed the rest. They partook of a quick breakfast of sweet tea and apples. Lillian packed up their belongings while John saddled the horses. Soon they were once more on the move.

"There's a small billabong that we should reach by midday. We'll stop there for lunch and fill up the canteens," John informed her.

Lillian frowned. "What about crocodiles?

He chuckled. "I'm surprised you don't recall that there are no crocodiles in New South Wales. They're only found in the very northern areas of Australia."

She thought for a moment and realized that no one had ever informed her of that fact. She'd always been told that water holes were dangerous and to keep away from them. As a sixteen-year-old girl, full of fantastic ideas, she'd assumed that crocodiles were the cause for concern. She told John as much.

He nodded. "No doubt your parents were concerned about the debris and snags hidden by the water. Weak swimmers can drown easily if they're not careful, but this billabong is remarkably clear."

It made sense and she was relieved, as their low water supplies had started to concern her. She'd heard more than one story of people dying in the outback from thirst. Such a death was a particularly slow and agonizing one. It was reassuring that John was an experienced bushman and that he was obviously familiar with their environment. She shivered, thinking about the possible consequences of not having John to guide her. She liked to believe that she was a strong, independent woman, but no amount of personal fortitude could have led her successfully through the harsh and unfamiliar terrain.

Sore, with the insides of her thighs throbbing, Lillian wriggled in the saddle. She didn't dare complain and she didn't want to ask John their expected arrival time in Byrock for fear of seeming weak and impatient. Instead, she focused her attention on their surroundings and tried to forget the pain and tension in her muscles. The morning passed quite quickly and they made good time. John soon announced their imminent arrival at the billabong. It was eleven o'clock, an hour earlier than John had predicted. She was beyond relieved to have a respite.

They dismounted and led the horses to the waterhole to drink then they filled their canteens and washed. The water level was low but it was cool, surprisingly clear and felt wonderful when she splashed her face and the back of her neck.

There was a shaded clearing not far from the billabong. There, they sat to rest and eat. Lunch consisted of the last of the stale bread, cheese and an apple each. It was basic fare but enough to keep up their strength and ward off the hunger pangs. They were eating the food that would spoil first. After that, they had tinned meat and Lillian had packed two pounds of flour to make damper.

They were quiet as they ate, each busy with their own thoughts. Lillian was thinking about how good it would feel to take a quick dip in the cool water.

"I'm going to rinse off our plates and freshen up," she told John.

"Fine, I'll wait for you here. I think we should lie low for an hour or so. It's the hottest part of the day, so the least amount of time spent in the sun, the better." He settled back, lying down and placing his bush hat over his face.

With John planning on a nap, Lillian would have some privacy. She rummaged through her bag and retrieved a bar of soap and a cloth, then hurried back to the billabong. She removed her boots and stockings and sat on a rock to re-braid her long hair, coiling it into a chignon at the back of head to keep it off her face and neck. She undressed quickly, whacking her clothes against a nearby tree and marveling at the clouds of red dust that billowed from the fabric. When she finally stepped into the cool water, she gasped in appreciation, walking in to hip depth before slowly submerging herself. The burning in her muscles instantly eased and she floated on her back for a long while, enjoying the sensation. She finally moved to the shallows, soaped herself all over and decided that she would wash out her under things, confident that the light cotton would dry quickly in the sun.

After laying out her rinsed items, she sat back in the water, relishing the cleansing experience. She hadn't realized just how much red dust and grit had been caked onto her skin. The ocher-colored earth had literally worked itself into every crevice of her body.

She lay like that in the shallows, listening to the sounds of the bush. The cicadas vibrated their song and the warbling of magpies combined with it to create a loud reverberation in the otherwise still atmosphere. So loud were the bush sounds that she failed to hear the figure approaching her from behind.

Chapter Thirty-Five

William had awoken early and left before first light. He'd slept fitfully, only managing to snatch an hour in total, his thoughts too wrapped up in Lillian and his fears for her safety. He was too anxious to find her to stay still.

In the early hours, he recalled a small billabong he was certain that John Steele would be aware of. Anyone local to the area, particularly horsemen and stockmen, made it a point to know where all the sources of water were located. He felt sure that Steele would have to recharge their water supply and that area would be a perfect spot to do it. William had no way of knowing when they would arrive at the waterhole, or even if they would stay for any length of time, but the faster he rode, the more chance he'd have of gaining on them.

William's instincts were all he was operating on. He had to anticipate Steele's movements and the probable course he was taking to Byrock. It wasn't hard. He just followed a route that he, himself, would have taken in similar circumstances.

He rode hard, picking up disturbances in the undergrowth that led him to believe he was on the right track. At nine o'clock, he came across the remains of a campfire. He dismounted Victory and crouched by the pile of ash. It appeared to be recent. Standing, he scanned the surroundings, his gaze immediately alighting on a scrap of soiled fabric hanging on a nearby tree branch. He strode over to it and snatched it down, his heart soaring with hope and relief when he noticed the familiar initials embroidered into the handkerchief — L.E.H. Until that moment, he'd completely forgotten Lillian's middle name, Elizabeth. He clutched the cloth to his face and breathed deeply, just able to discern her lingering scent. The action comforted him and gave him hope that she remained safe and well.

He stuffed the handkerchief into his pocket and remounted Victory. If he rode hard, he thought that he could make it to the billabong by midday. He was still confident that Steele and Lillian were traveling at a slower pace. Steele, of course, was capable of hard riding too and had a horse up to the challenge, but Lillian's mare was older and less accustomed to an intense pace. Moreover, Lillian was unused to long periods in the sun and being astride a horse. Even though he expected she'd be trying her hardest to appear unaffected, William knew she'd be hurting. This last thought sent another wave of rage coursing through him. The entire fucking scenario was unacceptable. He still couldn't believe this whole course of events had been instigated by Margaret Dawson's lies then perpetuated by her fool of a father. He felt like ripping the man apart, limb by limb, and he might be driven to do just that if anything happened to Lillian.

He took a few deep breaths to calm himself and focused on keeping Victory on track. His stallion was an excellent stock horse, built for endurance and agility, and they worked together well. But he still needed his wits about him, particularly when they were galloping through the countryside and he was keeping a keen eye out for anything that might lead him in a different direction.

He slowed Victory to a walk when he recognized that the billabong was close, not wanting to alert Steele to his presence — if he and Lillian were even there. He prayed that his intuition was correct and that they *had* stopped at the waterhole for a break. He approached cautiously, his ears and eyes alert for the slightest sound or motion.

* * * *

Lillian splashed water on her face and upper torso before reluctantly standing to make her way out of the billabong. She had no wish to be caught in such a state by Steele. That thought was positively mortifying. As she stepped out of the shallows and walked toward her clothes, a figure in the trees caught her attention. She froze, unable to make her feet obey her mind's command to move and get to cover. She peered into the foliage and was shocked then horrified to see that it was John Steele.

A shiver ran through her when she realized the import of what she saw. *How long has he been watching me?*

He stood from his crouching position and slowly walked toward her. He had a look on his face that made her blood run cold. She knew that expression now, recognized it for what it was — raw and primal lust. He licked his lips as he drew closer, his attention aimed at her breasts. And still she couldn't move, as if her legs were mired in quicksand. Her pulse thundered in her ears as she cast around her for a means of escape.

"Don't be afraid, Lillian," he rasped, hungrily raking her body with his gaze. "I'm not going to hurt you."

And that was all it took to shake her out of her frozen state. She stepped to the side quickly and groped for her clothes, managing to snare her skirt. She clutched it to her chest.

"John, this is highly inappropriate." She hated the tremor in her voice, knew that she needed to appear strong and in control, but she couldn't help it. She was shaken and worried about his intentions. The situation of being alone with John had always been a concern, a constant in the back of her mind, but nothing could have prepared her for the daunting reality.

"I've wanted you since the moment I saw you, Lillian." He moved closer and raised a hand to stroke her hair. "You're the most beautiful woman I've ever seen."

His gaze traveled from her face to caress her body visually. She shivered and clutched her skirt closer.

She tried to placate him, keeping her voice soothing but strong. "John, I'm very flattered, but please allow me to get dressed. Then we can talk."

He sidled closer still, snaked an arm around her waist and pulled her to him. She felt his undeniable arousal pressed against her stomach.

He dipped his head to hers and breathed deeply. "You smell so good," he murmured into her hair.

Lillian's heart spiked in alarm, beating so hard she felt like it was about to jump out of her chest. "Please, John. Don't."

She'd never before been in such a situation and she knew instinctively that it would be bad to antagonize him. Her mind raced as she tried to work through her options—there were not many. Perhaps if she could get him to talk to her it would buy her some time. But before she could follow that thought through, John wrenched her skirt out of her hands, rendering her once more completely naked, exposed—and absolutely terrified.

Chapter Thirty-Six

William dismounted and looped Victory's reins over a low-lying tree branch. He scanned the area as he slowly approached a nearby clearing. The billabong, he knew, was off to the right, but if they'd stopped, he assumed that they'd be resting in the clearing.

He heard the horses before he saw them, their soft snuffling and whickering unmistakable. He stilled, crouching and peering through the foliage in the direction of the sounds. He could see two horses, one a stallion and the other a smaller mare — his mare.

He hadn't realized that he'd been holding his breath and he exhaled slowly, relief and exhilaration coursing through his veins.

Thank fuck. I've found them. His thoughts were followed by feelings of caution. He didn't want to give Steele and Lillian an opportunity to run. Given that Lillian believed the lies of George Dawson and his daughter, she wouldn't be amenable to just getting on her horse and following him home. No, he had to handle the situation with care. He scanned the immediate area from his hiding spot and couldn't see

Steele or Lillian. He stayed put for a minute longer to ensure that they were not in the immediate vicinity, then he stood and approached the horses. His plan was to walk the animals some distance away and hopefully buy some time. He needed to delay Lillian and make her listen to him. Just as he was about to snatch up the reins, sounds to his right, toward the billabong, drew his attention. He stopped dead in his tracks and strained an ear toward the noises. Then he started running.

He sprinted toward the billabong and burst through the trees. The sight that confronted him was confusing, infuriating and startling in equal measures. It took a moment for his brain to catch up with what his eyes were witnessing. Lillian was naked at the edge of the water and John Steele was standing in front of her. The man was close, far too close.

William's vision hazed to red and his chest constricted. Anger and a fierce possessiveness coursed through him. He fisted his hands at his sides and trembled, as a rage he'd never previously felt overtook him.

"What the fuck is going on?" he thundered, advancing quickly on the pair.

Steele jumped and spun around to face him but William wasn't focusing on Steele. His gaze settled on Lillian's panicked expression.

He was unbuttoning his shirt and shrugging it off in seconds as he took quick strides to reach them. He shoved Steele out of the way and gripped Lillian around the wrist, wrenching her body against his and draping his shirt around her shoulders. He just hoped that the panicked expression on her face wasn't triggered by her guilt, but as he felt the shudders rack her body he knew it was fear causing her distress. He pulled her closer and wrapped his arm around her waist protectively.

"I'm here now, my darling," William reassured her, feeling like a heel for even doubting her for a second.

"Why the fuck are you here, Cartwright?" Steele interrupted. "Haven't you caused enough damage, sticking your nose and other...parts of your anatomy where they don't belong?"

William thrust Lillian behind him then turned to face Steele. Rage coursed through him and he took a couple of deep breaths. He wouldn't gain anything by losing control, even if it was a prick like Steele on the receiving end.

"Leave now, Steele. Before I do something that we'll both regret."

Steele chuckled, a low mocking sound. "Always the same supercilious asshole, Cartwright. Who died and made you God? You've caused Lillian enough distress. Don't you agree?"

Lillian's name spoken so easily and so familiarly from the other man's lips had William fisting his hands anew. *How dare the fucker! Who the hell does he think he is?* He breathed deeply, allowing the air to expand in his lungs for a few seconds before exhaling loudly. "Why don't you tell *me* why I found you here, with Lillian, while she was undressed?" he advanced toward Steele. "What were you planning to do?"

"This is no concern of yours," the other man snarled. "You negated your right to question whatever Lillian does after you got Margaret Dawson with child!"

"Enough!" William roared and stepped toward Steele. The other man feinted to the right. William spun around just as Steele grabbed Lillian by the arm and wrenched her toward him.

"Lillian, let's go," Steele ordered and started dragging her away.

Vaguely, William registered Lillian struggling against Steele and once again, he saw red. His gaze shimmered through scarlet and the thin hold he had on his control snapped. He reached out, grasped Steele by his collar and yanked him back—hard. The motion jolted Lillian backward and out of Steele's grip.

William saw his advantage and took it. "Lillian, move away." He spun Steele around to face him then released his hold on the man's collar.

"Now, are you going to go quietly? Or do I have to persuade you?" William asked, his voice ominously low.

"Do your best, Cartwright," Steele taunted. "Lillian and I have been doing just fine together. Then *you* come riding out to the rescue, to claim your gorgeous prize. What's the matter, one woman's not enough for you?"

William saw Lillian out of the corner of his eye. She looked to be just about to wade into the argument and he couldn't have that. If events took a turn for the worst, he wanted her to be out of the firing range. "Lillian, stay where you are," he commanded, giving her a stop motion with one hand to drive his words home. He risked a quick look in her direction and noted her furious stance, hands on her hips and her lush mouth set in an angry line. He turned his attention back to Steele, not wanting the man to get the upper hand on him.

"One woman is plenty for me, Steele, and that woman is Lillian. Whatever else you've heard is bullshit—not that I need to explain anything to you. Lillian is coming with me."

Steele's eyes narrowed. "Not if I can help it," he snarled. "This is one time that I plan to make things difficult for you." He started to bounce around on his toes. "For once in your life, you might not get what you want!"

William's boxing training kicked in. He automatically put his guard up and increased the distance between them. Steele was a swarmer—not a particularly good one at that—*and* he was out of condition. In-fighters in particular needed to keep fit to maintain their stamina and Steele didn't keep up with his training as William did, which would make Steele slow and sloppy. William was an out-boxer, quick footed with a fast, long-range punch, and he had won his fair share of matches, both in and out of the army. He had no qualms that he could take Steele easily and quickly.

William locked his gaze on Steele, assessing his every move to anticipate his next action. The man closed the gap between them and unleashed a flurry of body punches to William's torso. William grunted and took the punches, preferring to wear Steele down a little and assess his strength. Steele's blows lacked power and almost as soon as his flurry started, he backed off, breathing heavily.

William vaguely registered Lillian's frantic yelling in the background but he blocked her out, focusing entirely on his opponent.

Keeping his guard up, William stepped back, widening the gap between him and Steele once more. Steele moved in again and threw a right-left combination that William evaded easily, bobbing and weaving back up to face the other man head on. Steele tried again, dancing closer, crowding him before unleashing a few fast punches that William quickly blocked.

"Had enough yet, Cartwright?" Steele panted. "I think you've lost your edge."

William smirked, keeping his defensive stance and bouncing on the balls of his feet. "I'm merely warming up, arsehole."

He'd had enough of dancing around Steele and he wanted to end it, but the man was obviously not going to give up without a fight.

William dodged back a couple of steps, drawing his opponent toward him. Steele took the bait and lunged forward, ready to unleash another round of punches. But Steele was already tiring where William had barely raised a sweat. His reflexes were quick and, when Steele dropped his guard, William attacked. He unleashed a fierce right uppercut, taking Steele under the chin. The man was lifted off his feet slightly and taken off balance. Immediately William followed through with a powerful left hook. Blood flew from Steele's mouth and he staggered, swaying for a moment, an odd look of surprise on his face before he crashed to the ground.

Chapter Thirty-Seven

Lillian gasped and ran toward the two men. William was breathing heavily and looming over John Steele's prone form, his fists still clenched as if he was waiting for the man to jump up and continue the fight.

Lillian knelt next to John and felt for his pulse, terrified that William had killed him. She couldn't believe he'd survive a punch like that. Blood trickled from his mouth but she was relieved to see his chest rise and fall steadily in respiration.

"He's knocked out," William spoke from above her. "Interesting that you're so worried about him, my dear."

His voice dripped with sarcasm and she gazed up into his face. His expression was impassive but his eyes glinted dangerously.

"I was worried that you'd killed him," she snapped.

"He'll be fine. He'll come around in a couple of minutes." William studied her upturned face. "Did he touch you?"

"What?"

"You heard the question. If he touched you without your consent, you should pray that he never wakes up because I *will* kill him."

"No!"

"No, he didn't touch you? Or he didn't touch you without your consent?"

Lillian threw him an exasperated look. *Does the man honestly think I'd be intimate with another?* If she told him it was only his timely arrival that had stopped John's probable plans to molest her, there was no telling what he'd do. "No. He didn't touch me," she stated adamantly.

Suddenly the enormity of the situation sank in and she stood on shaky legs, swaying slightly as she tried to regain her equilibrium. William was at her side instantly, enclosing her in a protective embrace. Lillian melted against him, momentarily forgetting the events of the previous days and taking solace in his arms. She breathed in his familiar masculine scent and immediately felt comforted by his presence. Nothing had ever felt so good or so right as the feel of his arms around her. William smoothed his hands down her back in a soothing caress and for an instant, she submitted to the calming sensations.

"Do you know how worried I've been? How desperate?" he said into her hair.

Lillian stiffened and pulled away from his embrace, cruel reality suddenly intruding upon the intimate moment. She turned her back on him, glad when he didn't try to stop her, and engaged in a quick internal dialog with herself. She needed to harden her heart and her mind to what William had to say. She'd been surprised to see him. She'd already convinced herself that he was better off without her in what was no doubt a complicated situation. And she'd convinced herself that William would see things the same way. Now, here he was, having tracked her down. She couldn't imagine how hard he had to have been riding to catch her and John Steele. And how *had* he done that? How had he known where they'd been heading?

He was standing motionless behind her and she could almost feel the tension radiating off him. She turned and gazed up into his face, noticing for the first time the strain around his eyes.

"Why did you follow us, William?" she finally asked.

He let out a long breath and scraped his hands through his hair. "Why do you think? Did you really believe that I'd allow you to leave me with only that pitiful letter for an excuse?"

Lillian studied him and wondered if he was even aware of Margaret Dawson's state. George Dawson, she was sure, would've taken the first opportunity to enlighten him. Perhaps she'd been wrong about William after all. Perhaps he really didn't care about the consequences of his actions.

"It's beyond us now. You have to think about Margaret Dawson and the baby she is carrying — "

William cursed loudly. "That's a complete lie," he snarled. "I can't believe you'd take the word of a cad like George Dawson without even having the decency to talk to me! What sort of man do you take me for?"

Lillian blanched. For the first time, she worried that she'd been too hasty in her decision to leave. Her mind raced through her conversation with George Dawson and her subsequent reasoning. "But why would he say that? Why would he lie like that?" she whispered.

William's jaw hardened. "I don't fully understand the man's reasoning, but he did tell me that the combination of our two properties would be beneficial to the both of us. Perhaps that was his justification — pure, callous greed!"

Lillian paled. "But using his own daughter and risking her reputation? That's just despicable."

William laughed coldly. "Dawson is ruthless when he wants something. If Margaret *is* pregnant, it definitely isn't mine. Perhaps Margaret told him that I'm the father. I don't know for sure at the moment but I *do* intend to find out. My only priority was finding you safe and well. I didn't hang around the Dawsons' to ask about details, other than the direction in which you were heading."

Lillian suddenly felt ill and a dull throb had started in her temples. She wanted to believe William with every fiber of her being, but she just couldn't reconcile the fact that George and Margaret Dawson could be so calculating and cruel. She had so many questions, but a low moan jolted her out of her reverie, reminding her that John Steele was at that moment lying on the ground injured.

She knelt next to him. He moaned again and opened his eyes.

"He's coming around," William announced dispassionately. "I'll get his horse."

Lillian stared down into John's glassy gaze. "John, can you hear me?" she asked anxiously.

He blinked then focused his eyes on her face. "Lillian?"

"Yes. Are you badly hurt?"

"I'm fine." He gritted his teeth and struggled into a sitting position. "Has the arsehole buggered off?"

"No. The arsehole is still here," William snarled as he led John's horse toward them. "You don't seriously think that I'd leave Lillian alone with you again?"

John glared up at him and Lillian noticed a bruise forming on his jaw.

William turned his attention to her. "Lillian, I'd like you to go and wait for me in the clearing."

This worried her. What was he planning to do? "I'm not sure that's a good idea…"

William cut her off. "I don't plan to kill him, Lillian," he muttered irritably. "Trust me. I just need to speak to Steele alone for a moment."

Lillian wasn't sure about leaving the two men. She stood and studied William's face. He gazed back at her impassively, giving nothing away. Behind her, she heard John curse and struggle to his feet.

She sighed and picked up the remainder of her clothes. She still wore William's shirt and had hurriedly donned her skirt when the men had been busy arguing. "Fine. I'll wait for you in the clearing," she capitulated, too tired and irritated to protest further.

* * * *

Lillian returned to where they'd left the horses. Her underclothes were still a little damp and she hung them on a tree limb to dry.

She retrieved a blanket and the small bag of toilet items she'd allowed herself from her saddlebag and laid the blanket on the ground. She was still barefoot and was mildly surprised that her scamper through the dry undergrowth hadn't damaged her feet.

Her thoughts were with the two men at the billabong and she worried about William's intentions, and for that matter John Steele's too. Surely their ire had fizzled out by now and they could talk civilly to each other.

She loosened her hair from its braid and started brushing it, taking comfort from the soothing strokes as she pondered on her current situation. She didn't know where she'd go from here but she suspected William would want to take her back to the station. They needed to talk before she would go anywhere with him. She had questions and she wanted answers.

She heard the crackling of underbrush and a moment later William appeared. Lillian's breath caught in her throat as he strode into the clearing, his shirtless torso rippling with his movement and a light sheen of perspiration covering his chest. She had little experience with the male physique but even in her naïveté, she could appreciate William's perfectly masculine form. Her mouth watered as she studied his muscles, honed and sculpted from physical labor as well as boxing. Even his legs were powerful and well defined through the fabric of his work trousers. Trousers that sat low on his lean hips, exposing the distinct V of his pelvis and the trail of dark hair that snaked beneath his waistband.

She hadn't realized that she'd been staring until he chuckled. She looked up at his smirking face.

"Enjoying the view?" he asked, his lips quirking into a sly smile.

She blushed, feeling unaccountably embarrassed at being caught ogling him. After all the things that they'd shared, surely she should feel comfortable enough to look at him. It was the events of the past few days, she reasoned, that made her look at William in a different light, almost as if he was another man, virtually a stranger. The thought was disturbing and she pushed it to the back of her mind. William was the same man, she told herself. She would hear him out and try to make some sense of everything. Deep down, she knew that William was a good and honorable person. Up until this point, she'd allowed her head to rule her actions and it was time she gave her heart the lead.

Another, more immediate worry surfaced. "Where is John?"

William joined her on the blanket, one leg crooked beneath him and the other bent at the knee with an elbow resting across it.

He scowled at her question. "You two definitely became friendly in the short period of time that you've been together."

She huffed out an exasperated breath. "He *helped* me, William. Who knows where I'd be if it wasn't for him? Probably wandering aimlessly in the outback and on the brink of death through dehydration!"

He sighed. "That's exactly why I didn't do anything save for that knockout punch, which he was asking for. I just ensured that he had enough water and thanked him, albeit grudgingly, for helping you. He didn't leave without some vocal persuasion but, presumably, he's now on his way back to Coolabah."

William studied her intently, his face an impassive mask. "But if he'd touched you in any way, he wouldn't be *comfortably* sitting astride his horse right now."

A shiver worked its way down Lillian's spine at the unmistakable venom in his voice.

"Well, happily that didn't happen," she said softly.

As she bowed her head and traced the pattern on the blanket, she sensed William reaching toward her. He stopped short of stroking her face and instead curled a long tress of her hair around his finger.

"You have beautiful hair," he murmured, moving closer to her. "And I love seeing you in my shirt."

"William." She raised her head and looked him squarely in the eye. "We need to talk."

He cursed and pulled away from her. "What George Dawson told you about his daughter and me is a lie! She's *not* carrying my child, Lillian. That can only happen one way and I can tell you, I've definitely *never* been intimate with her."

"I just can't believe a father would lie about something like that at the expense of his daughter."

William studied her face. "Can't you?"

She inhaled sharply. Of course it was possible. Just look at her father and what he'd done.

"I'm sorry, I shouldn't have drawn a comparison like that," William apologized.

"You're right, though. I should have learned from my own father's unscrupulous behavior that anything is possible."

"Perhaps Margaret told George that I'm the father and he was just standing by his daughter. I don't know for sure, but I'm determined to get answers." He looked thoughtful. "I didn't tell you this before, but when I stayed at the Dawson property recently, Margaret crept into my room that evening and propositioned me."

Lillian gasped. "That's shocking. Why would she do such a thing?"

William's lips thinned into a grim smile. "She's obviously not as innocent as I'd first assumed and given the subsequent events, I'm now wondering whether she was trying to set me up. If I'd succumbed to her wiles, she could then claim that I was the father."

"I'm so sorry I left. I was overwhelmed and all I could think about was that if I stayed, my presence would interfere with you, Margaret and the unborn baby."

"Do you have any idea how desperate I've been? How terrified for your safety? When I read your letter, I felt like you'd physically ripped my heart out."

Lillian stifled a sob. She felt wretched that she'd caused William so much distress.

He closed the distance between them and wrapped an arm around her waist, pulling her into his lap. "Hush now," he whispered into her hair. "I found you. You had to know that I wouldn't let you go so easily."

She melted against him and breathed in his masculine scent, relaxed and happy for the first time in days. "I'm glad you did find me. How did you do it by the way?"

"I read your letter again and again and it didn't sit right with me. I couldn't allow myself to believe the words that you wrote. I was suspicious and I asked Mrs. Thompson if anything unusual had happened that day. She told me about George Dawson's visit. I drove over there immediately and confronted him. With some persuasion, he eventually told me everything."

She couldn't believe she'd just run off without waiting to speak to William. Of course, at the time she had thought she was doing the right thing, but it still didn't make up for her impulsive behavior. "I can't apologize enough for leaving the way I did. I can only say that I wasn't thinking properly."

He stroked a hand down her back soothingly. "We'll rest here tonight. I'll get a fire started."

He gently lifted her off his lap and stood. "Let's gather some kindling."

Chapter Thirty-Eight

William collected wood and tinder. When he arrived back at the clearing, Lillian was making dough for damper.

He dropped the bundle of timber and prepared a fire pit, arranging kindling, tinder and wood to burn slowly and thoroughly.

When the fire had burned down to coals, they cooked the damper, wrapping the dough around a stick and toasting it over the embers. The smell of baking bread floated on the still night air and made his mouth water. He'd had nothing decent to eat in days, just eating whatever he was able while in the saddle.

The damper was delicious, warm and doughy, and when dunked in tinned stew, it tasted like the best meal he'd ever consumed.

After dinner, they curled up together on the blanket. William lay on his side, his head propped on his left hand while he caressed Lillian with his right. He still couldn't quite believe that he'd found her and he felt compelled to touch her constantly. Her sweet scent of apples washed over him, making him desperate to taste her.

Her hair fanned out around her head in a beautiful silky mass and her emerald eyes glittered in the firelight. She'd replaced his shirt with a blouse of her own that he started to unbutton, working slowly and opening the fabric down the front with one hand. His cock stiffened when he saw that she wasn't wearing underclothes. Her pink nipples pebbled when the chill night air hit her breasts. Unable to resist any longer, he bent his head to her chest and sucked a rosy-tipped breast into his mouth. She gasped and thrust under him, forcing her plump flesh between his lips. He flicked her nipple with his tongue and massaged the other mound with his right hand, reveling in the feel of her silky smooth skin and her sweet taste.

Lillian moaned and wriggled underneath him. She wound her hands into his hair and tugged hard, sending desire unfurling down his spine and tightening his balls.

He released her breast with a popping sound and kissed a trail down her torso and across her flat stomach, licking a path above the waistband of her skirt. The firelight illuminated her body, bathing her skin in a warm glow.

He unfastened the garment and tugged it down, hissing and cursing under his breath when her legs were revealed to him. Harsh purple bruises covered her inner thighs in the arc of a saddle, looking stark and obscene against her pale flesh.

"Look at what you've done to your beautiful skin," he chastised, shocked at the extent of the saddle chafing.

"It doesn't hurt. It looks worse than it feels," she assured him.

He bent his head and planted soft kisses around the bruising on each of her thighs. He was appalled at the discomfort she must have suffered, particularly as the saddle she used was a stockman's saddle and definitely not designed for the smaller, female form.

She undulated her hips. "Please, William."

He dipped his head and inhaled her feminine scent, his mouth watering with his need to taste her. He cupped her knees and spread her legs wide, wanting to take things slowly and needing to draw out his own anticipation to touch her. The firelight flickered across the plump, wet folds of her sex, making it glisten enticingly. He used his thumbs to spread her lips then bent his head and licked her thoroughly and slowly through her center. She tasted divine, tangy, with a hint of apples. Fuck, he loved the soap she used. He'd have to ensure that she had a lifetime supply. He licked her again, lapping up her juices. She moaned and pumped her hips up, thrusting against his mouth. He speared his tongue into her hot, slick channel and used his thumb against her clitoris, massaging the taut little bud until she was panting and mewling.

"*Please.*" She gasped and gripped his hair, tugging his head closer against her.

Her skin was hot to the touch, burning up with the warmth from the fire and the lust that he was arousing in her. He grasped her thighs gently and pushed them farther apart. He locked his lips over her center and sucked, locating her clitoris with his tongue and tweaking the bundle of nerves as he thrust a finger inside her and massaged her front vaginal wall. She stiffened beneath him then cried out. His mouth flooded with her delicious juices and he sucked the pulses from her body as she trembled against his face.

Fuck, he was so hard his cock could cut glass. He needed to be inside her, couldn't wait any longer.

He shuffled back to undress, wanting nothing but the feel of Lillian's soft, naked flesh against his firmness.

He gazed at her a moment, drinking in the vision of satiated loveliness. She was flushed and glassy-eyed, her shapely legs spread open and offering an invitation to heaven.

He could hold back no longer. He lined his cock up with her entrance and thrust into her hard and fast, burying himself to the hilt in her moist, swollen flesh. She cried out and dug her nails into his shoulders. He stilled for a moment, reveling in the feel of her gripping him like a fist.

"I'm going to move," he said, his voice tight with restraint. "Are you okay?"

"Fine. Yes, please move." Lillian wriggled beneath him, gyrating her hips.

William supported himself on his elbows and pulled all the way out, brushing his cock on the outer lips of her pussy and spreading her moisture across her clit. He hovered there, rubbing the little nub with the thick crown of his cock, back and forth, dragging along her nerve endings and making her shudder beneath him.

Fuck. Her responsiveness constantly astounded and delighted him. She was sexuality and sensuality personified, wrapped up in one delicious, feminine package.

He tucked his elbows tight to her sides and dipped his head to her neck, latching onto the sensitive skin, sucking and nibbling. She arched beneath him and moaned his name, her voice broken and ragged.

He drove his cock back into her slick channel and started a pounding rhythm, his pelvis smacking against hers as he suckled and nipped her neck. Lust coiled down his spine and his balls tightened. He could tell that she was close. Her insides clenched and gripped him and little tremors erupted through her to massage his shaft. He swept his hand between their writhing bodies and found her clit, tweaking it to bring her closer to release.

She whimpered, dug her nails into his shoulders and wrapped her legs around his waist, gripping him tightly as she pumped her hips up to meet his thrusts.

"Come on, Lilly. Let go already!"

He felt her stiffen then shudder. Her pussy pulsed rhythmically in orgasm, milking his cock and sending him so close to the edge of that wonderful abyss. But he wanted to claim her, to mark her as his.

"I'm coming inside you," he ground between clenched teeth. "Let me know now if you don't want that."

She arched her back, mashing her breasts against his chest. "Please," she begged. "I want it."

He groaned loudly, her sweet assent sending him over the edge, and he thrust hard twice, shooting his seed deep inside her, his own release racing through him like a freight train.

He rolled off her, ensuring Lilly was closest to the fire, and lay on his back, breathing heavily. He turned to his side and propped his head on one hand, gazing down at her. She eventually opened her eyes and blinked lazily at him.

"And she's back." He chuckled and grazed his free hand down her arm.

She blushed prettily then frowned. "William, why didn't you want to—?"

He cut her off with a peck to her lips. "I know. I didn't withdraw." He continued to caress her arm lightly. "I should have, but I didn't want to. You're mine, Lilly, and I'm yours if you'll have me. Coming so close to losing you has made me reassess some things."

He tugged the blanket over them, tucking it securely around her body. "I want to make you mine in every way, so we belong to each other officially. But first I need some answers from Margaret Dawson and her father. It's only fair that you hear the truth, and not just from my lips."

She caressed his face. "I believe you, William. You don't need to prove anything to me."

He sighed and grasped her hand, turning it and placing a kiss on her palm. "Thank you, my sweet. But I need to get to the bottom of it. I won't have rumors and unfounded stories floating around. Sleep now. We'll talk more on it in the morning."

He lay next to her and drew her close to his body, spooning her, nestling his cock against her lush arse. The fire would last until morning warming Lillian's front while his body protected her back.

He buried his face in her hair and inhaled her scent, relieved and comforted as he hadn't been since she'd left. He hadn't realized just how desperate he'd been for her until he'd held her in his arms again. One thing was crystal clear to him—he'd never be complete without her by his side.

Chapter Thirty-Nine

Lillian's heart warmed when they eventually rode up to the homestead. It wasn't that long ago that she'd thought she'd never see it or its inhabitants again. It literally was a feeling of coming home. Emotion and anticipation overwhelmed her when she saw Mrs. Thompson and the children.

The children, having seen their approach, ran up the long drive to meet them.

William vaulted down from Victory and strode over to them, swinging Clara up onto his shoulder and taking Edward by the hand. They laughed hysterically and chattered non-stop, demanding to know everything that had happened since William had left.

"Father, you brought Lillian home," Edward exclaimed happily.

"I did, indeed. I told you that I would," William responded, leaning down so that Clara could scramble onto Lillian's horse. Lillian grasped the little girl around the waist and settled her firmly on the saddle in front of her. "Hello, darling," she said into her ear.

Clara grinned and turned her head for a kiss.

"And hello to you, Master Edward," Lillian greeted the little boy with mock seriousness.

"We missed you," Edward said, allowing his father to swing him onto the back of Victory.

Tears gathered in Lillian's eyes. "I missed you too." She couldn't believe she'd willingly left these sweet little children. She felt particularly guilty given that they'd lost their mother not too long ago. William had assured her that the children thought she'd gone to visit a friend and that he had left to retrieve her, but still she felt incredibly remorseful.

They set off once more down the drive toward the house, the children chattering happily and informing them of everything that had occurred in their absence.

When they approached the homestead, Mrs. Thompson was waiting on the front verandah. Lillian felt a spark of anxiety at seeing the housekeeper. What would she think of her abrupt departure? Would she be disappointed in her for causing William so much distress? Did she know what had happened, *why* she'd left? Lillian studied the older woman as they drew closer and was relieved to see no obvious look of ill will in her expression.

"I have a hearty lamb stew simmering. You must both be famished," Mrs. Thompson, informed them when they were within hearing distance.

William leaped easily from his saddle and helped the children down from each horse. "Thank you, Millie. I'll have Stan come and look after the horses. We'll be in, in a moment."

The housekeeper scurried inside with Edward and Clara close on her heels as William assisted Lillian from her horse. He grasped her around the waist and swung her from the saddle, allowing her body to slide slowly down his.

"Welcome home," he whispered in her ear.

Lillian melted against him, relief and happiness coursing through her. "It's so good to be back. William, I'm sorry for…"

He touched a finger to her lips. "Hush. Don't apologize anymore. What's done is done and thankfully we have you back now, where you belong."

"Is Mrs. Thompson aware of why I left?"

"She doesn't know the details, but she doesn't judge. She loves you and she'll understand that something must have happened to send you away. I'll tell her what she should know and keep the sordid specifics out of it."

Lillian breathed a sigh of relief. She loved and respected the housekeeper and would hate to think that the cruel story concocted by the Dawsons would interfere with their relationship.

After freshening up, they enjoyed a lovely meal of lamb stew. Once the children were in bed, William explained to Mrs. Thompson the basic details behind Lillian's leaving. Understandably the housekeeper was shocked, then furious to the point of demanding to confront the Dawsons herself.

"That won't be necessary, Millie," William replied grimly. "Although I do appreciate the sentiment. Lillian and I will be heading over there first thing in the morning. I'm determined to get to the bottom of it, so we can move on with no threat of unwelcome repercussions."

William turned toward Lillian and took her hand in his. "We'll be moving on together, Millie. Lillian belongs here. This is her home, if she'll accept it—and me."

Mrs. Thompson clapped her hands and shrieked in glee, immediately jumping from her chair and enfolding Lillian in a close embrace. "I'm so happy for you both," she said through tears of joy. "I can't imagine two people better suited to be together."

Lillian laughed and hugged her back, pleased beyond words that the older woman would accept her so readily into their family.

"Now," William announced. "I think Lillian needs to bathe and sleep in a comfortable bed. We'll be leaving early tomorrow."

They said their goodnights and William escorted Lillian to her room. "You need to rest tonight, sweetheart," he advised and kissed her chastely on the cheek. "Sleep well and I'll see you in the morning."

Alone in her room, Lillian contemplated the events of the past few days and couldn't quite believe that she was back. Her heart warmed at the feeling of belonging and love that radiated from everyone. But there was one thing that confused and worried her. While William had intimated in every way possible that he loved her and wanted to be with her, he hadn't actually asked her anything. He'd basically told Mrs. Thompson that Lillian would be staying and that this was her home but he hadn't officially asked her to marry him. He hadn't yet asked her to become Mrs. Cartwright and she was unsure if he ever would.

Chapter Forty

Lillian had relished the opportunity of washing the red earth from her hair and body. She'd been tired the previous evening but hadn't been able to stand the thought of going to bed coated liberally in the outback, so she'd taken the time to give herself a thorough sponge bath.

Earlier that morning, she'd slipped downstairs and shampooed her hair over the tub in the washroom, ensuring to lather and scrub her scalp liberally, determined to rid herself of the ocher-colored dust that had permeated her very being. Now, for the first time in days, she actually felt clean.

"Lilly, are you awake?"

She opened the door to William and smiled. He was freshly shaven and smelled deliciously masculine — a combination of spice and the outdoors. He'd dressed in a crisp blue linen shirt, left open at the neck, and dark gray trousers. It wasn't his usual working attire but it was more casual than a suit and made him look dashing yet restrained.

Unsure what to wear to an outing like the one they were just about to embark upon, Lillian had decided on a light cotton and lace dress in a pale floral print that hung to her calves. She'd pinned her damp hair into a mass of curls atop her head and powdered her face lightly, applying a pale pink shade to her lips.

"You look beautiful," William murmured, raking his gaze over her body appreciatively.

"Thank you, but I don't know if it's exactly appropriate for our visit this morning."

He grimaced. "I'm hoping that the unpleasantness will be over and done with quickly. Then I have a surprise for you."

She raised an eyebrow in inquiry. "A surprise?"

"Just wait and see." He smiled mysteriously and held his hand out for her. "Come."

* * * *

As the Dawson property came into sight, Lillian's belly quivered with nervous tension. She glanced at William and the hard set of his jaw told her that he wasn't looking forward to the impending confrontation any more than she was.

William turned onto the long driveway and slowed down, coming to a stop not far from the house's entrance.

Apart from the dinner dance she'd attended not long after she arrived in Australia, this was the first time she'd been to the property. She looked around, unsurprised that the house and the immediate surroundings were not dissimilar to those of Mulga Creek.

William opened his door and stepped around the front of the automobile to open hers too and assist her from the vehicle. Lillian removed her headscarf and checked her reflection in her compact. It was silly, she supposed, but she didn't want to confront Margaret Dawson looking less than her best.

William took her arm, led her to the front door and rapped the knocker abruptly. A moment later, Margaret Dawson opened it, surprise and anxiety suffusing her features when she realized who had come calling.

"Hello, Margaret," William greeted her. "May we come in?"

Margaret looked at them, indecision in her eyes, but William pushed past her. "Thank you," he said, pulling Lillian along with him.

"Who is it, Margaret?" George Dawson appeared in the hallway and stopped dead in his tracks, his face turning an alarming shade of red when he caught sight of them. "Cartwright," he sneered. "You have the audacity to come back into my home *and* bring your whore with you?"

Lillian gasped in shock as William growled and stepped forward.

"You're lucky that I'm not in the habit of beating on weaker men, otherwise you'd be a dead man for that insult."

Dawson paled and took a step back.

William glowered menacingly and Lillian laid her hand on his arm in an effort to calm him.

"William," she implored quietly.

He took a deep breath and wrapped his arm around her waist, pulling her close to his side. "We need to talk, Dawson. I want some answers. Surely you're not surprised that I'm here?"

George Dawson gave a curt nod and led them down the hallway to a drawing room. He entered and poured himself a whiskey from a decanter on a drink trolley, motioning with his glass for them to take a seat.

William led Lillian to an armchair but he remained standing. Margaret Dawson entered the room cautiously and took a seat to Lillian's left, looking warily between the two men.

George Dawson finished his Scotch in one gulp and turned to face them, looking directly at Lillian. "I'm surprised at you, young lady. I thought we were of the same opinion...that you and I agreed it's for the best for my daughter, William and their unborn baby that you leave."

Before Lillian could respond, William slammed his fist on a nearby table making them all jump in alarm. "That's a lie, Dawson," he roared. "I've *never* been intimate with your daughter. These lies have to stop. Now!"

Lillian was quickly reassessing their decision to confront the Dawsons. She glanced at Margaret and found her studying her lap intently. She wondered at the woman's apparently calm demeanor.

William's jaw was clenched tight and Lillian knew he was working hard to maintain control of his temper. When he next spoke, he kept his voice modulated and his words were addressed to Margaret Dawson. "Does your father know the truth? Is he in on this façade in an attempt to gain control of my land?"

The young woman looked up from her lap and stared at him, her bottom lip quivering.

"Answer me!"

When she finally spoke, her voice was barely above a whisper. "I told him that you were the father."

Lillian looked quickly at William. His eyes were blazing and boring a hole into Margaret Dawson, ordering her silently to continue with her explanation.

Her voice trembled. "I knew that my father wanted a connection between us. He thought that it would be beneficial to join the two properties. He spoke about it often and I knew his hope was that we'd be married." She looked up and met William's stare. "It was my hope too," she finished quietly.

George Dawson blustered from the other side of the room, "Margaret. Don't let him intimidate you. He needs to own up to his responsibilities —"

William cut him off with a glare and a growl.

"He can't be fooled, Papa," she cried. "He's right. There is no possible way that he could be the father. I lied to you!"

A deafening silence fell on the room. Up until that point, they hadn't even been sure that Margaret *was* pregnant.

Lillian looked at William and noted the expression of utter relief on his face. She understood now why he'd been so determined to have the truth exposed. It worried him that in the back of her mind Lillian would always have a level of uncertainty. She understood it, because until that moment, she suddenly realized, she *had* harbored a flicker of doubt.

Margaret Dawson was speaking again, her voice low. "I couldn't keep the pretext up any longer. I knew really, when you spurned my advances, that it wouldn't be possible. I guess it was just wishful thinking that you may have come to my rescue and claimed the baby as yours. It was silly and irresponsible. I'm sorry."

Lillian couldn't find it within herself to be completely unsympathetic. Obviously, the woman thought herself to be in love with William and had clearly gotten herself into trouble with another man. It was an unenviable situation and she found herself feeling sad for her.

"Who the hell is the father?" George Dawson snarled at his daughter. He was now a livid shade of purple and obviously not nearly as comfortable with this new status of his daughter's condition.

Lillian stood quickly, not wanting to be privy to a discussion about Margaret Dawson's intimate liaisons.

"We'll take our leave," William said quietly, grasping her elbow and guiding her to the door.

Neither of them spoke until they were ensconced in William's automobile and heading up the driveway. William exhaled a long breath and grasped Lillian's hand, raising his voice to be heard above the engine noise. "Well, that was awkward. I can't say that I'm unhappy that Margaret Dawson finally admitted the truth, although I wouldn't want to be in her shoes at the moment."

"The poor girl. I feel for her," Lillian said, her voice ripe with sympathy.

William looked at her askance. "Are you serious, Lilly? Her actions and those of her father caused you to leave. I know you thought that you were doing the right thing at the time, but you could have been killed or badly injured." He shook his head. "No. It was a self-serving thing for her to do. At no time did she think about the consequences of her actions and her father was so besotted with the idea that he might get his hands on my land that he didn't even question her."

"I think it was much more than the lure of your land, William. You are a respected member of the community, a decorated war veteran and successful in your own right. Any man would be proud to have you as a son-in-law."

He glanced her way and gave her hand a soft squeeze. "Your opinion of me warms my heart, my love, as does your sweet disposition." He brought her hand to his lips and kissed her palm. "I'll try to see matters through your eyes. At any rate, George Dawson has been served his due. No doubt the father of Margaret's baby is one of the property workmen. It would be next to impossible for her to have been...indiscreet with anyone else."

Lillian scanned their surroundings and wondered where they were going. She said as much to William.

"Remember I told you that I have a surprise for you?"

She smiled. "Yes. I've been wondering what that is all about."

He pulled off the main road and onto a dirt track. "Well, we're nearly there."

Lillian had no idea where they could be going. On either side of the vehicle was thick brush. They bumped along the road for a few miles, the noise making any further conversation impossible. Then William stopped the vehicle.

"We're here." He opened his door and walked around to her side. He assisted her out of the automobile before collecting a blanket and a basket from the back seat. William took her hand in his. "Come."

They wandered a short way through the bushland until they came to a lovely clear billabong. Tree branches swayed and hovered over the water and fat lizards sat sunning themselves on the rocky ledges.

"William, it's lovely," she breathed.

He smiled. "It is, isn't it? It's not full all year round, but we've been lucky, weather-wise."

He led her over to a shady clearing and laid the blanket down. He sat and tugged her to sit next to him. "We have a picnic lunch," he announced, unpacking the basket with a flourish. "We have cheese, eggs, cold lamb, fresh bread and wine."

"A veritable feast," Lillian laughed, delighted.

She was famished and ate ravenously, enjoying the fabulous food and their peaceful surroundings. They chatted amiably, both of them avoiding the subject of the Dawsons. Lillian had taken off her shoes and stockings and relished the freedom of fresh air circulating around her legs and feet.

William had grown quiet. She turned her head to look at him and her breath caught in her throat. He was kneeling before her on one bended knee, a box open in his palm.

"Lillian, my love, will you please do me the honor of becoming my wife? I love you more than life itself. I'll do anything for you and I can't imagine my life without you in it. Please marry me?"

A lump formed in Lillian's throat and her pulse soared in exhilaration. For so long her heart had ached for this man before her, ached for a love lost. Then when she'd found him again, fate had thrown so many challenges in their direction that she'd almost lost hope that they'd ever be together.

A sob worked its way up her throat and she held a trembling hand out to him. "Yes," she whispered. "Yes, I *will* marry you."

She looked into his eyes and saw such tenderness and adoration that it took her breath away. He steadied her trembling and slid a beautiful diamond solitaire onto her ring finger. She looked down at her hand and fluttered her fingers, allowing the diamond to catch the light and sparkle magnificently. It was elegant and lovely and exquisite in its simplicity. "William, it's beautiful," she said reverently. "I love it."

He smiled. "I'm glad. I'm beyond ecstatic that I'm finally able to put it on your finger."

She raised an eyebrow questioningly. "Oh?"

"I bought it for you ten years ago." He caressed her face. "I've kept it ever since. I could never bring myself to part with it, even though you and I were separated. It felt like, however small, I had a piece of you with me."

Tears filled her eyes and her heart swelled in her chest. How she loved this man! "I'm the luckiest woman in the world," she told him, tears of happiness trailing down her cheeks.

He grasped her around the waist and lowered her gently to the blanket, resting his weight on his arms. His thick arousal nestled between her thighs and her pulse rate spiked in anticipation.

"Thank you, my darling," he said, his voice thick. "You can't know how happy you've made me."

"I do know, William," she breathed. "I feel the same way."

He groaned and took her in a possessive kiss, his tongue tangling with hers as their mouths connected desperately. He nipped at her, sucking, nibbling and bruising her lips in his urgency.

His solid erection throbbed deliciously against her sex. She whimpered into his mouth and gripped his shoulders, thrusting her hips up shamelessly and grinding them against him, using his hard cock and the seam of his trousers for friction.

He cupped her head with one hand and her backside with the other and pulled her tighter to him, slanting his mouth across hers and deepening the kiss. High on his passion, a headiness assailed her, sending lightning bolts of pleasure to her pulsing core.

He pulled away suddenly, leaving her breathless and wanting.

"Undress," he demanded softly. "I want you naked."

The raw look of lust in his eyes as he raked her body with his gaze sent hot desire rippling down her spine. She shed her clothes quickly and soon she was standing totally exposed before him. He took his time examining her, until his scrutiny rested at the juncture of her thighs. He licked his lips and started to undress himself, staring at her intently. Within seconds, he was naked. His beautiful, muscular body gleamed enticingly in the dappled sunlight and made her mouth water.

Abruptly he bent and swooped her into a cradle hold. She shrieked in surprise and threw her arms around his neck, laughing in delight. He supported her easily and strode to the edge of the billabong, walking in waist deep and slowly lowering her into the water.

Lillian gasped at the initial change in temperature and clung to William, her arms around his neck. He tugged her close, dropping his hands to cup her backside then wrapping her legs around his waist.

"You're mine," he whispered, skimming his lips over her neck. "You'll not leave me again, Lillian." It was a demand, not a request, and one to which Lillian was all too willing to concede. She arched against him, relishing the feel of her breasts and tight nipples mashing against the hard contours of his chest.

The water lapped gently against their bodies as William ran his nose along the column of her throat, nibbling and sucking the sensitive flesh.

She moaned when he drew back and entered her swiftly, stretching and filling her with his thick arousal. He pumped in and out of her with long, languid strokes, cupping her backside and manipulating her body roughly. "This. Is. *Mine*." He punctuated each word with a hard thrust.

"Yes, yours," she gasped. "Always." Ecstatic beyond words that this man, this handsome Light Horseman was finally hers and that theirs was a love reclaimed.

About the Author

Jasmine's alter ego lives in Sydney, Australia with her husband and their Border Collie.

She loves reading all genres but in particular she enjoys erotic romance novels and thrillers.

Jasmine loves writing and is always looking for new ideas for stories that will provoke inner passions, stimulate the senses and ignite the imagination.

She has won some short story competitions and is now excited to have started publishing her erotic romance stories through Totally Bound Publishing.

Jasmine Hill loves to hear from readers. You can find her contact information, website details and author profile page at http://www.totallybound.com.

Totally Bound Publishing